SPOT

BONESTEEL

COLD
as *ice*

A.C. BELLARD
AND EUGENE L. WEEMS

COLD AS ICE

Published by: Celebrity Spotlight Entertainment, LLC
www.celebrityspotlightentertainmentllc.com
FIRST EDITION: 2015

Cover Design: Marion Designs/www.mariondesigns.com
Editor: Terri Harper/Terristranscripts@gmail.com
ISBN 13: 978-1500959562
ISBN: 1500959561

Library of Congress Cataloguing-in-Publication Data:

Celebrity Spotlight Entertainment, LLC

Printed in the United States of America

DEDICATION

To our parents, families and friends who are living or have gone on to a better place. The love remains unconditionally in our hearts.

Sincerely,
Alec Bellard
Eugene L. Weems

ACKNOWLEDGMENTS

A special thanks to my sister, Earline Sweet, may she rest in peace.

Thanks to Annie Rienhart, my creative writing professor from Hartnell College; the incomparable Jack Bowers of Santa Cruz, jazz musician and composer; Renee Adams-Barnes, my academic counselor who read almost everything I wrote. To my co-author, the magnanimous Eugene L. Weems. To my daughter, Tabora Kimani, with love. And finally, to my Creator for blessing me with the courage and wisdom to write.

Peace Out
Alex Briggs
Aka A.C. Bellard

ACKNOWLEDGEMENTS

ALDINE WEEMS...My grandmother and mother, the woman who holds both titles, my world, my heart. The loving and caring spirit that intoxicates my soul. The foundation of my temple. The queen who remains at the top of the pedestal of my realm. The woman who raised such a handsome, respectful, successful man. How can I ever show or express my gratitude for being blessed with you? Such words of appreciation don't exist in this world. Memories of you, your unconditional love, kindness, and beauty remain alive through me. I will continue on my journey toward achieving all your unfinished goals as well as my own aspirations until I conquer them all. As you used to say, a person will never accomplish nothing with hopes and wishes, but only through believing in self, hard work, dedication and devotion to the things you want to see happen. My success is living proof of your teachings. Love you, momma, with all my heart and beyond my last breath.

My love goes out to the following people: My sister Melissa Gina Johnson, my niece Micaiah and nephew Micah.

Finally, my deepest appreciation and warmest friendship is extended to all those people who have been supportive. Thank you for the love. I will keep bringing you hot page turning novels. So if you missed out on any, go cop them and experience the excitement of an electrified heart throbbing read. Let me continue to take you into worlds beyond your imagination.

Eugene L. Weems

Contents

THE CITROEN

Friday, April 15th
William Street Park
San Jose, California: 7:00 a.m.

"HEY, FAT-BOY! You's early as a motha'. Is you hidin' from the police? Talk to me. I talks back!"

Newman pretended not to be perturbed by Adam's loudness. He was too busy scoping the area like a sergeant on a SWAT surveillance team. "Get in the friggin' ride, Adam Ant. I ain't got all day. My shift starts at three-thirty."

"Ga-Haw!" squawked Adam. "What the hell is you drivin', some kind of kidnap vehicle?"

"Miss me with the funnies, Ant, I'm not in the mood," said Newman with a frown that caused his coarse black eyebrows to merge across his forebrain.

"A'ight, a'ight, but I still got to know what kind of spaceship we ridin' in," said Adam, climbing into the front passenger seat and craning his neck like Stevie Wonder. He's wearing black Ray Bans and is looking the car over from every angle except down.

The auto was factory painted crimson and a metallic charcoal gray with silver trimmings. It could have easily been mistaken for a reject from a Volkswagen assembly line. It was all grill, big headlights and a sloping roof line. Its fat seventeen-inch tires held the auto's metal work about two inches above the ground. It looked awkward and dorky, like a lunar landing vehicle.

"It's a Citroen," said Newman, as he flipped the ignition switch and let the engine purr.

"A Citroen? What the hey?" yapped Adam, while attempting to light a generic nonfilter cigarette.

9

"It's made in France, it's expensive, and you can't smoke because it's my brother's car and he ain't havin' it!" croaked Newman.

"Aw, man! You sho' you don't want me to fire up this cocktail?" Adam Ant's beady gray eyes glow from a pocked brown face, lips stretched wide to reveal two spaced out rows of yellow tinged teeth. "Yeah baby, it's laced with rockettes. Jimmy figured yo' ass was coming, so he hooked us up a couple. The shit is fresh as filet mignon."

Again, Newman's eyebrows meet and his plump cheeks are ruddy. "Just hold up till we get to his place. And did you shower this morning, 'cause you're funking up my air space. You smell like doo-doo."

Adam is sporting a burgundy colored watch cap pulled snugly against pointed Spock-like ears. He's wearing a brown and beige Pendleton that's two sizes too big, a pair of gray Dockers loaded with fast food grease stains, and a pair of canvas black and white bubble yum tennis shoes. He reeks with a fowl musty mothball odor like he's been sleeping in somebody's closet.

"Fuck you, fat-boy! How you twist yo' mouth to say that shit. You wearing a nasty ass Polo shirt that's three sizes too small, some dookie-green, wrinkled-up Bermuda shorts, and a pair of geek Rockports with no socks. You're sweatin' like a Chihuahua in heat and it ain't even seventy degrees in the shade, tah-hee-he!"

"Kiss my fat white ass, you Cheetoes lookin' muppet," fired Newman.

"Ta-hee," Adam Ant runs right over Newman's comeback line and continues his taunt, "Charlie Chan, pork chop eatin' ugly mutha fucka'. Once you get a blast of this shit, how I'm smelling ain't gonna matter one bit. Ya' pimple butt. My weenie is gettin' hard just contemplatin' yo' plump ass, ta-hee-he."

"Oh, look who's the comedian now. You think you can abuse me with the funnies. You must be forgetting who I am, you sorry excuse for a turd."

"What you talkin' about, Willis?" said Adam, showing mostly gums and saliva. "Why, you the county coroner, ain't cha'?"

"Wrong! Try again!" barked Newman starting to lose patience. He put the car in gear, checked his mirrors and made a U-turn. "I'm the C.M.E., you loud mouth lemonade kid. That stands for Chief Medical Examiner, and you don't want to get on my bad side this morning 'cause I'll have you stabbed, slabbed and drop-kicked into a barrel of hydrochloric acid."

Newman is messing with Adam Ant's high. Adam relaxes a bit, ceases the clowning, and tries to get serious. "So what's the difference, Papa Smurf? Coroner, M.E, ain't they representin' the same function?"

"The difference goes like this, egg sandwich. A coroner is not always a doctor. Most are undertakers and tow truck operators. They're into the body transportation business. Often a coroner hires a doctor to do an autopsy. If the doctor isn't trained in forensic pathology, then they're apt to make a lot of mistakes, and those mistakes can place an innocent person on death row or allow a guilty person to go free.

"Now as for me, yeah, I'm a medical examiner, but I'm a certified forensic pathologist. I'm a doctor whose patients are dead. I'm a detective of death. I'm trained to know everything about suicides, homicides and accidents. I can analyze traumatic injuries, stab wounds, gunshot wounds, poisoning and blunt force. I can tell you which bullet hole was the entrance or how the knife went in, and I can tell you where the perp was standing when he did it!"

For a brief moment Adam is captivated by what Newman has just said. He's contorting his face, pretending to be unimpressed. "Miss me with the shenanigans, Newman. You make it sound like you're some kind of asset to society. Why, you're just another nerd whose momma happened to pay his way through an ivy league medical school. Hey, you is a pipe smokin' crack addict same as me, tee-hee."

"That's what's wrong with you, crispy critter," replied Newman, "you haven't got a clue about what you should do with your life and you haven't got a purpose, so you wanna dis somebody who does."

"I got a purpose," said Adam, folding his arms across his chest. "I'm the playa' who's been supplyin' yo' porky butt with a safe place to hibernate just so you can smoke up a gang of crack. You're in my hood and it's my business to see that you don't get your cap peeled. You know what I'm sayin'?"

"Sounds like a plan, Stan," replied Newman, still in a festive mood and displaying a row of jagged white polished teeth. He realizes Adam is right. "Hey, you didn't forget to tell Jimmy about the girls, did you?"

"Don't worry, trick daddy. Tahoe and Niecee don't need no prior notice. Them skuzzy-ass bitches got a nose for dope, especially when it's free. They'll show up before the next cock crows, unannounced, like clockwork. You dig?"

The maple tree lined streets were narrow. Blue jays were screeching and sparrows were chattering up a storm. It was an old residential neighborhood on the southwest side of town with modestly priced hacienda style homes. Jimmy's spot was a three storied gray and white shingled Victorian on a corner lot. Adam wanted to park the Citroen in a carport around the apartment's rear, but Newman was adamant about keeping the curious looking vehicle within his sights. They agreed to park on a patch of sidewalk and front lawn.

Climbing wooden porch steps, they entered the foyer. On the first floor someone was cooking. The smell of fried bacon was mixed with Lysol and fresh paint.

They ascended a narrow stairway that led to a carpeted hallway on the second floor. Music from an oldies radio station could be heard as they shuffled past an open door. Jimmy's apartment was the last one, directly across from the bathroom. The door was ajar. Adam pounded on the frame and someone yelled, "Just push it open!" They entered and the hoarse voice continued, "Don't forget to block it!"

Adam Ant picked up a gray cinderblock and placed it flush against the door's frame. Next, he picked up a two-by-four and propped it under the doorknob. A homemade barricade, the loft was secure. The single room had only one window, which provided a birds-eye view of the Citroen and the comings and goings in the street below. Despite the window's shutters being flung open, the room still had a stale and dusty odor.

A large steamer trunk occupied the floor's middle. It was lying flat on its side, covered with an assortment of dope smoking paraphernalia, a tarnished metal spoon, a freshly used syringe, a stale box of Arm & Hammer baking soda, a rusty box cutter blade, a coat hanger wire, and a green ceramic ashtray filled with marijuana butts. There were three straight-backed vinyl kitchen chairs, a plastic pillow and five cotton blankets propped on a bare mattress. An old Westinghouse refrigerator took up the remaining space. Other than sunlight, an overhead forty watt bulb was the only alternate light source.

Jimmy emerged from behind a plastic shower curtain which covered a storage closet that was converted into a bedroom. His graying mousy brown shoulder length hair was disheveled. Bloodshot retinas peered from a gaunt and angular face, with lint particles trapped in a natty billygoat beard. He'd just finished shooting up and was wiping a trickle of blood from his forearm. He had missed a vein on his first and second try. Jimmy was normally a jovial five-foot-five. He didn't have a short man's complex, but at the moment he was a little perturbed.

"Hey, Jimmy Mac," said Newman, offering Jimmy a high five.

"Hey, Boss Hog," answered Jimmy, narrowing his pale blue eyes. "The eagle must be flying high this morning?"

"Right you are, Jimmy Mac. I got the cash, if you got the stash."

"We'll have to take a short one down the street," replied Jimmy, his pale blues glistening. "My folks ain't got that order ready yet, but it will be by the time we walk over."

"Can we text 'em?"

"No can do. Landline maybe, but it's got to be from a phone booth."

"Are you still without a phone?"

"Tah-haw," hawks Adam. "He had three, but he fed 'em to the crank monster."

"Shut the fuck up!" spat Jimmy. "One of them phones came up missing the last time you were here. Your shit stinks, Ant!"

"I told him the same thing just a while ago," interjects Newman, trying to glaze over the tension with light comedy.

"Come on, Jimmy Mac. I wasn't the only one here," argued Adam. "What about Tahoe and Niecee? I bet you didn't sweat them about no missing phone!"

"Miss me with the bullshit, Adam. You're staying here until we get back. And don't go fuckin' around my personals, you got that?" said Jimmy, looking Adam square in the eyes and poking a finger into Adam's pecks.

Adam slaps Jimmy's finger away and pleads his case, "Eh, you talkin' to ya boy, Jimmy Mac. Don't I always look out for you?" said Adam, rocking on the heels of his tennis shoes and stretching his arms out like he's preparing for an embrace.

"Hold up," said Newman, "where's that musical chime coming from?"

"What music?" croaked Jimmy as his gaunt complexion wrinkles, "I ain't got not radio."

"IT'S A RINGTONE!" howls Adam.

Adam walks over to the refrigerator. The door handle is broken. Jimmy keeps a set of vice-grip pliers handy to open it. Adam pried the refrigerator open and removed Jimmy's cell phone from the second shelf. Newman's jet black pupils take on the shapes of twin crescent moons as he holds his breath to keep from laughing out loud.

Jimmy's face looked like a red bell pepper as he snatched the phone from Adam's outstretched hand. "Gimme that, shithead!"

Adam flails his arms and does a shimmy. "See what I'm sayin'! I'm on your team, Mister Jizzat. How you like me now?"

As Ant continued to jabber, Jimmy Mac stomped out of the funky little room with Newman close behind, reminding Adam to keep an eye on the Citroen.

Ten minutes after Jimmy and Newman's departure, the girls, Niecee and Tahoe, showed up. They were brash and full of rancor. Adam could hear them cutting up way before they arrived. He stuck his head out the loft's window and yelled at them to get away from the Citroen.

"Fuck you, munchkin! This ain't yo' ride!" alleged Tahoe. She was leaning and trying to look cute with a slim brown cigarette dangling from the corner of her mouth. She had ebony pixie cut hair and was built like a pink flamingo, nothing but mop handles for legs and arms. She was decked out in Wrangler cut-offs, Birkenstock sandals, and a Tweety Bird T-shirt.

"That's right, it ain't mine, but I'm being paid to look afta' it, so step away from the merchandise, woman. And Niecee, why you holding your purse like you got a live monkey in it? Girl, let it loose. It ain't done nothin' to you! Tah-hee-hee!"

"Don't start with me!" scoffed Niecee, "ya friggin' Tasmanian. You know I can be your worst nightmare!"

"How you figure that?" howled Adam.

"Cause I'm a bitch that can shoot!"

"Right on, girl! Check his punk ass," prodded Tahoe as she slapped Niecee's outstretched palm with a low-five like tag team wrestlers. They continue ogling over Newman's car.

"Yeah, this ride is freaky. It's drippin' in chrome," marveled Niecee.

Niecee wasn't pretty. She was a big red-boned gal with a tiny head. She sported a petite blond afro on a neutral colored face with a pall parrot nose. She was taller than Tahoe, but you couldn't tell because her posture was hunched. She had a buffed butt and cabaret dancers legs. Her calves and ankles were muscular and thick. They were laced in glistening gold and silver bracelets, quite striking as they jangled when she walked, mimicking an old Nigerian custom once used on women by the men of the culture, legs laden with heavy brass wire to make sure their women couldn't run.

Jimmy Mac and Newman returned to the loft with each man sporting a new straw fedora and a fresh pair of Ray Bans. They looked like the Blues Brothers. They're talking smack and saying nothing that makes any sense. Jimmy's got a beer keg under his left arm. He jams it in the refrigerator and disappears behind his curtain to shoot up. Newman hands Adam a bag of groceries, then tosses a quarter-ounce Ziploc pouch of rock cocaine atop the steamer trunk and pulls a baggy of powder from his Bermuda shorts pocket.

The adjacent apartment is belching out Lauryn Hill's Zealots CD... *"Whether Jew or Gentile, I rank top percentile..."*

Adam spills the grocery bag's contents onto the steamer trunk. Twelve packs of cigarettes, four different brands, a quart of Hennessy and two bottles of Cisco. Apparently, Newman knows what everyone likes.

Tahoe is pestering Jimmy. She wants to shoot dope with him, but he's not having it. He hates all crack smokers, because he figures they're just wasting good dope. Tahoe likes doing a little of both, but before they can get the party started, other dope fiend tenants are banging on the door making up excuses in hopes of getting invited in.

Jimmy Mac is going berserk. He's mainlining and once again is having trouble finding a vein. He instructs Adam to monitor the door and cautions him not to let anyone in.

"Come on, Jimmy. Just a little taste, baby boy," coos Tahoe.

Jimmy is chomping on a piece of gum, his jaws going ninety miles an hour. He's tweaking with a mirror and using tweezers to pick hair bumps off his chin. He points Tahoe to a quarter spoon of coke that's laid out on a dresser. He peeks over her shoulder to make certain she's using her own rig.

In the meantime, Adam is testing out the brand new pipe that Newman brought with him. It's a tiny glass globe about the size of a golf ball attached to a five-inch stem. Adam loads the bowl and Newman grabs his arm and hands him a half dozen brass screens. Adam doesn't want to use screens but Newman insists. Adam fires up

15

and takes a monster hit. His cheeks are ballooning like a professional trumpet player. Newman's watching him intently. He's thinking Dizzy Gillespie. Niecee's smoking a cigarette and flicking her fingernails, anxiously awaiting her turn.

"Break out your hardware, Niecee, and let me bless you with a little sumpin'," said Newman.

"Oooh, you's a nasty white boy!"

Newman frowns, "I'm talking about your pipe, your straight shooter, crazy woman." Newman tosses her a half a gram of rock. Niecee's hazel eyes glisten. Her smirk breaks into a smile. With her baby finger she examines the cocaine.

"Why's it so yellow?"

"I think it's the cut," offered Newman, "it's probably procaine."

"Whaddaya mean, not enough cut or too much?"

"Heck if I know. I'm a pathologist, I'm not a chemist."

Niecee removed a broken piece of an auto's antenna that's hidden behind her left ear and burrowed in her afro. It's a hollow chrome plated tubing about four inches long. She crumbles the rock and shoves a few granules in the opening of one end, tilts her head to the side and lights up. The dope sizzles and sparks. She inhales, her eyelids shut tight, then she exhales a stream of stinky yellow smoke and makes an ugly face. She scrunches her nose and grinds her teeth. "Ugh! This shit taste like that pharmaceutical crap."

"You can't rock pharmaceutical coke," decreed Newman. "Your pipe just needs to be cleaned. It's probably got some trash in it." Newman hands Niecee a coat hanger wire. "Here, try running this through it and then blow out the residue."

"Tah-hee-hee!" cackles Adam, grabbing hold of his crotch. "When you get tired of playin' with that, come blow on a real mutha' fuckin' pipe, girlie."

"POW-smack!" Niecee shoots a stiff jab upside the back of Adam Ant's head and finishes with a swift kick to his right shin. Adam flinches twice but doesn't have time to counter. Tahoe is finished shooting up and she swoops from behind Jimmy's curtain and attacks Adam from his left flank. The girls swarm on him like wasps protecting a hive. Niecee's got him in a headlock and Tahoe has got a vice-grip on his groin.

Adam squeals in a shrill voice, "I'm just playin'! Ya'll let me go!"

The trio are entangled as though they're dancing a pasodoble across the squeaky hardwood floor. Adam finally breaks their hold, but the girls are not relenting. They chase him as he tries to escape the loft. He's got half his body through the open window. One foot is on the roof and the girls cling fast to the other. These chicks aren't playing. They're as serious as two storks fighting over a bull frog. The commotion draws Jimmy Mac away from his curtained room. He and Newman are grinning and howling.

"Crack that, sucka'!" yowled Jimmy, "make him pay!"

"Don't let him get away!" heckled Newman, "tie his slick ass in a sailor's knot!"

Still clinging to the window's frame, Adam starts to wail, "Stop! Stop it!" His voice is strained. He sounds like he's having a stroke. The girls release their grip and Adam scrambles back inside. Everybody is on freeze frame. Adam is sweaty pale like he's either seen a ghost or he's about to croak. He's short of breath.

"Swa...Swa...SWAT!"

"Swat?" the girls echo.

"Swat what?" snickers Newman.

Adam is sprawled on the floor with his back bracing the wall, still gasping for air. He points to the window. Jimmy jostles over and takes a peek.

"Oh shit! It's a raid!"

Cloaked in black windbreakers, dark jeans and combat boots, the SWAT team wore forbidding blank expressions. Two officers, one a hulking figure weighing some three hundred pounds, were crouched beside the Citroen. The remaining seven member crew were sprawled strategically around the Victorian home.

The point jimmied the building's front window, sending the dogs, two Dobermans and a Rottweiler, through. They slid across the hall's linoleum floor and parked themselves at the manager's door. The point opened the front hatch and four deputies rushed in.

Back in Jimmy's loft, the girls were frantic. They had juvenile records and neither could afford an arrest, but it was their turf and they knew all the hideouts and the quickest routes for an escape.

Bolting for the back porch stairway, Adam synchronized his moves alongside the girls'. His target was the bathroom across from Jimmy's apartment door. His mission, flush the dope down the toilet. But Adam Ant was notorious for capitalizing on someone else's misfortune. Just as Newman gave orders to run, Adam had already activated his plan of deceit. He darted past the girls, skidded across the back porch banister and hit the ground running.

When the back door slammed shut, the Rottweiler streaked down the second storey hallway. With the power of a ferocious black baby rhino, he crashed through Jimmy Mac's door, overturned a chair, tore through some bedding and leaped on top of the steamer trunk as he continued to growl and bark.

But the loft was empty. Nobody was home.

SUNSET INVESTIGATIONS
Old Town Village
Los Gatos, California: 10:00 a.m.

LIKE MOST SMALL California cities, the village's population had turned into a jungle. Los Gatos had plenty of everything except mere space. Everything was connected and atop of everything else.

Across from the Old Town plaza was Aliya Bonesteel's Cashmere Properties Realty, and hitched to an awning between two white posts was another sign, Sunset Investigations. The new tenants occupied two quaint offices on the building's second. floor. The frosted glass door advertised divorces, accidents, missing persons, surveillance, and the phone book's yellow pages told a lot more: eavesdropping, child custody, court room evidence, insurance claims. Bonded, insured, and licensed twenty-four-hour service, confidential and reliable. Investigators: Rob Bonesteel and Sunny Jordon.

Dressed in a business white blouse with her kinked blond hair tied in a bun, It was Sunny's job to greet clients and screen all incoming calls.

"Good morning, Sunset Investigations, how may I help you?

"Rob Bonesteel," said the voice in a whisper.

"Excuse me?"

"Rob Bonesteel. Tell him it's Harry."

Sunny pushes one of several buttons displayed on the phone's console, "Rob, some friend of yours is on line two."

"Who?"

"All I got was Harry. He's whispering."

"Harry?"

"Yeah, Harry. And Rob, you've been fartin' rainbows for the last

19

twenty minutes. Gee whiz, crack a window or something."

Rob ignores Sunny's comment. "Hello, Newman, what can I do for ya, pal? And why are you whispering?"

"I've got no time to explain but I'm in a bit of a jam. I need you to meet me at the bus stop in front of the Optometry Building on 14th and Santa Clara. And call Bob's Towing. Tell them you'll be picking up a Citroen in about an hour."

"A Citroen? Ain't that your brother's car?"

"Yeah, here's the license number."

"This is gonna cost you, pal. You're on the clock."

"Don't worry, I'm good for it and you know it."

When Rob hangs up, Sunny skips into his office. "What gives, Robbie?"

"That was Newman, in case you didn't know."

"Oh, Harry Newman, the medicine man."

"He's not a medicine man, silly. He's the chief pathologist for Santa Cruz County. He and his brother Randy bring us most of our business."

"So what's he got for us, a new case?"

"I'm not sure yet, but here, call Bob's Towing. I gotta run. I'll check back with you before noon."

Rob hands Sunny the Citroen's license number. She's familiar with the routine, she knows what to do.

When Rob arrived at the Optometry Building, Harry Newman was nowhere in sight. Rob parked his Subaru Tribeca in a loading zone, which gave him free parking for about fifteen or twenty minutes. The high-rise had eleven floors. He took the lobby elevator to the third floor and found Newman hugging a stool at a snack bar counter. He's stuffing his face with a huge muffaletta sandwich. There's lots of mortadella cheese oozing from it and some has attached itself to the side of his neck. Rob taps his hunched shoulders just as Newman gets into his second bite.

"You need to step away from the counter, Newman, 'cause you're puttin' some hurt on that sandwich."

Newman ignores Rob and chomps down on the sandwich for the third time. He's serious. His lips are swirling and the food is trying to escape from his mouth, "Don't fuck with my mojo, Bonesteel. This is a real man-sandwich. Here, have a taste."

"Thanks, but no thanks." Rob's forehead wrinkles and he pushes Newman's sausage fingers away. "What's the biz-zap, Newman? Why did you insist that I plow through lunch hour traffic when I could be kicking back in my office eating my own lunch?"

Again, Newman ignores Rob's grumble and takes a swig from a Styrofoam cup. It's a counterfeit 7-Eleven Big Gulp soda. He burps, wipes away the drool from his bottom lip, and levels Rob with a blank-eyed expression. "Did you call Bob's Towing like I asked?"

Rob's staring back. He's looking at Newman's huge forehead. He's thinking, lobotomy. "No, Sunny made the call. The tow company says there's no such animal on their lot."

"What? Hell no! He took it!"

"Well, why didn't you stop him, and where did this happen?"

"I was seeing a client down in Williams Street Park."

"A client?" Rob is in disbelief. He knows the area is a drive-thru drug infested neighborhood. It's near the university, but it's not likely Newman was doing any moonlighting at ten a.m. "Sounds like you're up shit creek, pal. You're gonna have to file a stolen auto claim."

"Stolen my ass!" barks Newman with spittle leaping from his plump lips in two different directions. "It's my brother Randy's car, and those eggheads better find it!"

Rob bobs and weaves to avoid getting hit by Newman's spit. "You already told me that. No sense in going fifty-one-fifty on me. We can drive down to Bob's and check it out. If you say it's there, then it must be there."

"I can't go with you."

"What?"

"Look, just take me down to Hertz and I'll get a rental. I've got to get back to Santa Cruz. My shift starts at three-thirty."

"All right, have it your way. Is there anything I need to know before I go down there and embarrass myself?"

"Yeah, you know Randy is a classic auto collector. Your brother Houston has done a ton of restoration work for him."

"Right."

"So the Citroen is the prize of his collection. It's in mint condition, a 1934 model, made in France, and fresh as the day it rolled off the assembly line. You get it back for him and I'll see to it that you get a ten percent finder's fee."

"Oh, yeah. What's it worth?"

"Oh, about three hundred and fifty thou'."

Rob whistles.

"And another thing," continues Newman, "if they ain't got it, then check the county sheriff's garage. I'm suspecting they have it and they're playing me."

"Kill game, Newman! You're workin' me like a rib sandwich. What's up with that?"

"I'm not shitin' ya, Rob. Remember, I once worked for Santa Clara County Sheriffs. Bob's Towing works for them and they're a bunch of thieves!"

Newman is getting animated and Rob's losing patience. He's thinking about his Subaru getting towed from a yellow loading zone. "Okay, slow down a minute. What's with the sheriffs? It's becoming apparent that they've got a bone to pick with you."

Newman sighs and runs his hands through moppy black hair. "I used to be an assistant to their chief pathologist. While my boss was on a sabbatical, two county jail prisoners died of heart attacks, according to the jailhouse doctor's report, but the deaths were really due to police chokeholds. I peeped it and refused to supply a death certificate that said cardiac arrest."

"Bullshit!" said Rob, only half believing him.

"No, that's real talk, Holmes."

"Can you prove it?"

"Come on, Rob. Why do you think I switched counties? I wasn't a team player so they made me a deal. I became Santa Cruz County's chief medical examiner, and the promotion made me more enemies than friends. I've had to watch my back ever since. And that's the snizoid," said Newman, grinning from ear to ear.

By the time Tahoe and Niecee stopped running, Adam had streaked down an alley, jumped two fences and cut through a sleeping pitbull's backyard. Sweaty and short of breath, the girls took a foot bridge on the south end of Williams Street Park and followed a jogging path that led to the back entrance of a Paul Masson Winery. Without haste, they quickstepped across a parking lot and entered a neighborhood shopping center.

"Slow down, girl," cried Niecee, "this ain't no triathlon, and I ain't Marion Jones."

"You need to ditch them ankle bracelets, Niecee. They're out of style."

"Excuse me? Out of style?" Niecee is looking like she was about to throw a case of wine bottles, if she had some, at Tahoe's head.

"Girl, I'm just playin', chill out. Let's go kick back at Ruthy's Place and have us a couple wine coolers. My treat, okay?"

Ruthy's Place was a minibar, pool table and phone booth. It was a check cashing pub known best for its frosty beer goblets and greasy take-out food. The mini-menu boasted tuna fish sandwiches, French fries, Louisiana sausage, hot Texas chili and microwave pizza. The pub was a popular employee break spot for several local businesses, including the dock workers from Paul Masson.

Ruthy had recently had some remodeling done, a new sundeck which fronted the left side of the shopping center's parking lot. The deck was terraced and provided enough room for several pine park benches and a couple canopied lawn tables. Ruthy was having a cigarette break. She had her designer laptop with her when the girls strolled up.

"My, my!" she hollered. "Where ya'll coming from? Is somebody chasin' ya?"

The girls leveled her with a look, and their eyes flitted from Ruthy to the laptop and back.

"That's my intellectual property. It's a Mac Notebook, in case you didn't know," exulted Ruthy, eyeing the girls cautiously and taking a slow drag from her cigarette.

"I knew that," quipped Tahoe. She immediately kicked off her sandals to let loose some gravel that had gotten trapped under the arches of her feet, while Niecee plopped herself on the nearest bench.

Niecee Edwards and Tahoe Holloway were inseparable. They were childhood friends. Niecee knew how Tahoe looked before her teeth were straightened. Both were outspoken and would never suffer from the bullying of men. They were girls who could drink most folks under the table. They kept each other's back and they were full of frolic and fun.

"Looks like you girls could use a drink!" apprised Ruthy. She pulled a cell phone from her apron pocket and diddled a text. Seconds later, a lanky white girl in pink coveralls appeared with a cold pitcher of wine, a bowl of diced fruit, and three sparkling glasses. The slim white girl smiled, set the tray on the table and split. Ruthy poured and the threesome quenched their thirst.

Ruthy was an older gal. Her exact age was anybody's guess and she wasn't volunteering. Her complexion was a smooth ebony black on a baby doll face with looming brown eyes. Her heavy heart shaped hips and thick lips were sensual. She was the sole proprietor of the beer joint she named Ruthy's Place.

"Ruthy, this Kool-Aid is the bomb! What you got in it, girl?" raved Tahoe.

"I'm not giving up any of my trade secrets," she huffed, "I don't need no competition. By the way, in case you didn't know, your boss lady, Brenda, left a message. She says she's layin' ya'll off."

"That heifer got her nerve!" erupted Tahoe.

"Yeah, she too chickenshit to call us on our cell, so she using you to do her dirt," attested Niecee.

Ruthy is not the least bit alarmed. She returns a polite smile. "Brenda owes you some money, right?"

"Damn skippy, she owes us money!" screeched Tahoe.

"She ain't paid us a cent for none of last month's shows," clamored Niecee.

Ruthy reached into her apron pocket, pulled out the cell phone and diddled another text. Two minutes later, the same white girl stepped out, smiled, handed Ruthy two brown business envelopes and exited the same way she'd come. Ruthy passed out the envelopes and each girl peeked inside. Their faces lit up and Tahoe shrieked.

"Oooou, you da' shit, Ruthy!"

"Shama-lama-ding-dong!" cheered Niecee.

"There ought to be enough to cover your fees for last month. Brenda said she'd hire ya'll back in a couple months, and not to forget you owe her twenty percent. And in case you didn't know, I've got a vested interest in Cheesecake Productions. I've got Brenda's back, so you best enjoy this little vacation and try and stay out of mischief because there's always another girl waitin' to take your place. By the way, where did you say ya'll was comin' from, Niecee?"

"We was just smokin' some herb with -- Ow!"

Tahoe cut in by stomping on Niecee's big toe. "We was just hangin' out with Adam. "

"Adam? Did you say, Adam?" probed Ruthy with a frown. "A little beady eyed midget that wears a dingy watchcap and smells bad all the time?"

"Yeah, that's him."

"I gave up a fifty to haul some trash that's piled along the backside of my lot. He started the job but never finished, and that was a week ago."

24

"Don't worry," consoled Tahoe, "he's hiding right now, but he'll soon show his lizard brain before the day's end, and me and Niecee will sock it to him!"

"Ya damn Skippy!" crowed Niecee.

Ruthy is tickled and laughs heartily. Her eyes are tearing up. "Don't put hands on him, girls. Just get him to come over and finish the job."

The girls left Ruthy's place feeling completely ecstatic and thrilled. Their good fortune couldn't have arrived at a better time. Two years ago the girls were involved in a serious workplace accident. They were employed with Deluxe Dry Cleaning in San Jose. Tahoe was a press operator and Niecee was in charge of drapes and alterations. The boiler room explosion occurred during a morning coffee break, while the girls and two other employees were assembled in a back room. One employee was killed instantly, another suffered third degree burns on the right side of her body. Niecee's hip was fractured in two places and Tahoe received retina damage to her left eye.

Initially, the Deluxe Dry Cleaning insurance policy was liable for all doctor and hospital expenses plus an additional five thousand to Tahoe and ten thousand to Niecee, part of an injury benefit clause. The girls refused the offer and hired a private attorney.

A lawsuit was filed asking for ten million dollars. The lawyers assured the girls that after several preliminary courtroom appearances, each girl would receive no less than three million. The lawyers insisted the case was a slam dunk, but after three months no agreement had been reached and Niecee and Tahoe were ready to give in and accept the original offer. In order to regain their client's confidence and trust, the law firm started issuing the girls a check in the amount of fifteen hundred a month. So, along with their unemployment benefits and working part-time for Cheesecake Productions, the girls had a steady flow of income until their case was settled.

On their return trip to their cottage, the girls took a shortcut and jogged part of the way before reaching Guadalupe Creek, a rocky and shallow riverbed which meandered alongside Williams Street Park and the back fence of the girls' home. It was just last March when they stumbled across a body wrapped in plastic and stuffed under a bluff. The corpse was female. She'd been on a missing person's website for eighteen months.

The coroner's initial findings stated the corpse showed signs of poisoning. The woman's body was relatively fresh as though death bad occurred only a couple days prior to being found. Harry Newman did the autopsy. Although it was no longer his jurisdiction, it was done as a favor to a friend of a friend. Ice crystals were found in some of the tissues, mostly the liver and a portion of the lungs. It was Newman's guess that the woman had been killed eighteen months prior to the body being hidden in the creek.

The cadaver was fresh. The victim was cold as ice.

SUMMIT LAKE
Berryessa District
San Jose: 2:00 p.m.

BOB'S TOWING WAS situated on Old Oakland Road, just parallel to the Nimitz Freeway on the north side of town. It was one of the more popular wrecking yards and the third largest in Santa Clara County. Rob walked up to the rustic wooden counter wearing oil stained khaki coveralls and a Giants baseball cap. A screwdriver was tucked in his top front pocket and he carried a crescent wrench in his left hand. There were three clerks servicing customers, so Rob waited his turn. Finally, a young clerk who'd been restocking supplies greeted him.

"Can I help you?"

"Sure can. I'm in search of a couple items," said Rob as he patted himself down until he located a folded piece of paper that was stuffed in his rear pocket, then handed the list of auto parts to the clerk.

Nodding his head, the clerk said, "Oh, yeah, we got everything you're looking for. The Cadillac grills are back on the east lot. There's a light pole with a letter 'F'. You'll find the parts about three rows over next to a mechanic's shack. Will you be needing tools?"

"No thanks. I brought my own, but I'll need a push cart."

"All right, there's several carts parked on the left side of this building. Just walk straight past that side exit."

Rob continued with his role play. He thanked the clerk and greeted a few other wrecking yard customers. He toured the huge lot and disappeared around several stacks of foreign cars piled about eighteen feet high. Two dusty isles to his left was a barrage of banging and high speed drill noises coming from a tin-roofed workshop. Rob hadn't seen anything resembling a Citroen, but he knew the mechanics

27

workshack was one of the places he needed to check. It was next to a fenced-in yard of what appeared to be a batch of freshly towed autos.

Rob was peering through an open window when he sensed he was being watched. Some guy resembling a three hundred pound defensive lineman was trying to creep up on him. Rob reacted to the crunch of gravel from a pair of fourteen inch motorcycle boots, and without a second's haste, Rob's reflexes went into play as he sidestepped the burley tattooed figure. He smashed the guy's left kneecap with his crescent wrench and kicked the creep's right leg from under him.

"Whoa!" said the hulk as he toppled like timber. Rob held the giant at bay by shoving his snakeskins under the man's chin. By then, two mechanics rushed out the building to see what the commotion was about.

"Hey, Tony!" said the skinny guy holding an acetylene torch, "have we got ourselves a problem or what?"

Tony looks up at him with a strained expression as Rob applies a little more pressure to the man's throat. The disabled brute glares at the skinny guy and his shorter companion. The shorter guy is built low to the ground. He's got arms like an orangutan and is just about as ugly. He's clutching a four-foot crowbar like he's itching to do something nasty with it.

Rob's thinking is one step ahead of everyone. He reaches inside his coveralls and whips out a .380 revolver. The mechanics flinch and take a step back. The skinny guy grumbles something which no one but he understands. He flips open a cell phone and makes a call.

Bob's Towing & Wrecking Yard was owned by three Indian brothers, Billy Bear, Frank Dean and Bob Wayne George. Billy Bear and Frank Dean were the work horses of the family run business, and Bob Wayne called the shots. Although their ages differed, they were all once football standouts, linebacker, nose tackle and defensive back at Saratoga High, a rival of Rob's alma mater, Los Gatos High. Bob Wayne showed up wearing a gray sports shirt, a navy blue blazer and a pair of faded skinny legged jeans stuffed into suede bike boots. He was six-four, two-seventy, pure beer. Light on his feet, he jostled over with big teeth grinning and switching a toothpick from one corner of his mouth to the other.

"Everyone back to work! I got this," commanded Bob Wayne. Glaring at Rob, he asked, "Bonesteel, why are you harassing my employees?"

"Excuse me, but I think I'm the one who's being violated here."

"You can't blame my crew for being a little rough. Three months ago they found a body stuffed in the trunk of an '89 Buick. Since then we've become leery of anyone snooping around, even if they're a customer. So what's your beef, homeboy?"

"I got a client who says one of your drivers towed away his Citroen from Williams Street Park this morning."

"Yep, sure as hell did, but the sheriff had us drop it off at their garage. It's standard procedure when impounding a vehicle for what they call a forensic drug inspection. If the auto turns up clean, they'll call us soon enough to pick it up."

Rob hands Bob Wayne a business card. "Well, my client would appreciate it being handled with care. I'm to return it to him as soon as possible. It's a classic."

"Yeah, we know, a 1934 Citroen. It's a beauty. Don't worry about it, Bonesteel. We'll get back at ya' as soon as we get the call."

When Tahoe and Niecee arrived at their cottage, they found Adam chilling out on their back porch. The girls seemed to come from out of nowhere and Adam was spooked, so he stuffed a crack pipe he'd just torched down in his sock. The girls were winded but Niecee spotted him first.

"Why you hidin' out like a turtle that's lost his shell, Adam?"

"Ya damn trick!" crowed Tahoe, "You oughta be downtown gettin' your grind on, mista'!"

"I got plenty of time for that, sweet cheeks, tah-hee. Besides, don't ya'll want your cut?"

"Hell no!" squawked Niecee, "You scuzzy-ass, bastard. You know that's Newman's dope."

"Yeah, what kind of friend are you?" erupted Tahoe.

"Ta-hee-hee, I'm the fiendish kind, girlie," yelped Adam as he clutched his crotch just to antagonize the girls.

"Instead of playin' with yo' little pee-pee, you need to toss that pipe before you burn up your socks," warned Tahoe. Adam's face had frozen. He looked like he'd just got his finger caught in an electrical socket. His sock had caught fire. His chicken legs were smoking. In a panic, he kicked off his tennis shoe, yanked off his torched sock and screeched, "You owl-eyed, pall parrot lookin..."

"Hey, hey, Mister Bojangles," jeered Niecee, "don't even try and go there, 'cause we got you now, munchkin!"

"Yeah, that's right," rallied Tahoe, "we'll kidnap your ass and torture you like a Taliban."

"That's real talk," howled Niecee, "you'll be speakin' in tongues when we get through with you."

Adam Ant finally gathers his composure and grins broadly. He loads up his crack pipe and hands it to Niecee. "I'm just playin' girlie. You not gonna sodomize me for having a little fun?"

"Fuck you, ya little pervert! We're cool," announced Tahoe. "Besides, we gotta get cleaned up 'cause we're doing a hitch tonight."

"Oh, yeah? Where?"

"Summit Lake, you turtle shit. So you need to find someplace else to hibernate, you dig?"

Adam left, but planned to return later after the girls had gone. He'd hidden a serious stash of crystal meth in their attic. Tahoe and Niecee weren't stupid. They kept Adam's so-called secret amongst themselves.

"Summit Lake? Why did you lie like that?" whined Niecee. "Girl, don't you know that once you start a lie you have to finish it? Anyways, I heard that there's this huge party jumping off in Santa Cruz this weekend. If we can find us a trick on wheels, then we can do what we always do."

"Oh, don't tell me. Get in, get out, and get some head!" Tahoe and Niecee echoed simultaneously.

"Hey, Tahoe," said Niecee still contemplating, "I think I know why Brenda laid us off."

"Okay, genius, so now you're gonna tell me something I already know," said Tahoe.

"I'm being serious, so listen up. At that last bachelor party we did, you gave the groom a private lap dance. I bet you somebody blabbed about it and somehow it got back to Brenda."

"Damn Skippy Peanuts!" howled Tahoe in agreement. "And Brenda said we owed her twenty percent, which means she knew it was a five hundred dollar quickie."

"Yeah, but you can't be doing that side show shit, Tahoe. It could cause Brenda to get her business license pulled. Remember, teasing is legit, but beyond that..."

"It's a crying shame! Put some ice on it, Niecee. We still got paid and nobody got played. All I want to know is what lucky sucka' is gonna be my sugar daddy tonight?"

Back in Santa Cruz, Newman's at the county morgue. He's on his dinner break, snacking on egg rolls and a quart of wonton soup. He'd just completed an autopsy on a female corpse. Two minutes into his meal his cell phone warbles.

"Santa Cruz County Morgue, you stab 'em, we slab 'em," chimes Newman.

Rob cringes. Of course Newman can't see him, but he's hoping to rattle whomever is on the end of his line. "How in the world do you get away with answering the phone like that, Harry? Aren't you at work?"

"Why, certainly," chuckles Newman, trying to do his best improv of Curly and The Three Stooges.

"Okay, wise guy, but suppose I was the mayor, or better yet, the chief of police! How would you know?"

"Hey, you've called me on my private cell, bird brain, not my business line. And it just so happens I've got a couple city hall detectives observing me; it's procedure. But for now they're in the little boys' room, 'cause they were looking kind of pale. Enough with the formalities, Bonesteel, tell me you've got the Citroen."

"Yeah, I got a solid lead, but you're not going to like what I'm about to say."

"Should I be sitting down for this?"

"No, nothing like that. It's been impounded. Bob's Towing was instructed to drop it off at the Santa Clara Sheriff's garage."

"I told you they were in cahoots!" howls Newman.

"Cahoots? What the hell is a cahoot?"

"The hell with you, Bonesteel. You know exactly what I'm saying. So what's our next move?"

"Well, according to your story, it's a grudge thing, so I expect they're messing with you. They know the car is registered to your brother, Randy. They just might call him and ask him to pick it up."

"That's exactly what I don't want to happen, ya numbskull!"

"Why's that?"

"Because I didn't get permission to borrow it in the first place."

"You know you're intelligent, Harry, but you're still a nut. Is that formaldehyde you're sniffing, 'cause the stench is coming through the phone."

"Oh, you're really with the funnies this evening, Bonesteel. Matter of fact, I just filleted a female vic that was found over in Scotts Valley."

"Oh, yeah?"

"Yeah, and she's another poisoned cadaver similar to the one that was discovered in Guadalupe Creek last month, but this one's been poisoned with arsenic."

"Well, I know you're just itching to explain, so I'm listening. And if you don't mind, I'm going to punch my record button."

"Why would you wanna do a thing like that?"

"I'm an investigator, remember. Besides, this knowledge may be useful."

"That's fine with me, Bonesteel, but the problem with you is you're lacking common investigative experience."

"You don't say."

"I do say. For instance, if you worked in a jailhouse, you'd have a better insight into human nature and criminal mentality."

"So?"

"Hold it, I'm not done yet. And if you'd worked a beat, you'd have a little black book with all kinds of juicy information about this and that."

"Harry! Sorry to interrupt you, but I haven't got time for this lecture. So for now, let's just get back to the autopsy, okay? Besides, my military reconnaissance experience counts for something."

"I know what this is about," whines Harry, "You're just using me to get yourself some on-the-job training."

"Something like that," chuckles Rob.

"Okay then, here goes. Arsenic has a different effect depending on the degrees of ingestion. It's absorbed from the bowels and into the bloodstream and then the organs. The liver takes up the toxins where most of it accumulates. And if it's in a large enough dose, it quickly freezes the brain function. Of course, small doses over a period of time affect the nerve endings in such a way that the vic will feel prickly heat like hot needles and the outer skin will blister, then comes nausea, severe headaches, and fatigue."

"I'm right with ya, Harry. So, two female bodies found dead approximately fifteen miles apart, one in March and one in April. So, I'm thinking like you must be thinking. This is not coincidental, right?"

"Exactly, but even more so when I add another tidbit of information." Harry pauses. He's waiting for Rob to ask a question.

"Okay, I give," quips Rob, "what's the tidbit?"

Newman clears his throat, "Actually, there's two. I did the autopsy on the first victim."

"And?"

"And she also died of poisoning, but it wasn't arsenic. The other poison was succinylcholine."

"What kind of jabberwocky are you telling me, Harry?"

"It's the ingredients found in anti-freeze."

"Anti-freeze?"

"Yeah, that's what I said, anti-freeze. Tastes sweet when drank. It mixes well with wines or citrus drinks. The chemical crystallizes the liver and lungs and creates breathing and blood flow problems. A large enough dose will cause paralysis in the internal organs, causing suffocation, then it dissipates. Unfortunately, if it dissipates, it can't be traced."

"Hmm, so what's the other tidbit?"

"The corpse that was done by the anti-freeze poisoning is still fresh. Somebody killed her and put her on ice."

"No shit? How long?"

"That, I couldn't tell you. Sliding a thermometer into the liver trick hasn't given me a clue. But this is all theoretical, Bonesteel. I'll be waiting on lab reports for at least a couple months before I can validate my findings. Besides, we won't know who she is until her teeth impressions get back from the dental lab, but that should happen sooner. So, if you want to help out on this, Mister P.I., I'll fax you her stats along with a snapshot of her face."

"That, I can do!" replies Rob with enthusiasm. "I've got the police missing persons database file logged into my computer. How far should I go back?"

"Try anywhere from six to eighteen months."

"Gotcha! And don't worry, Harry, after talking to Bob Wayne, I think he's anxious to get your car back so he can get twice paid."

"Dumbass, you didn't mention the finder's fee I'm paying you?"

"Relax, Harry. Sometimes you've got to invest some to win some."

Rob fights through Nimitz Freeway traffic and takes the Los Gatos Boulevard exit. He parks, then rushes into the atrium of Cashmere Properties. Before he can reach the stairwell leading to his second floor office, Aliya Bonesteel interrupts, "Hey Rob, you got a minute?"

"Not now, Sis, I'm on a mission."

When Rob enters his office, Sunny's got her feet propped on a chair. She just finished putting on a coat of nail polish and she's fanning the air while watching the Wendy Williams Show on her video cell.

"Sunny, did you get Harry's fax?"

Sunny picks up a sheet of paper from Rob's desktop. She holds it gently between her forefinger and thumb.

"Bingo!" said Rob after snatching it.

"Boy, you're a bundle of enthusiasm. We got a new case?"

"Not exactly. I'm helping Newman on an unsolved murder."

"Well, your desk misses you, Robbie. And it's piled with unsolved cases. Cases that pay the rent and our expenses."

"Ah, we don't pay rent, remember. Aliya owns this building as well as our apartment. All we've got to do is help pay utilities and taxes."

"Oh Robbie, I love it when you talk dirty to me," teases Sunny as she rolls her eyes to the left and then to the right. "You're so hilarious. You got me breaking out in hives."

"Quit being ridiculous," replies Rob. "Where are we having dinner tonight?"

"I knew you'd ask me that, so I made reservations at Khartoum's."

"Isn't that a pub?"

"They were, but they did some remodeling. There's a new addition. It's called The Black Kettle Steak House."

"Sounds good. I wonder what kind of desserts they've got listed?"

"Oh, don't worry about that, Robbie," replied Sunny as she crosses then uncrosses her legs, "I got your dessert right here."

Rob froze. He sees a flash of black lace undergarment with a patch of blond hair peeking back at him. It's Sunny's crotchless panties.

Sunny giggles, "I see you peekin' but you ain't speakin' Robbie."

Sunny is five-two and weighs one hundred and ten pounds. Rob snatches her by the waist and hoists her atop his mahogany desk. Her legs are cocked at quarter past twelve. In a flash, he's already in and humping.

"Silly rabbit," decrees Sunny, "aren't you gonna lock the door?"

"We ain't got time," answers Rob huskily, "because, I'm about ready to explode."

By dusk, Tahoe and Niecee had dressed and were ready to roll. It was a chilly night. The patchy sky and quarter moon were pale. They hitched a ride to Race Street and The Alameda, one of the city's main boulevards. Boarding a crowded number 22 bus and crossing the Nimitz Freeway overpass, Tahoe reached up and tugged on a cable. A bell dinged twice and the driver pulled over. The girls exited from the rear and jaywalked through bumper to bumper traffic to the other side of the street.

The Bell Motel was one of several tucked between aging apartment buildings and a variety of nine-to-five businesses that stretched along the boulevard. There were shady oaks and elms, narrow sidewalks and patches of neatly trimmed lawns. An old residential neighborhood bordered the back fences of the business district. Facing traffic with their backs toward the motel, Tahoe lit a long brown cigarette and Niecee waved at drivers that honked. The girls chose the location because the area was safe, a short block from the freeway, and a perfect spot to hitch a ride or maybe meet a guy who wanted to party.

Frank Dean George was the owner of the Bell Motel. The same Frank Dean whose brothers, Billy Bear and Bob Wayne, ran the wrecking and towing yard on Old Oakland Road. While Tahoe and Niecee were waving at cars, Frank Dean strolled up. He'd just finished having dinner at his favorite neighborhood restaurant. He was wearing a burnt sienna suit with tan pinstripes running through it. His shoes were two-toned, white and brown Stacy Adams, and a charcoal brown brim was worn ace-cock-duce, leaning to the side. His shirt was tan, starched, and the sleeves were rolled up to his forearms. His suit jacket was slung over his left shoulder. A lean six-two with high cheek bones and leathery skin, Frank Dean peered at the girls through bottle thick wire rimmed glasses. Niecee's bodacious butt in pink spandex was the neon sign that brought Frank Dean's gallop to a halt.

"Now that's what I'm talking about!" he shouted as he propped his hand under his chin and struck a pose.

Niecee, with arms folded across her ample bosom, flashed Frank Dean a coy smile, but when Frank glanced in Tahoe's direction, she looked back at him like she'd just caught him going through her purse. Tahoe's fierceness didn't faze Frank Dean. He knew what the girls were up to. He'd seen their kind in the area many times before. He played it safe and gave them the benefit of the doubt.

"My name is Frank Dean, ladies, and some of my friends call me George." He tipped his brim and smiled. His thin caramel lips stretched from one ear to the other, and the muscles in his clean shaven face seemed to ripple when he spoke. His voice was soothing. His eyes were not evasive. His years were measured in hangovers. "If you're waiting for the bus, it's not gonna arrive for another hour, and I've got a nice big heater and a couple six packs on ice if you'd care to keep me company for a spell."

"We're not waitin' for the bus!" decreed Tahoe as she flicked ashes from her brown one.

"Aw, girl," cried Niecee, "he's just being nice. And hey, you got a car, Mista George?"

"I've got a truck," he replied cheerfully.

Niecee winked at Tahoe and hooked Frank's right arm with her left. "Okay, Mista' George, show us the way."

Tahoe was indifferent. She let out a sigh, flicked her cigarette toward the pavement and sauntered a few feet behind.

The Bell Motel was three buildings, two rectangular and the third was square. The pair ran parallel and on opposite sides of a graveled driveway with parking spaces out front. There were eighteen units total, nine in one building, eight in the other, and the last unit occupied the square building by itself. A Pakistani manager and his wife lived in the office unit with a kitchenette. Their shades were open when Fran Dean and the girls walked by. The couple was up and about. They spotted the trio and waved, and Frank Dean yelled, "Namaskar!" which is Hindi. It means both hello and goodbye.

The third building was positioned at the rear of the parking lot. It was Frank's unit, number eighteen. It had a private carport, storage room, and utility shed. Upon entering the humble abode, the girls were surprised by the apartment's coziness and warmth, and they marveled at the colorful arrangement of Indian ornaments and artifacts that it contained. At first, the girls were composed and played it cool, but after a few sips of beer they hit their host with an onslaught of questions.

Frank Dean's great grandfather was a chief of one of the Cherokee tribes that was forced to give up their land in South Carolina and move to a reservation in Oklahoma. The new land was worthless until someone discovered oil. Realizing their grievous mistake, the government tried to buy back the deeds. Chief George held out for the highest bid, then took his family and two brothers and headed west.

Together, they purchased more land and settled in the Santa Cruz Mountains. When the Chief's squaw passed away, he took up with a young black girl, who became Frank Dean's great grandma, Anna Mae George.

The girls were completely mesmerized as Frank shared his private world and the intricacies of his family's past. When the beer ran out, they switched to wine. Frank Dean made his own wine from ripened grapes in his cool dark cellar. He said he owned property in Morgan Hill as well as a lake between Lexington Reservoir and Summit Road. He believed that wine was a delight and a challenge and never meant to be drunk too quickly.

"Wine should be savored," he told Niecee as she was feeling a little frisky while gulping the sparkling pink vin rose'. "Don't gulp, Princess, savor it," he coached.

Niecee was fawning over Frank's attentiveness and obvious affection, but whenever he left the room or diverted his focus, Tahoe would roll her big brown eyes, stick her finger down her throat and feign a gag. The girls giggled and laughed, and Frank was fine with that. He'd often laugh right along with them or he'd come back from whatever he was doing and prop himself between them and teach them some more.

"All the senses are awakened when you drink wine," he'd preach. "You drink with your eyes, tongue and throat." And he'd go on and on, "Notice the colors the wine makes in the glass."

His ceaseless chatter did not annoy the girls. They loved getting smashed and they knew that they could drink this old fool under the table. But like so many lonely men, Frank Dean had a dark side the girls knew nothing about. After a while, his bloodshot eyes became more bleary. His posture became hunched and his chest appeared slightly concave, yet he was still chatty and alert. He slipped from one conversation and oozed into another, and this night wasn't a night he'd allow his dark character to show.

"Well, ladies, are you still interested in making it to that party? Where'd you say it was?"

"Santa Cruz," proclaimed Tahoe. "We've got to meet some friends at the Boardwalk and they're expecting us." Once again, Tahoe was telling half truths, but she wasn't one to be telegraphing her moves with just anybody.

"Well, let's get going," said Frank, "and, Princess, grab a case of that vin rose'."

"Let me help you with that," said Tahoe.

Niecee was tipsy. Frank grabbed her around the hips just to balance her, but he got himself a feel. Frank Dean continued to be the perfect gentleman, generous, hospitable, and a man of his word, but the truck he'd told the girls he had was actually an RV. It was a twenty-foot recreational vehicle with all the amenities.

They drifted down the Nimitz, Highway 17, with ease. The RV hugged the road like a Cadillac, and Frank had a vast collection of jazz and oldies CDs. When he dropped the girls off, *"You've Got Me Hypnotized"* could still be heard belching from stereo speakers. As he made a U-turn, his red tail-lights vanished into darkness. Grinding a gear, he drove away.

At twilight, Summit Road was bleak and foreboding. Only the night stars and a few county roadside lanterns cast a shadow of light through · the thatch of black forest. Summit Lake was on the west end of a creek that spilled into Lexington Reservoir. The two bodies of water were severed by the treacherous cliff windings of Highway 17, just a couple miles beyond the city of Los Gatos and a stone's throw from a village called Boulder Creek.

The lake was on private property, a citrus ranch owned by the George family for nearly a century. In the early days, the ranch supplied the locals with crops of lemons and oranges, and much later, tangerines. For a brief period the Georges hired and housed field workers. The laborers were mostly Mexican families and a few were black. The laborers' quarters were still intact, oblong bungalows made of iron and tin about seventy-five yards from the lake's north shore. A hundred yards beyond, camouflaged by a cluster of white pine, were two warehouses and an abandoned well with an underground stream. Thirty yards to the right of the main road lay a three storey graystone mansion which hadn't been lived in for several years. It was shrouded by a dozen towering redwoods and a pair of giant oaks. Six twelve-foot pillars supported its five-hundred foot porch and two dilapidated terraces.

Since the death of the George's father, Frank Dean, the eldest son, became the sole owner of the Summit Lake property, while brothers Billy Bear and Bob Wayne took over running the wrecking yard and leased out a hundred acres of farm land just outside the city limits of a town called Morgan Hill.

When Frank Dean dropped Tahoe and Niecee in Santa Cruz, he made a stopover at Summit Lake. Since he'd taken over ownership about fifteen years ago, the once thriving citrus orchard had become strangled with stockpiles of lumber, old refrigerators, washing machines and hot water tanks. There was also one rusted out bulldozer, two tractors and a flatbed truck. Tall grass and brush weed had engulfed the unused machinery. The land and lake were in a hollow overlooking the highway about a mile and a quarter below.

Frank Dean had to drive up to his place with caution. High-beam headlights were a valued light source, and since the early Spring brought heavy rainfall, fallen branches and debris would often block his path. Eventually, he found a clearing where the ground was hard like clay and the grass wouldn't grow. There was plenty of room for a U-turn, so he cut the engine and parked.

Frank Dean was familiar with every path, tree and rock, and knew the best fishing holes in the hollow. The land had become a cavalcade of adventure for him and his brothers at the height of their youth. Using a heavy duty utility flashlight, he followed a path away from the mansion and down to the lake. The patchy fog had cleared and the quarter moon, with help from a spatter of stars, gave the lake an ominous glow. It was an unusually dry winter; the rainy season had been sparse. The bank's sandy slopes were barren for about four feet.

Frank Dean stepped onto a short pier where a rowboat was moored to one side and an aluminum raft to the other. With the beam from his flashlight he traversed the water's edge and stopped when he caught the glimmer of what he thought were bits and pieces of metal or white wood. On closer examination, he identified them as fish. Two dozen bloated fish. He'd found several of the same on a prior trip, although he hadn't taken time to figure out what was killing them, and he was puzzled because he didn't recognize the breed of fish. The lake was once rich with striped bass and trout, and most of them had swum back towards the reservoir. Yet the dead fish worried him. He decided to gather a few specimen and have the game warden check them out.

The lake and land calmed him, and despite the fact he was a functioning alcoholic, Frank felt he was always in control. Yet he knew it was alcohol that had shortened his father's life and made him the miserable bastard that would beat up his wife during a drunken stupor and strike his kids when they got in the way. It wasn't until

Frank and his brothers got older and decided to strike back did the beatings stop. He recalled his father's Jeckle and Hyde personality quite vividly, hard working, gentle and kind, or lecherous, vile and destructive.

Actually, Frank Dean was never in complete denial about his own disease. There were plenty of episodes of bloody fistfights that sprung up amongst he and his brothers whenever they attempted to drink together. And outsiders best not interfere or they would become the brother's target of hate during a brawl.

What Frank Dean did do was fool himself into thinking his state of alcohol abuse was less severe than what he'd witnessed from his father. He'd tried AA but couldn't get past the fourth step. He'd always give up on the fourth; at least, that's what his sponsor said. "Take a fearless moral inventory, Frank. I assure you, you'll feel lots better." But for Frank Dean that would never happen, and his nightmares were getting worse. He needed to take his inventory before it was too late.

Frank suffered from blackouts. He'd disappear for a day or two. No one knew where he'd gone or what he'd done, and when asked, he'd lie. He'd fabricate because he was afraid. He was afraid he'd done something awful, just like the werewolf in horror movies. At times, it drove him angry and shaken, just because he couldn't remember. What havoc had he perpetrated? He just couldn't remember.

When the last bullfrog stopped its bellowed croak, Frank Dean heard the warehouse generator's whine. He was puzzled at first, yet, the sound was so familiar that it didn't strike him as odd. As far back as he could remember, the generator's refrigeration machines were set on automatic timers. They ran for five-hour cycles and shut down for one hour, twenty-four-seven, until someone shut them off. The refrigeration was once a necessity. The icy cold preserved the abundance of citrus crops. But there were no citrus fruits in storage anymore. There hadn't been any for years. Frank recalled buying and placing a heavy padlock on the door to the generator room, but he couldn't recall where he'd stashed the key. Perhaps the generator was activated due to some power line surge? Frank decided the hell with it. He'd leave it alone and eventually it would shut down on its own.

TROY

Khartoum's
Campbell City limits: 7:00 p.m.

ROB AND SUNNY ARRIVED at their dinner date ten minutes late. The restaurant's parking lot was full. They couldn't find a close alternative, so they parked the Subaru two blocks down the street. Khartoum's was jammed packed. It was Friday, payday, and way past cocktail hour. A lot of the after work crowd were too drunk to leave. Many patrons were ordering mugs of coffee just to sober up. The hostess checked the log and confirmed their reservations, yet they still had to wait an extra twenty minutes before their table was cleared.

Khartoum's decorum was antique furniture, tiffany laps, lots of oak and stained glass, a "Cheers" atmosphere. The Black Kettle was thirty feet beyond an archway and up one floor. Their theme was similar. The help dressed casual. The only uniformity were white monogrammed shirts and waist high apple green aprons. There were private booths in the smoking section and that's what Sunny had reserved.

Sunny wore an emerald colored dress with jade accessories. Her natural blond hair had red highlights in it, credited to her beautician trying out a new technique. Rob wore his signature blue on blue outfit, although he mixed it up a bit too much. Powder blue shirt, navy blue trousers, and a sapphire dinner jacket, with gray leather boots and a kufi to match.

The restaurant used a tag-team system. Each table was waited on by sets of three. The first waiter served the bread, butter and water. The next came with salad and eventually a selection of wines. And the third waiter took their order and delivered the main course. Rob refused the salad. He wanted it served along with the main course.

41

Sunny was amused by his request.

"Ooou, that's the stizzle," chimed Sunny. "Which do you like, Robbie? The waitress says one thing and you automatically choose another."

"You must know me by now," replied Rob, "I gotta do what I gotta do."

"Thanks for reminding me, I do what I gotta do," teased Sunny. "By the way, what's up with you and Newman?"

"Huh?"

"Like every time he comes up on a new case you put our cases on a back burner. I know he's a funny and mysterious kind of guy, but we're not the homicide division and you're not a C.S.I. 'Cause if you are, then it's something you forgot to mention when we decided to start this business."

Rob sets down his fork and dabs his mouth with a napkin, "I'm sorry, babe, and you're absolutely right. I just like to mix it up a little bit. I might learn something. You know what I'm sayin'?"

"That's fine with me, Robbie, but I'm gonna need some help 'cause we're about to lose our clientele, ya feel me?" Sunny bugs her eyes and punctuates the phrase just to get her clown on, and Rob bursts out laughing.

They were done with dinner a little before nine. After eating dessert, a spumoni and Neapolitan ice cream combo, Sunny smoked a cigarette and Rob polished off a double Brandy Alexander. Before leaving the restaurant, Rob texted his Uncle Floyd and Aunt Elizabeth and made arrangements to stop by.

The ride lasted an hour. The late evening traffic was sparse. Sunny became the designated driver and she loved to drive fast.

They pulled into the driveway at eleven o'clock. The Monterey mansion's motor court had gone through a redesign. An eight-foot tall marble fountain had been installed with a thick ring of multicolored petunias encircling it. Miniature palms were planted in huge ceramic pots, which were stationed along the path that led to the home's front doors. Sunny parked between a Cornice and a brand new Mercedes. Rob wanted her to park in front of the gazebo, but the space was already filled by a vehicle that was covered with a burgundy colored tarp.

Floyd opened the door and Elizabeth hugged them as they walked through the terra cotta tiled foyer and into a spacious step-down living room. The room was also refurbished with a lime green and soft yellow decor. There was a fragrant odor of apple blossom paint.

"Egad!" shrieked Sunny, "I like this new look, Aunt Liz. You've got an Asian flavor goin' on."

"I'm glad you like it," said Elizabeth, smiling, "I'm not quite finished with it. I'm still browsing through a variety of shops and magazines. I want to add some pottery pieces and an antique oriental screen."

"So where did you two love birds have dinner?" asked Floyd, rubbing his palms together then stuffing his hands inside his cardigan sweater pockets.

"We ate at the new Campbell Courtyard. You know the one that used to be called The Factory," replied Rob

"Hey, that place was once a hot night spot. Liz and I used to go there from time to time."

"Oh, I remember," Liz affirmed, "but I liked Sebastian's best. That was in Campbell's Prune Yard Shopping Center."

"That's right. It was a glass office high-rise restaurant with a fantastic view from the eleventh floor," exclaimed Floyd.

"Sounds romantic," cooed Sunny, leaning her head on Rob's left shoulder. "Well, Robbie and I ate at this new addition called The Black Kettle Steak House, not so romantic but the food and service were really good."

"HEY FLOYD!" came a bombastic voice from Floyd's library office, "I found something!"

Everyone cringed.

"I'll be right there!" yelled Floyd.

"Who was that?" moaned Rob.

"Why, it's Newman."

"Newman?"

"Yeah, Harry Newman. Isn't he a friend of yours?"

Rob's eyes widened and his jaw sagged. He looked like he was about to cry.

"Oh, wow!" chuckles Sunny, "wouldn't you know, Rob was on a case to get Harry's car out of hock."

"I know," said Floyd, "he already got it. It's parked outside."

"Where?"

"I think he parked it in front of the gazebo," added Elizabeth.

"Come on, Uncle Floyd," said Rob. The two men zip past the women and make a beeline toward the library office.

When Rob enters the office, he finds Newman hacking on Floyd's computer number two.   "Okay Harry, what gives?   Aren't you supposed to be at work?"

Newman dips his beefy right hand into a jumbo bag of microwave popcorn. He shoves some in his mouth before he begins talking. "Hey Bonesteel, glad you could make it." Newman reaches inside his coat pocket and hands Rob a check.

Rob grabs the check between his right thumb and forefinger, holds it up toward the light, and whistles, "Holy Moly! You feeling all right, Harry, because I'm not sure I deserve this!"

"Hey, you earned it, pal. I took your advice and paid those two George brothers off. They nearly broke their necks trying to get that Citroen back to me."

"Huh, money talks, bullshit walks," countered Rob.

"How right you are, pal. Hey, Floyd, let's show Rob what we've been up to."

"Sure thing, Harry." Floyd gets situated at computer number one and both he and Harry are clicking away on their keyboards. "Okay, I'm ready, Harry."

"Rob, take a look at Floyd's map simulation. It shows every state park on the West Coast. Now look over here at my map. It targets Oregon, Northern and Central California, and Nevada's Reno and Tahoe area."

"What are the red triangles for?" inquired Rob.

"Each triangular area designates where a corpse was discovered over an approximate twelve year span."

Rob begins a count moving his index finger across the screen.

"No need to count," said Floyd, "there's thirty-two total."

"Yeah, twelve males and twenty females," intoned Newman. "Fourteen have bullet holes in them and eighteen are dead by various causes, and some show traces of some type of poison."

"So how do all these deaths relate to your two latest vics?" quizzed Rob. "One was found under a riverbed near a residential park and the other was found in a Scott's Valley forest, right?"

"Exactamundo," decrees Newman, "and I believe they're related to some of these other cases but I need more facts. Lots more facts," he concluded by throwing another handful of popcorn into his mouth.

At four a.m. the sun's rays crept over hilltops and darted through the foliage of Boulder Creek's forest. A red-tailed hawk hovered and

Troy Dominique made a right turn from Maple Hill Cemetery's driveway and merged into Highway 9's two-lane traffic. He drove a silver-gray hearse Cadillac. The back end was chopped, the windows and roof remained. A metallic three-foot CB antenna was stuck to a fender near the windshield's passenger side. A rusty green industrial wood chipper was bob-tailed to its bumper.

About half an hour into his drive, Troy entered Santa Cruz city limits. He continued south, switching over to Highway 1, and fifteen minutes later he made a left onto Highway 152. By five a.m. he was headed north on Highway 140. He sailed through the city limits of Merced and Mariposa until he reached the perimeter of Yosemite National Park.

Troy took an off-shoulder roadway and followed a fire trail that veered into a marshy ravine. The gulch was smothered in foxtails, tall sticky olive grass and clumps of short and stocky bamboo. Once he was certain his vehicle was hidden from the traffic of prying eyes, he cut the engine, crawled over the front seat and opened the side panel doors.

With the doors flung wide like the wings of a giant butterfly, he muscled out a white heavy duty Glad Bag. With ease, he hoisted it onto his left shoulder and trudged deeper into the forest. After a hundred yards, he was ankle deep in orange sticky mud. He flipped the hefty bag off his shoulder, and using a hunting knife, he slit the bag from top to bottom, severed the knotted end, then suddenly, he stopped. Standing still, a light breeze slashed his face. The sleeveless khaki coveralls displayed his twenty-inch biceps and a web of bluish veins that ran the length of his arms.

Once the caw of crows and screech of blue jays started up again, Troy reached into his hip pocket, removed a brown handkerchief, and wiped the sweat from his brow. With what seemed like a burst of new energy, he snatched the open end of the Glad Bag and flung it like a track and field contestant doing a hammer throw. The contents whistled through the chilled morning air and traveled for about seventy feet. It exploded off a massive redwood and split into several parts. The remnants of the shredded bag was still stuck to Troy's fingers.

He remained still for about ninety seconds, then he cracked the knuckles of both hands and trudged back through the bush the same way he'd come. Re-entering the hearse through side panel doors, he maneuvered into the front seat, cranked the engine and checked the Cadillac's console. It was six-thirty a.m. That gave him plenty of time to get to his jobsite, the trimming of twenty-five palms on an apricot farm just eight miles outside the city of Merced.

Troy Lester Dominique is a skilled landscaper who has owned a tree trimming business since he was seventeen. Now at age twenty-nine, he worked jobs as far north as Eureka, Redding, Ukiah, and a few areas to the south. As a boy, he perfected his skill by doing trail work with loggers in the Santa Cruz Mountains.

Troy's family moved from Haiti to the Boulder Creek area when he was twelve. His father, a mortician, took over the area's lone cemetery and mortuary service. Troy was a bright and adventurous kid, a lanky six-foot-three with big green caterpillar eyes. He was a popular kid amongst his classmates, although he disliked attending Montessori, a private Catholic school. He hung out with almost anyone and tried to impress no one. Yet, when approaching him, Troy would nod his head or smile rather than speak, due to a speech impediment. He was born with a tongue that was half the normal size.

In his spare time, he liked to rock climb and explore the Santa Cruz Mountains because it reminded him of similar mountain ranges from his Haitian home. He loved to hunt and the ritual of killing animals was never a problem for him.

Around age eleven, Troy killed a human being. He was playing in a Haitian forest and stumbled upon a camper who reeked of alcohol and was curled into a sleeping bag, obviously trying to sleep it off. Pulling what he thought was a harmless prank, Troy set fire to the foot of the camper's sleeping bag and hid out in the bush to observe the reaction.

Unfortunately, his prank turned ugly when the sleeping bag erupted into flames and the camper panicked in his attempt to escape. Troy became paralyzed as the camper began to scream and the sleeping bag jittered recklessly across the earthen floor like a flailing fish desperately seeking water. Troy snapped out of his stupor and tried stomping out the flames. In the end, the fire is not what killed the camper. He died of fright because his heart gave out.

Even though Troy understood the gravity of what he'd done, he didn't have the ability to process his emotions like ordinary people. The screams of the camper reminded him of something he'd seen on a Saturday morning cartoon, an image that would intrigue his impressionable mind, dangerous and forbidden, yet somewhat magical. As years passed, it ignited a craving in Troy. The boy grew up to devalue human life.

Troy was only fourteen when he committed his second murder. It was not premeditated. Only an experiment, a fantasy he was trying to fulfill. He had an interlude with an older woman, a female pedophile, although he didn't know it at the time. She was a woman he'd met on a secluded Santa Cruz beach. Her plan was to have sexual intercourse inside a beach cave.

At first, the woman was in complete control, but Troy didn't care about sex. His stimulus was something quite different. After smoking a joint, he got her to eat some hallucinogenic mushrooms that had been laced with a poisonous extract from puffer fish, an old Haitian formula used to create deep sleep. Troy had stolen the mushrooms from his grandma and was eager to try them out.

Suddenly, the lady keeled over. Her silent mimed screams were never heard. Within seconds, her heart stopped and a minute later it started up again. Her wide sad eyes never shut. The woman was alive but completely paralyzed. There was an antidote but Troy had no knowledge of it. Maybe his grandmother knew, but he had no time to find out. Troy did what he thought was his only alternative. He hid the woman in a cold storage unit, a neighboring farmer's industrial freezer. The same freezer that was on Frank Dean George's land. He kept her there for several days and would check on her from time to time. Troy expected the lady to come back to life and just walk away with no memory of what happened, just like his grandmother once told him. Yet, the risk of keeping her there was too great, so he stripped her naked and dumped her into a wooded ravine where mountain lions roamed.

While Troy Dominique was out canvassing California's state parks, Tahoe and Niecee were drinking fat mugs of coffee on a friend's houseboat along the Santa Cruz Harbor. The bash they'd heard about was only a house party, so they spent the night. It was Saturday morning and they were exactly where they were supposed to be. Tahoe had scheduled an appointment with their attorney that Niecee knew nothing about. Besides, Niecee was too engrossed with the texts that Frank Dean kept sending to her phone.

"Who's that?" asked Tahoe, sipping her coffee and filling the boat's galley with cigarette smoke.

"It's Mista' George."

"Again? Isn't that his fifth text?"

"Fo' real!" replied Niecee, pouting her lips and tilting her head to one side, "I think he likes my loose booty."

"Girlfriend, spare me the nickel and dime conversation. Tell him you're a square broad and you can't control the shake," quipped Tahoe.

"Tahoe, he really does like me, 'cause I told him I would play with his Jolly Ranchers."

"Ding dong! Cock-a-doodle-do! That's more than like. I'm telling you, girl, that dude will soon be stalking you. You'd best be careful with him, 'cause he's old enough to be your daddy. Besides, you won't be needing to pursue his dollars anymore 'cause we're about to be rich!"

The law firm's receptionist frowned and Tahoe ignored her and continued with her loudness. Finally, after a thirty minute wait, the receptionist stood, straightened her skirt and made a gesture toward the lawyer's office, "Mister Hines will see you now," she said in a nasal tone. The girls quickly rose from their seats and marched past the receptionist like they were dignitaries from Ghana.

The oversized windowless office walls were plastered with certificates, photos and awards. A polished leather golf bag complete with monogrammed irons was leaning on the edge of a cluttered mahogany desk. The obese baldheaded lawyer held two cell phones. He signed off on one and continued chatting on the other. When the girls strolled over to his desk, he ended that call as well.

"Hello, girls," he said, grinning like a jagged toothed shark sizing up a meal, "please get comfy and take a seat. As I told you over the phone, we've reached a respectable settlement with the opposing firm and if you agree to accept this offer, then we're ready to cut you a check this afternoon."

The girls were bug-eyed, leaning forward at the edge of their seats. Tahoe's left hand was clasping Niecee's wrist. They appeared to be holding their breath.

"A check?" chirped Niecee.

"Yes, a check," the lawyer replied.

"How much?" crowed Tahoe.

"Three million," said the lawyer, still grinning.

The girls were stunned. They glanced at one another, then back at the lawyer. He smiled some more and continued. "That's three million minus the firm's customary thirty-three and a third percent, as well as the twenty thousand we advanced you over the last eight months. In addition, it's taxable income. So that would leave you with, ah, let me see." He takes a moment to fiddle with a hand held calculator. "Ah, one point seven million split. Would you like separate checks or shall I write you a lump sum?"

"Oompa loompa! Of course we want separate checks."

Completely startled, the lawyer jumps to his feet because Niecee had just fainted. She fell sideways from her chair with a thud, like a two hundred pound sack of brown rice. The right side of her head met the plush carpeted floor, but Tahoe's quick reflexes softened the blow. The lawyer took nothing for granted. He called 911 and ten minutes later Niecee was examined by a team of EMTs. She was given a clean bill of health, but the lawyer still referred her to the firm's personal physician.

The one point seven million was split down the middle and wired to two different banks. The process was much quicker than waiting on the checks to be written that afternoon. Niecee's eight hundred and fifty thousand went to her Wells Fargo account, and Tahoe's equal split was deposited with Chase Manhattan Bank.

The girls were ecstatic. It was five past eleven in the morning. They couldn't agree on what they needed to do first. They were only a couple blocks away from the Santa Cruz Boardwalk, so they headed in that direction. Along the way, they ran up to a Foster Freeze and Niecee ordered a root beer float while Tahoe decided on a banana split covered in chocolate chips. Their orders were taken from a walk-up window and they ate at a canopied table near the parking lot.

"Just quit it, Niecee."

"What?"

"Relax, girlfriend, 'cause your jitterbug knees are causing the whole table to shake. You shouldn't be eating ice cream if you're cold."

"I'm not cold, silly, I'm just excited. Hey, let's call Brenda and tell her the good news."

"Hmm, I was just thinking the same thing. She's a smart business woman."

"Yeah, a smart one she is!" counters Niecee with an owl-eyed expression.

"I thought I just said that." Tahoe removes her cell from her blue jean's front pocket and makes the call.

"Good morning, Cheesecake Productions, Brenda speaking."

"Hey dawg, guess what?"

"Tahoe, is that you?"

"Hell yeah, it's me. We're rich, Boss Lady! We got paid!"

"Ahh!" shouts Brenda. "No, you didn't!"

"Yes, we did!"

"Ooou-Wee. Okay, let me calm down. How much you get?"

"A million point seven."

"Apiece?"

"No, split down the middle."

"Hot damn, bitch! What are your plans? Are you still gonna work for me?"

"No way! We're gonna start our own striptease business."

"Really?"

"Nah, I'm just kiddin', Boss Lady. But first we need to buy a house, cars, and a whole bunch of stuff. Got any ideas?"

"Well, the last thing you wanna do is go on a spending spree and telegraphing your moves. The whole world doesn't need to know that you came into some dough, you dig? So, you and Niecee put your heads together and slow it down some. Look, I've gotta do a deal with some clients this afternoon, but give me a call back this evening and we'll celebrate, my treat."

"Alright, that sounds cool."

"Hold up a sec. Let me give my sister-in-law, Aliya Bonesteel, a call-back. I was just talking to her. You know she's a real estate broker out in Los Gatos, and she just happens to be showing a place down on Ocean Avenue as we speak. Sit tight, I'll have her call you in about five minutes. Does that sound cool?"

"Ya damn skippy!" shouts Niecee as she leans on Tahoe's shoulder with her ear to the phone.

Aliya's arrival didn't take long. She pulled up in a champagne colored Beemer convertible 650i. The girls watched in awe as the driver's door swung open and a pair of glass stiletto heels touched down on the graveled lot. Aliya was a statuesque brunette sporting a short and wavy shag. Her business pantsuit ensemble was polymer white on white. She wore a pair of platinum framed designer shades with a platinum necklace and bracelets to match. She held a silver cased cell in her right hand and a slim lit cigarette in her left. Smiling, she approached the two girls and extended her jeweled right hand.

"Hi, I'm Aliya. You must be..."

"Niecee and Tahoe," they chimed, with each girl pointing a finger at the other.

"Well, I'm pleased to make your acquaintance. I offer my warmest congratulations. Brenda gave me an update on your situation. I hope I can be of some help."

The girls both started jabbering at once and Aliya could barely make out what they were saying. Their enthusiasm was infectious. Aliya threw up her hands and waved at them to stop.

"Girls, girls, just listen. I have an idea. First, you'll be needing some transportation, and that's my brother Houston's department, although he's out of town on business at the moment. I'm assuming you both have a driver's license?"

The girls were clinging to every syllable that came from Aliya's mouth. They stared at her perfect sparkling teeth and nodded their heads as she continued to speak.

"I've got a car I keep at my brother's garage. It's in mint condition and, yes, it's insured. I'll loan it to you until you figure out what kind of car you'll want to buy. Brenda is right, you need a guide, and I'll be just that if you'll let me. When my husband died, I became the beneficiary of his million dollar life insurance and his real estate business. At the time, I didn't own a business license nor the knowledge of how to run it."

For the first time in their lives the girls were silent and polite. Aliya was taken by their attentiveness. They were so young, she thought, Niecee, twenty-one, and Tahoe, twenty-two. They were definitely intelligent and strong willed. They reminded Aliya of herself when she was just starting out. "Okay, enough with the small talk. If you're ready to do some house hunting, then follow me."

They piled into the BMW. Niecee took the front passenger seat and Tahoe sat in the back. The cloudless sky was a perfect pale blue. It was almost noon, seventy-six degrees. It was going to be a warm afternoon. Aliya turned on the sound system and slipped the gear into reverse, as Jill Scot's melodic whisper breezed through the state-of-the-art speakers. They got on the Nimitz freeway and streaked towards The Cats, the town of Los Gatos.

Troy was thirsty, and he'd just finished trimming his third desert palm. It was his fourth day on the Merced farm, twelve trees down with thirteen to go. Not a bad pace for a job that paid two hundred dollars per tree. The giant palms were at least fifty years old and hadn't been trimmed in the last twenty years, or so it seemed. It was risky and dangerous work for a person working alone. One had to be strong, especially in the legs. Troy used a variety of ropes, hooks, fasteners and saws. There were only certain types of sailor's knots he trusted with his life. Fifty feet up in the air was pretty high. A fall would probably kill him or break most of the bones in his body.

The heart of the palm clusters were full of treachery. They were home to creepy things from bats to poisonous spiders and rodents. On occasion, it could be the home of a family of opossums or maybe some raccoons. Troy was never amazed at what he'd find hiding in a tree. He wore a goggled mask and thick workman's gloves. He was prepared for anything and accustomed to working at a torrid pace.

At eleven-thirty, he climbed down and took an early break. He'd planned to take half an hour for lunch and his day would be finished by two o'clock. About eight hundred dollars for seven hours, a nice fat salary for a short day's work.

He ate inside the hearse with both driver and passenger doors flung wide open. In his cooler was a gallon of papaya juice, five apples, a half dozen bananas and several other fruits. He kept a battered GE portable radio that ran on six 'D' sized batteries. He had it rigged up so he could piggy back a Sony CD player. He carried a collection of fifty New Age albums: Yanni, Enya, Pure Moods, Deep Forest, and Healing CDs, the ultimate and most relaxing music one could buy.

The farm he was working at was one of the oldest in the area. Three hundred acres of apricots, prunes and plumbs. The harvest season was two months away, so there were only a handful of laborers monitoring the fields.

After lunch, Troy scoured the grove. He kept a pair of army field binoculars in his glovebox. He'd scope the area by lying flat on the roof of his hearse. For the past two days he'd been zooming in on one of the farmer's daughters sunning herself atop a fruit drying shed. Her bikini was the spaghetti type, colored lime green. She had natural shoulder length auburn hair and dark olive skin. Her torso and legs were muscular and sleek. Troy determined her height to be about five foot-eight. He sensed she knew he was watching, because at the end of each day she'd zip past him in her red Mustang convertible and honk.

Troy set the binoculars aside and proceeded with his knuckle cracking ritual. His mind was moving at warp speed. He knew the exact location of the garage and where all the cars were parked. He moved with the swiftness of a cheetah and the grace of a gazelle. He was a hunter and he had a plan.

By two o'clock, Troy had gathered his tools. He'd just shoved the last palm leaf into his wood chipper when the red Ford zipped past and, instead of honking, she waved. Seconds later, his boss drove up from the opposite direction. He pulled up to the wood chipper's rear and let the truck engine idle and spoke to Troy from the cab. "Hey, nice work, buddy!" He made a thumbs up gesture and Troy smiled. "I realize that this is your weekend, but I really need you to come back tomorrow."

Troy frowned, "Maybe, but it's Sunday."

"I know, I know. But if you can take down a half dozen tomorrow, I'll double your pay."

Again, Troy smiles, a little broader this time. "Hey, I can do that. No problem. I'll be back tomorrow around six."

The owner drove toward the main house and Troy fired up the hearse and headed for the highway. About five miles into his drive he pulled off the roadway and slid behind a parked car. It was The red Ford Mustang. The hood was up and the farmer's daughter was leaning against the auto's front fender with her arms folded. Troy got out and offered to help.

She said she didn't know what happened. The car had been running fine when suddenly there were grinding noise and smoke and she lost power. She said her gas tank was at least half full, so she knew she hadn't run out of gas. Luckily, she had been driving in the slow lane and was able to steer off onto the shoulder of the highway.

Troy told her wasn't a mechanic, but it wouldn't be going out of his way, so he offered to take her home. She agreed since she had forgotten to bring her cell phone and Troy told her he didn't have one. She climbed into the hearse front seat and smiled when Troy slipped behind the wheel. Troy had to travel another two miles before he could reach an exit that led them over the freeway and back the direction they'd come.

After making the exit, Troy detoured down a dusty wooded road, then he cut the engine. The hearse glided for a moment then stopped. The girl was calm, yet curious. She bad no reason to panic. If it was an invitation for spontaneous sex, she was willing. She didn't mind because she was very much attracted to the guy behind the wheel.

Troy flipped a switch. There was a thunk. A hidden latch had bolted the passenger side door. The girl instinctively pushed, but the door wouldn't budge. She searched for a handle, but there was none. She couldn't roll the window down. When she returned her focus back to Troy, he was wearing a mask with goggles and an oxygen canister. There was something in his hand.

He sprayed her in the face. Her hands flew up, but it was too late. The amyl nitrite was a fancy version of nitroglycerin. It was stored in a cylinder receptacle instead of a capsule. It diminished the supply of oxygen to her brain. Within seconds she began to weaken. Her eyes narrowed. Her vision was blurred. She tossed her head from side to side and kicked at the windshield. She was frantic but not giving up. She flipped into the back seat and dove headlong for the side panel doors.

Troy caught her by the heels as the doors flew open. The girl was athletic, a goalie on her college soccer team. She managed a quarter spin and kicked him in his face. It twisted his mask and for a moment he couldn't see. He released his grip and the girl bolted. Her heels dashed the roadway. She was in a dead sprint.

Troy didn't panic. The girl had made a crucial mistake. She'd run deeper into the woods instead of towards the freeway. He knew eventually she would get disoriented and tired. The wooded area was an abandoned orchard. The land hadn't been worked for the past five years. The farmer had sold out to some industrial firm. There were signs posted about trespassing and warning hunters to keep out. Troy was a hunter. Seeing the signs made him smile.

Troy disconnected the wood chipper and started the hearse's engine. He cruised along the roadway for three-quarters of a mile before he spotted her. She was zigzagging from one tree to another and running out of steam. The hearse crept up on her. Her stamina had drained. She had no power in her limbs. She tumbled to the ground, spread eagle. Troy got out and grabbed her like a ragdoll by the collar of her blouse. She thrashed her legs wildly, similar to an injured frog trying to reach water but stuck on dry land.

Troy wielded a sledgehammer and smashed her upside the head, knocking her unconscious. He tied her hands and feet and tossed her in the front seat. He drove back to where he'd left the wood chipper and reconnected it to the vehicle's rear. He turned on his police scanner and drove off the roadway, moving further into the field.

By five o'clock, be had driven into town, cashed his check and eaten a quick meal. Then he located a self-service carwash and cleaned the chipper as well as the hearse and a couple of tools. He towel dried the sledge hammer and a pair of long-handled shears and placed them in a cargo box. Then he shut down his scanner and continued westbound on Highway 140.

OOMPA LOOMPA!

Bell Motel
Saturday, April 16th

FRANK DEAN FELT HIMSELF sliding into a funk. His day had started okay with Niecee, exchanging text messages back and forth. This went on for quite some time, but suddenly his texts weren't being answered. Puzzled, he shrugged it off and went forward with his plans. He made a seven o'clock dinner reservation for two at Palo's Fine Cuisine. He called Navelet's Florist and placed an order, a bouquet of twenty red and yellow roses. He planned to pick them up on his return trip from his doctor's appointment later in the afternoon. He needed a drink, but that would have to wait.

For now, a quart of apple juice was followed by a short bottle of castor oil. He had awakened with a sore throat. It was the wrong time to be sick. After downing the oil, he scarfed up a lemon and two grapefruits. Then he walked over to the kitchen sink where he gagged and spat. After of a couple deep breaths, he took a toilet break. He showered and shaved, primped before a mirror, and proceeded to get dressed.

The attire be chose was black. Everything was black. Black satin boxers, a sleeveless undershirt and rayon knee-high socks. His Levi's were jet black with a perfect crease and adjustable button flaps on each side. He didn't need a belt; his Asian laundry lady added just enough starch so the trousers could almost stand upright. Black moccasin boots adorned with two gray tassels to tie them. Before putting on his dress shirt, he snapped on a modified back brace which touched the top of his hip bone and stopped an inch beyond his diaphragm. The wide elastic band fit snug against his lower ribs. It was tailored in layers of pleats resembling a tuxedo cummerbund.

It was here that Frank Dean stashed his I.D. and a wad of cash.

On his right side a cell phone was placed, and in the middle of his spine he hid a Smith & Wesson, an ivory handled .22. Over his black silk dress shirt, his jacket was a black corduroy fabric with a reversible lining, water repellent and squared off at the bottom. It reached the top of his thighs. He wore a rawhide string tie around his neck with a mother of pearl slider. His curly salt and pepper hair reached the nape of his neck, and set snuggly over it was a black short brimmed Panama hat with an indigo band.

Frank Dean was driving a Dodge Ram pickup. He had direct access to whatever came through the salvage and towing yard. This one was painted black and practically new. His brothers' tow policies were strict. They'd hold a vehicle for no more than two months, then it was off to the auction block if no one made an effort to pay the storage fees and claim the vehicle. The storage was fifty dollars a day. It didn't take long for a claim to reach the thousands, and in most cases the fee was greater than the vehicle's worth.

The doctor's office was no more than a couple miles from the Bell Motel. He took the scenic route, the back streets of a business and residential area. Down the Alameda, a left at Taylor. Taylor ran parallel to Julian and Julian later became McKee. McKee Road was on the east side of San Jose. It ran parallel to Alum Rock Boulevard, which meandered into the hills of a golf and country club with a picnic area and hiking trails.

The doctor's office was on McKee Road, somewhere between the 101 Freeway and King Road. The building was two storey, rectangular and brick. Frank Dean parked the Dodge. He was fifteen minutes early, so he took his time getting up to the second floor by using the outdoor stairwell. The doctor's office was a drug and alcohol treatment center. APOR was the acronym that was posted on the door. It was posted that way by design to provide the patients with some measure of anonymity.

The receptionist was blond, curvaceous and friendly. Her pink cotton blouse stretched across her ample bosom. Upon seeing the girl, Frank Dean's eyes widened and his eyebrows arched from behind coke-bottle lenses. She smiled broadly and welcomed him in. She seemed to be pleased to have someone admiring her. The waiting room was full, about nine clients thumbing through magazines and drinking coffee from Styrofoam cups. The doctor was behind schedule, but Frank's wait wasn't long.

Dr. Denardo was a psychiatrist. She was tall, five-foot-nine, thick bodied, large boned. Her strawberry blond hair was disheveled. She had friendly gray eyes, a wide mouth, thick pale lips and tea stained teeth. She spoke in a raspy voice as though she were hoarse from shouting at someone one too many times.

"Mister George, good to see you today. Glad you could make it."

Frank Dean was not in a talkative mood. He shook hands with her and took a seat in the lone chair that was centered in front of her desk. He removed his brim and placed it over his right knee. Dr. Denardo continued with her cheerful chatter.

"You seem to be fit and in good spirits considering your dilemma."

Frank feigned a smile. He had no prior experience with therapists. She was a nice enough person, but there was no place for therapists in Indian culture. Besides, he had a migraine and was wondering why Niecee hadn't called nor made any effort to return his last texts.

"Your attorney sent me a copy of your file. Give me a moment to review it."

Frank had received his third drunk driving offense. His attorney advised him on this therapy thing. Clock a few hours, is what he advised. The judge would be more lenient if Frank was already getting help from an outpatient program. Frank Dean couldn't BS this woman. She verbally chin checked him a couple of times. She told him he was a classic bipolar manic depressive and that he needed to quit drinking. She said he inherited the disease and that the older he got, the more serious the bouts of depression and erratic behavior would become.

She pleaded with him. "Blackouts are dangerous, Mister George. Please, for God's sake, don't play Russian Roulette with your life or perhaps someone else's!" She prescribed three hundred milligrams of lithium carbonate, morning, noon and night. He thanked her, took the prescription, shook her hand and walked out.

It was two-fifteen p.m. and Frank still had several errands to run. He did pick up his prescription, read the label, then tossed it in his glove box. He never broke the seal. From his waistband he yanked out his cell and sent another text:

MADE REZ AT PALOS FOR 7
LET ME PULL UP IN YOUR GARAGE GIRL!

He paused for thirty seconds and Niecee texted him back.

OOOOOO DADDY!

YOU CAN WASH MY CAR ANY TIME!
Niecee said she was busy but she'd text him back around five.

At five-fifteen, Frank Dean picked up the floral arrangements. By six, Niecee still hadn't called. He sent her another text, and then another at six forty-five. He was headed for the restaurant and his gut was telling him he'd be eating alone and that he'd wasted the day making plans on someone who was too busy to care. Yet Frank still had a full night ahead of him and he wasn't about to waste it. He tried to remain positive and bury his hurt. He didn't eat. He left a fat tip and took a stroll to the Cinnabar, a pub directly across the street.

Jim the bartender was working that night. He set Frank up at his favorite table. The jukebox was right next to it. Frank Dean loaded it with quarters and picked his selections before the sad song that was already playing would end. No one, especially not Frank, could pinpoint when the blackout started, nor when it would come to an end. Frank chose one bluesy medley that was followed by another, then another. No one in the bar seemed to mind. The room was slightly dank and semi-dark. The only thing that glittered, besides the glass being held in each customer's hand, was the menagerie of liquor bottle reflections from the beveled mirror that ran the length of the bar. Someone fell from their bar stool, another yelped and someone else howled. There were utterances when the fallen one rose to his feet, after repeatedly refusing help. Those who were able to cheer, cheered, and those who were able to clap, did so. Then Frank George shrieked. The words came out as if he were crying or about to die.

"CAN A MAN GET A FUCKIN' DRINK IN THIS JOINT, OR DO I HAVE TO SPEND MY CHEESE SOMEWHERE ELSE?"

Bartender Jim was possibly the only person who could pinpoint which drink took Frank Dean to the abyss. Jim knew it was time for his patron to quit. Get him up and get him out. Frank's blank stare told Jim he wasn't the same personality that had walked inside the bar less than an hour ago. Perhaps it was after he downed his third White Dragon, or was it the half dozen Flaming Gorillas he doused? He seemed to be doing just fine, rocking to the tunes coming from the jukebox and sending text after text.

Frank Dean left the Cinnabar of his own accord. He located his keys, the parking lot and his vehicle. A major but almost improbable feat for any human in his condition. By ten o'clock he was driving, bound for nowhere on Highway 580, ending up in Manteca, a town with a population of about ten thousand just off Highway 99.

He parked his Dodge Ram in the shadows of an enormous willow. It was a new development. Fifty acres of tract homes where the fertilizer was still damp and the lawns hadn't yet sprouted. At midnight he shut off his headlights and shut down the engine. Then he stumbled out from the passenger side and took a leak. When he climbed back in, he released the hand brake. The pickup coasted downhill for several yards, then it came to a stop and blocked the driveway of a home. There were no cars parked on the streets because most of the homes were still empty. They had been sold but their occupants hadn't yet arrived. It was quite dark. Some of the street lamps were not on. The electrical wiring was incomplete. Other than the pulsating wings of tiny gnats and short gusts of wind blowing sheets of paper in several directions, the new neighborhood was deathly quiet.

Frank Dean sat motionless behind the Ford's steering wheel. After twenty minutes passed, he finally moved. He removed his jacket, turned it inside out, and put it back on. He slid the .22 from his waistband and swung open the passenger side door. It needed a lube job, so it made an eerie creak. In the dead of night sound travels, and before he could set his black moccasins on the pavement, the home's porch light came on.

Frank Dean was startled. He didn't realize it was an automatic timer device which was set to turn the porch light on and off at forty-five minute intervals. He climbed back in and gently shut the truck's door.

In his attempt to start the engine, the alternator whined and the plugs wouldn't spark. The carburetor was flooded. After a couple more attempts, Frank slammed his palms against the steering wheel and sat motionless for another three minutes.

Suddenly, out of nowhere, a dark clothed figure was approaching from the vehicle's rear. Frank glimpsed the reflection of a flashlight in his side mirror. He gave the gas pedal two successive pumps and turned the key. The engine coughed then sputtered to life. With enough force to bust the truck's door hinges, Frank flung his driver's side door open. The good Samaritan neighbor who carried a flashlight didn't have a chance to get within ten feet. Frank Dean fired three bullets from point blank range, one in the man's neck and two in the face.

In their wildest dreams, Niecee and Tahoe never thought that someday they'd be buying a home in the city of Los Gatos, a rustic development with backyard creeks and loaded with evergreens. It was built on slopes and hills with an elevation average of three hundred feet, a place where doctors, lawyers and celebrity sports figures lived.

They fell in love with the location of the third home Aliya showed. It was four blocks down Hull Street, right off Bascom Road and less than a mile from the Nimitz Freeway. A twenty-four hundred square foot wooden A-frame, built on a quarter acre lot sometime back in the sixties. It contained three bedrooms, a bath and a half, cellar, attic and a two car garage. The asking price was two hundred and fifty thousand dollars, which was quite a steal considering the neighboring homes' current market appraisals were well over half a million. Yet, there was still some fixing up to do, like a new roof, window repairs, minor problems with plumbing, a fresh paint job, and a heap of foliage and trash needed to be cleared from the backyard. After touring the home, the girls weren't sure they wanted to invest in a place that required so much work in order to bring it up to speed. They challenged Aliya to make a stronger pitch.

"Girls, you're right. Besides repairs, there are other costs that have to be considered. There's closing cost fees, fire insurance, and I recommend that you buy some life insurance as well."

"Life insurance?" squawked Tahoe.

"Yes, it's the smart way to go. Remember, insurance is what gave you the funds that are going to change your status in life."

"Hell, we're cool, Miss Aliya," insisted Niecee. "After that accident, ain't nothin' happening to us."

"How can you be so sure?" countered Aliya. "Life comes with many twists and turns."

"Fire and life insurance I can understand," proclaimed Tahoe, "but you want us to pay cash money for this old house? If it's such a deal, then why hasn't anybody bought it?"

Tahoe posed a good question and a smart one. Aliya had to change her tactics to try and win back the girls' interest. "Look, here's the deal, girls. Are you listening?" Tahoe was filing her pinky finger and Niecee was looking at a crack near the ceiling as though it were about to collapse.

Aliya continued with her pitch, "Yes, you're right, Tahoe. This is a depressed property, which means its condition is bringing down the value of the neighboring homes, and if it were up to them, they'd pay to have a demolition team come in and tear it down. But it's really a diamond in the rough. I'll help you get the right people to make repairs, and I'll guarantee the neighbors will sing praises because their property values will automatically increase with yours."

Aliya regained their attention by being brutally honest. "Niecee, you don't want to pay for any home in the full amount. You pay the required twenty percent, your closing cost, insurance and so forth. Once you've invested twenty to thirty thousand in repairs, your property value will automatically increase. In two to five years this home will be worth close to half of a million, maybe even more, and you will only have invested about a quarter of that amount. You can sell it and walk away with your original investment and perhaps a two hundred and fifty grand profit."

Although the real estate market wasn't an exact science and was dependent on other factors, Aliya knew that despite thousands of foreclosure casualties, the market was rebounding. The location of the Hull Street home was a prime one. Aliya never told the girls she actually owned the home. It was getting late and there were multiple forms to fill out, as well as a trip to the mortgage house and banks that would have to be done the following day. The girls agreed to allow Aliya to arrange the sale, so they drove back to Santa Cruz and made a stop at Houston's garage.

Niecee and Tahoe raved over the sports car. It resembled an old Porsche. The engine was in the rear and its chassis was low to the ground. The Karman Ghia was a discontinued Volkswagen model. It looked expensive but it actually was not. The only problem with it was the transmission. It was the standard type and neither Tahoe nor Niecee knew how to handle a stick shift or use a clutch. Aliya gave each girl a quick parking lot lesson, up to the street corner and back. Tahoe was easily frustrated, but Niecee caught on quick.

Before Aliya's departure for Los Gatos, she told the girls she'd give them a holler on Monday afternoon. By then she'd have a list of master craftsmen assembled to do the house repairs and a timetable to better estimate when the home would be ready for moving in. She also advised the girls to consider furnishing the home with inexpensive antique furniture rather than pricy stuff that glitters, because the value would depreciate much too rapidly. She could tell by their blank expressions that the girls didn't comprehend a word she was saying. She told them they could talk more freely about the idea on Saturday. She'd planned to spend the entire day at the Hull Street house and the girls were invited as long as they promised to stay out of the workers' way.

Afterwards, the girls gave Brenda a call to find out where she wanted to party. Brenda said everything was set. They'd be partying in San Francisco and she'd pick them up about seven-thirty. Now the girls were on a mission. They needed to get home in a hurry so they could change their clothes and get cleaned up.

"This is not gonna' work, girlfriend," said Tahoe, fiddling with the auto's radio dials and trying to get a clear station. "First thing tomorrow, I'm going shopping for a new car and a new wardrobe, and you betta' come with me!"

"What, thought I wasn't?" giggled Niecee. She slipped into the freeway traffic in third gear, then smoothly shifted into fourth. Merging with traffic, she was grinning the entire time. "Yeah, I'm coming," she joyously added, "I'm right with you on the wardrobe thing, but I like this car. I betcha' Miss Aliya will give me a sweet price on it too!"

"Huh, I ain't so sure about her. She's a smooth talker. She seems to always know exactly what to say when it comes to overcoming an objection."

"Ha! She's a saleswoman, silly. That's what she's trained to do. That chick knows how to make money. If we follow her advice, we'll be rollin' in dollars forever!"

"Well, maybe and maybe not, but I do like the location of the home. And once we get it fixed up, I know I'll like it even better."

"Yahoo!" yelped Niecee, "I'm so excited!"

"Ya damn skippy!" whooped Tahoe.

They bumped fists, then elbows, and finished the ritual by snapping their fingers twice. Tahoe finally tuned into KDON, a hip hop station broadcasting from Santa Cruz. They barreled down the Nimitz and took the 280 Freeway offramp and cruised into San Jose.

When they arrived at their Margaret Street cottage rental, their driveway entrance was lit up with three police cars and a small gathering of onlookers. At first, the girls thought their landlady had another stroke until they saw her standing near a uniformed officer. She waved the girls over as soon as she spotted them.

"They caught a burglar hiding in the attic of your cottage," said the landlady, her pale blue eyes widening.

"What?"

"A burglar?"

"Yeah, your next-door neighbor called the police about a prowler and when she called me on the phone, I saw him go around the side and climb through your kitchen window. Then he came out through the front door and sat on the porch, smoked a cigarette and went back in."

"That's Adam!" shrieked Niecee.

"Adam? You mean it's someone you know?"

"That sorry no good for nothin' motha."

"Yeah, we know him," said Niecee, cutting in on Tahoe, "but he had no right to break into our house."

Then a sergeant took a slow walk to where they were standing. He had a pencil and pad in his right hand, all his brass was sparkling. His tan uniform was starched and creased, and weighing no less than three hundred pounds, his watermelon sized belly hung way below his belt line.

"Miss Wisekoff, are these ladies your cottage tenants?"

"Yes, they are."

The sergeant turned his attention to the girls, "Do you know that man? He told us he's a friend of yours." The sergeant was pointing at Adam. Adam was standing next to a deputy about twenty paces away. He was in handcuffs and they really couldn't see his face because his shoulders were drooped and his head hung between them, but the girls didn't need to see his face. His funky Pendleton shirt, watch cap and trademark bubble yum tennis shoes were the only articles of clothing he apparently owned.

"Yeah, we know him, and he ain't no friend of ours if he's breaking into our house," declared Niecee.

The sergeant looks Niecee square in the eyes, "Well, that might be true, madam, but we've got a bigger problem here." The sergeant calls out to another deputy and he jostles over quickly and hands two Ziploc baggies to the sergeant. One contains dirty white powder and the other contains two fresh syringes. The sergeant clears his throat, takes the baggies from the deputy, and holds them up to about eye level so the girls can see them.

"We found the syringes lying on the kitchen table and the crystal meth was in your attic. Of course we found your friend in the attic as well, and he claims the items do not belong to him."

"That no good son of a..." Niecee stops in mid-sentence because Tahoe just pinched her at the hip.

"He's lying!" declared Tahoe. "As you can see for yourself, he broke into our house to do whatever and ya'll busted him."

"She's right!" cosigns Niecee. "He's a liar! We don't use drugs and we don't keep needles or anything like that in our house."

The sergeant was seriously thinking about letting the girls off the hook and just charging Adam with the burglary as well as the drug possession, but the smirk on Mrs. Wisekoff's face made him change his mind. It was obvious she wanted the girls out of her cottage and removed from the property.

"Ladies, I'm sorry," said the sergeant, "I can't prove or disprove your statements, nor the burglar's. We'll have to leave that up to a judge, so I'm placing all of you under arrest."

Tahoe's face turned three shades of ugly. She was so angry she couldn't find words to speak. She curled up her fist as though she we're about to shoot a jab upside Mrs. Wisekoff's head or perhaps punch the sergeant in his watermelon belly, but she was distracted and perplexed when Niecee began to cry.

"Please don't take me to jail!" she wailed, falling to her knees as the deputy was trying to place handcuffs on her. Somehow, Niecee escaped his grasp by twisting and rolling on the ground. It surprised everyone when she jumped up and ran. It took two more deputies another fifteen minutes and the quick responses of three more to catch her. Niecee high-jumped two front yard fences and ran through several neighboring yards before they cornered her and tased her to the ground.

Tahoe was pissed. She was already handcuffed and had been rushed to a patrol car as the ruckus and chase began. She watched the finale from the backseat. Her rage became so fierce that she shattered both of the patrol car's side windows with the heels of her boots. Once everything was back under the officers' control, they loaded up in cars and whisked the felons to city hall.

Brenda showed up at the Margaret Street cottage at seven-thirty sharp. She pulled into the driveway and honked three times. The house was dark, yet she still expected the girls to come rushing through the front door. After waiting for a moment, she decided to try knocking on the door, but before she reached the cottage steps Mrs. Wisekoff called out to Brenda from her back porch. Based on the woman's body language and the strained expression in her face, Brenda knew that whatever this woman had to say, it wasn't going to be good.

"There's no parking back here," said Mrs. Wisekoff in a condescending tone, "and this cottage is unoccupied, so you need to leave." She was combing her rheumy eyes over Brenda's attire.

Brenda was dressed in a black leather waistcoat, a pink satin blouse and maroon leggings with fire engine red booties. Brenda was familiar with the woman's type, so she made an attempt to woo her with a little Southern charm.

"Sorry for the intrusion, ma'am, but I'm here to pick up Niecee and Tahoe," she said, smiling from one ear to the other. Brenda glanced at her cell phone log to make sure she had the correct address. "They do live here, don't they?"

"As I said, there's no one inside that cottage and those girls are no longer tenants of mine. The last I've seen of them, they were being carted off to jail."

"Jail?"

"Yes, that's what I just said. Now please leave before I have to call the police."

"Excuse me, Miss Lady, landlady, whoever the hell you think you are. You need to check yourself before you break somethin'!" Brenda's smoldering brown eyes made Mrs. Wisekoff take two steps back and her thin lips turned into a crooked line. She quickly spun on her heels and rushed back to the front of her home and disappeared. Brenda didn't budge. She stood her ground and diddled some digits on her cell.

"Hello, Karrene?"

"Yeah, sister-in-law, it's me."

"I need your help."

"Okay, what's this about?"

"Two of my employees, Tahoe Holloway and Niecee Edwards, were arrested today, possibly within the last hour, and I suspect they're being booked at the Santa Clara County Jail. I don't know the details, but whatever it is, I want them bailed out. Do your magic, sis, and don't worry about the cost. I got your back."

Karrene Bonesteel was a lawyer who specialized in family law and most of her cases were heard by municipal court judges. Karrene wasn't concerned about cost. When it came to any type of family situation, she relied on her Uncle Floyd to back her decisions. Right now she needed his influence and connections to aid her in this dilemma. Logging onto the county's computerized judicial file, she scanned for Holloway and Edwards. When she discovered the girls had juvenile files, she assumed their present arrests were drug related. She'd have to convey the information to her uncle because he would need all the facts. The actual charges were possession of drugs and drug paraphernalia, destruction of county property, and evading arrest.

Niecee Edwards and Tahoe Holloway grew up in Sunny Hills, a district of Milpitas, a small city between Fremont and San Jose. During the fifties and early sixties, hundreds of black families migrated from Oakland and San Leandro to work at Fremont's General Motors auto plant and the Ford Motor Company in North San Jose. The girls grew up on Valmy Street, along with their older brothers. Tahoe had two and Niecee had one. The boys became pals, but were instructed by parents to take their kid sisters along with them wherever they went. The girls ran the streets just to keep up with the boys. They picked up all the boys' bad habits, cursing, smoking, and they joined in all fights. When Tahoe's oldest brother Wade got his first car, the boys decided they didn't want their kid sisters hanging around. The parents had a voice in the matter. The girls, now twelve and thirteen, were becoming young women. It became a disciplinary gesture that the girls would grow to despise, but in the end it saved their lives.

Wade Holloway's first car was a canary yellow Volkswagen Beetle. One Friday evening, the Edwards and Holloway boys piled into the freshly washed and waxed auto and headed for a house party in San Jose. The auto's stereo speakers were blasting a popular tune, weed was being passed and beer had been guzzled. Wade was determined to make it to the party in record time. He was confident he'd be able to jet across the railroad tracks ahead of the oncoming freight train. His auto slid perfectly past the guard rails right before they dropped down, but somehow Wade missed a gear and he couldn't find third.

The boys died on impact when the gas tank exploded.

It was nine p.m. down at the county jail booking. Niecee and Tahoe were whisked through processing, fingerprinted, photographed and given lime green jumpsuits, underwear, a bedroll and blankets. There was only one public phone in the holding tank and it was out of order, but the deputy allowed each girl to make a call from their cell phones before confiscating them along with their jewelry and personal clothes.

Niecee called Frank Dean, although she wasn't able to get a clear signal. Perhaps the power on his phone was turned off or Frank was out of range. She couldn't make sense of his earlier texts, and she didn't have time to reply. She surmised that his cell batteries were low and just weren't printing out the characters correctly. She wished she would have tried calling him back sooner to let him know that she wouldn't be able to make it to his dinner invitation. She would have liked to put it off until tomorrow, but everything was happening so fast, the house hunting, the sports car. Now she really needed him and she knew it was her fault. She couldn't blame him if he didn't answer her text, because he had every right to be upset.

Tahoe had no plans to stay in jail overnight. She called the first bail bondsman that she saw posted on the holding tank wall. Aladdin Bail Bonds agreed to work with her after they checked out her credit rating, and based on the information she gave, it was apparent that she was a credible risk. They promised to have her out by midnight, but even a three hour wait seemed much too long.

The girls were escorted from the old jail to the new one. It was right next-door. The transport tunnel was underground. The new jail had eight floors. The women were housed on the eighth and the men were housed on the third through seventh floors. The first two floors were the culinary, the hospital and infirmary. The jail was overcrowded. The governor's realignment program forced low level state criminals to be returned to county jails, so the county and city facilities were bursting at the seams. They needed state funds so they could build larger facilities to accommodate the influx of inmates.

The cells on all floors were double bunked except for inmates accused of murder, who had cells by themselves. The gay men were given a choice, single cell or double with another gay man. The lesbian women had no choice. They were all lumped together with the general population. When Tahoe and Niecee arrived, there were twenty girls lying on floor mats in the dayroom, a combination TV lounge, game room and eating area. The inmates were scheduled to be transferred to Elmwood, a lower custody facility in Milpitas. The move would take place at four a.m. Guards removed a pair of girls from cell 817 and put

Tahoe and Niecee in it.

"Damn, that fuckin' Adam!" howled Tahoe, "after all we did for that fool. Just wait till I get my hands on him, that lyin' scuzzy bastard."

Tahoe was lying on a naked bottom bunk mattress. She slammed the upper bunk with the bottom of her jap-flaps, black jail house slippers made in China. The same type Bruce Lee wore in most of his Kung Fu movies.

"Hey, hey!" shouted Niecee, "quit doing that! I already got a headache and you're making it worse. Besides, it's your turn to stop whining. We always knew Adam was an untrustworthy piece of shit. He'd lie on his own momma if he thought it would save his dumb ass."

"Hey girl, that was crazy!" said Tahoe, rolling out of her bunk and smacking Niecee on her thigh. "Where in BeJesus did you think you was gonna run to?"

"I know," said Niecee, looking down at her and laughing at the same time. "I don't know what got into me, but I'm just glad those police didn't have them mean-ass German shepherds chasing after me!"

"Ha! They didn't call the dogs but a helicopter showed up."

"For reals?"

"If I'm lyin', I'm flyin', girl. That's how I knew they tased your butt, because that big-ass search light was beaming right down on you."

"Uooo, that taser was somethin' vicious!"

"I know. Your booty was bouncing like one of J-Lo's commercials!"

"No it wasn't!"

"Oh, yes it was," accused Tahoe, still laughing.

Suddenly, the guard unlocked their door and read from a sheet of paper he was holding, "Holloway and Edwards, roll up your gear and follow me."

"Oh, shit," said Tahoe, "they must be rehousing us."

The deputy led them to the same elevator that they had just ridden about an hour ago. He took them to the second floor and ordered them to step out. "Now, follow that yellow line and dump your linen and blankets in those carts at the end of the hallway."

The girls followed his instructions and continued down the hall, which took them to a stairwell and down to the basement floor. Once again, they ended up in booking. The clerk behind the desk handed each girl a large brown paper bag.

"Dump the contents out on the counter. We're going to make

certain everything that belongs to you is there." The girls gawked at him with dumbfounded expressions, eyes wide with mouths cocked open. They didn't move as the deputy glared back at them. "Your bail has been posted and paid, so let's get moving. Sign here, here, and initial there," he said, pointing to a section on a form. "When you're done, you can take your personals and change in the back." This time he was pointing to a wide open area next to the shower stalls.

"Hot damn, Niecee, it's not even eleven o'clock. That Aladdin bail bondsman sure works fast."

They had to pass through two locked steel doors, gates that shift changing deputies were coming through, so the girls had to wait. They ended up at the bottom of a driveway tunnel. When they reached the top, they were at street level, and just several paces to their right was a bus stop waiting booth. They made the turn and a woman wearing a dark blue jogging suit with tennis shoes to match was staring at them. She was carrying a Samsonite attaché case and she walked towards them.

"Hi, my name is Karrene Bonesteel. I'm Brenda's sister-in-law and I'm your lawyer." The girls stood frozen. Karrene continued being cordial and smiled. "You girls look hungry. Want to grab a bite to eat?"

They nodded their heads in unison and Tahoe finally spoke up, "This is Niecee and I'm Tahoe. We'd like you take us home first, because..."

"Ahh, not such a good idea, girls. I'm afraid the police have secured your pad and everything that's in it for the time being, but we'll deal with that tomorrow. Brenda told me to look out for you and she's family. That means you're family too, so that's exactly what I'm going to do."

KARRENE
Sunset Investigations
Los Gatos
Sunday, April 17th

ROB WAS AWAKENED by the sound of three alarms. The first was his sister's front office doorbell, the second was the bedroom clock radio, and the third was a cell phone. Rob ignored the first, Sunny rolled over and slammed the button on the second, and Rob flipped the cell phone's case open to answer the third. "Yeah, who is it?"

"It's me," said the voice in a whisper.

"Excuse me, but you'll have to talk louder."

"Who's that?" said Sunny, stretching.

"That's what I'm trying to find out," said Rob, while using a portion of the sheet to rub something from his eye.

"It's me, Harry. I was trying not to wake everybody in the house."

"Friggen, Newman! Well, you just did. Don't you ever just chill on a Sunday morning? And what is that you're chewing on, 'cause it's all up in my ears?"

"Marmalade on biscuit with a strip of turkey bacon, and man is it delicious!"

"Bacon? Okay, so I haven't had breakfast yet and we were planning on sleeping in, so what's up?"

"I got a tweet from a fellow pathologist up in Stockton. He'd just done an autopsy on a corpse that was brought in last night. It was a male, age sixty-three. He took three twenty-two calibers in the face. The vic's name is Joe Sunseri. He's a well-known real estate development contractor in Northern California. I know his son, Terry. We once were dorm mates at USC."

"I know this drawn-out conversation is leading up to something,

73

Harry, so get to the point."

"You remember the map assimilation on state parks that I ran by you at your uncle's place?"

"Of course I remember."

"Well, fourteen of those vics died of gunshot wounds."

"And?"

"So I spent most of my Saturday calling up coroners around the state." There's a moment of silence and then Rob hears Newman slurping something through a straw, then he burps.

"Quit bustin' my balls, Harry." Sunny giggles. She's playing with Rob's left earlobe and trying to listen in.

"Uhh, excuse me. Ten of those vics were shot dead with a twenty-two."

"From the same gun?"

"Nope, I didn't say that and ballistics is not my bag, so I wouldn't have a clue on how to prove it, but I got a hunch, and that's where you come in."

"Me?"

"Uh-huh, you. You're an investigator and the Sunseri family will be needing yours and Sunny's services. And I'll be your corner man so all your bases are covered."

"No way, Harry. I already got Sunny working on that missing person database and I'm not familiar with -- where did you say they live?"

"Stockton, the Sunseris live in Stockton and the shooting took place in Manteca. But you can pull Sunny off my project because you'll be needing her help on this."

"Oh." Rob rubs his forehead. He hasn't had his morning coffee. He feels a migraine coming on. "Well, let me think on it, Harry."

"Sure, Rob, but think fast because it's about an hour and a half drive from where you are, and I already told Terry you'd be up to see him around one this afternoon."

"You did that?"

"Yeah, I did, so get a pen, 'cause here's the address."

Rob clacks the phone's casing shut and watches Sunny roll out of bed. She climbs over a pile of books and magazines that she keeps on her side. Sunny keeps her area like a squirrel's nest. Everything she thinks she may need is within her grasp. Their office would look much the same way if it weren't for Rob's tidiness. Rob's a little OCD, obsessive compulsive. He claims he's just detail orientated, skills the military drilled into him.

"I know you're watching me, Robbie," alleged Sunny, "I feel your eyes trying to peer inside my brain."

"Your brain is fine, woman. It's your booty I'm looking at."

Sunny's wearing a loose pair of cotton flannel pajamas that are at least two sizes too big. She buys them that way for comfort. She pulls the material to one side and looks over her right shoulder to make sure there's nothing stuck to her butt. She finds nothing so she rolls her baby blues at Rob, "Okay, Robbie, give me the shiznits?"

"What?"

"You heard me. What's wrong with my butt?"

"Nothing's wrong with it," chuckles Rob, "other than it's getting mighty plump."

"Uooo, Robbie, you're despicable. Plump is just another word for fat."

Sunny pretends to fluff up her pillow, but instead she slaps Rob across his head, then leaps on top and tries to smother him. They wrestle for a good minute, which leads to some passionate necking, then they're abruptly interrupted by three clangs from Aliya's kitchen cow bell.

"If anybody wants breakfast, come get it now before it gets cold! This is your first and final call!"

Since her son Jake was away at college down in Atlanta, Aliya seldom ever cooked a complete meal, but when she did she'd go all out. Sitting at her kitchen table is like having a feast: Scrambled eggs, cheese omelets, smothered potatoes, beef sausage, baked pastrami strips, fresh green chilies, sliced tomatoes, biscuits, homemade peach and apricot jam, pineapple juice, milk and a huge pot of coffee. Whatever is left over she gives to her gardener or the paper boy's family.

Like the kids they are at heart, Rob and Sunny beat up on each other as they claw their way to the bathroom shower. After a short hot one, they clamber down the staircase.

Sunny arrives first. She's wearing red shorts, a yellow T-shirt, and there's a lavender turban towel wrapped around her hair.

Rob follows. He's still in his pajama bottoms and a robe. Aliya had every dish assembled buffet style and within a matter of seconds the trio was digging in.

"What's on your agenda?" quizzed Aliya, eying the pair from the rim of a huge mug of coffee that she was holding with both hands.

"We're headed up to Stockton, Sis."

"Stockton? Who do you know in Stockton?"

"It's a case, a new client."

"Oh, really. What kind of case?"

Rob thinks on it for a moment. He pauses a little too long so Sunny volunteers. "It's a murder case," she replies excitedly.

"A murder case? Since when did you two start investigating murders?"

Rob frowns. Sunny's eagerness to tell has put the spotlight on him. "Well, actually, we haven't, and we really don't know if we can be of any help with this case, but Newman seems to think so."

Aliya's dismayed. "Sunny, tell me he's joking, or is my brother on crack?"

Sunny giggles, "Heck, I don't know, but this is more exciting than a hootenanny. It beats sitting around the office and waiting for the phone to ring. I'm now officially a field agent, huh, Robbie?"

Rob grunts and yields a sly grin. He's not sure he wants Sunny involved with gumshoe work. He doesn't know how she can be useful to him until they meet the clients and find out what they're really expecting to gain from a private investigation.

"Hear me out, Sis. What I'm about to discuss with you stays at this breakfast table. Agreed?"

"Okay, lil' brah, I hear you," chirps Aliya, anxious to hear whatever secrets her brother has to share.

"Newman is trying to get a bead on a series of unsolved murders that carry back for at least twelve years. There was a murder up in Manteca last night, a friend's father, so Newman thinks that there may be a connection of some kind."

"So what's the connection?"

"It may have something to do with the type of weapon used." Rob throws his palms up. "Hey, that's all I got."

"You mean that's all you're going to tell me," smarts Aliya.

"Come on, sis."

"That doesn't sound so cool, you two. Do you think you can handle that kind of work?"

"He's my Jack and I'm his Jill and I'm just in it for the thrill," pipes Sunny, throwing hand gestures like she's a gangster or a premiere rap artist.

"No, I'm serious. You two are crossing a line here and it's a dangerous one. One that should be left up to the police. Rob, I think you should stall on this until your brothers get back."

"Sorry, sis, but this can't wait. Besides, what are Johnnie Ray and Houston supposed to be doing in Texas?"

"Ha! If you really want to know I'll tell you, but I'm not sure I can run this by you in the time allotted because I need to get ready for church."

"Well, give me the short version."

"Okay. Houston located *TreasureHunters-dot-com* on the web. He stumbled across it when he was helping Jake out with a geography term paper. There was this Spanish ship back in, I don't know, 1600's I guess, and it lost its shipment of gold bullion somewhere between Houston and Galveston. You know the inlet that runs into the gulf."

"Yeah, go on," urges Rob.

"Anyway, the treasure was supposed to have spilled along the beach of a riverbed, but the land that needs to be crossed to do the prospecting is owned by a group of cattle ranchers. Now, there's a constitutional law, I think, that gives any citizen a right to treasure hunt on government land and in this case a public beach. They can hunt as long as they stake a legal claim to it, and of course the government gets a percentage of whatever is dredged up."

"So they're stuck between a rock and a hard place?"

"No. Houston got his claim papers cleared, but the ranchers want in on whatever he and Johnnie Ray find, so they're prospecting while that conflict of interest is being dealt with by the courts."

"So Houston's got himself a dredging crew but he only trusts Johnnie Ray and he needs him to watch his back."

"Exactly!"

"Such a deal. I kinda wish I was with them."

"No, you don't!" snaps Sunny, elbowing Rob in the ribs, "because Ho money is slow money and I want mine in chunks."

Neither Rob nor Aliya can figure out what Sunny's talking about, so Rob whistles the first chorus in Yankee Doodle Dandy and marches out the kitchen. Aliya laughs heartily, but Sunny is perplexed.

By ten-thirty Rob and Sunny are on their way to Stockton and Aliya is dressed and ready for church. After the death of her husband, Aliya joined the church where his last rites were held. The Prayer

Garden was located near Taylor and Fifth Streets on the north side of San Jose. The main portion of the Sunday service would begin at eleven o'clock and break for lunch at twelve-thirty, to finish out by three.

Earlier, Aliya had texted Tahoe and Niecee. She wanted to invite them to the service, but they never replied back. She knew that last night they'd planned a celebration with Brenda and they were supposed to go on a shopping spree today. Aliya was anxious to get some people in place to do work on the girls' first home. While leaving to pick up her auto, she ran into her gardener. He was doing work on the front yard of an insurance company just two doors down.

"Good morning, Mister Jio."

"Hello, Miss Aliya. Good to see you again. Oh, how nice you look." He stopped his raking and took a step back, "You're all dressed up!"

"Why thank you, Mister Jio. Yes, I'm going to church this morning."

"Ah, yes, very good." He gave her a polite practiced smile.

"Mister Jio, I've got some tree stumps that need to be removed on one of my properties. Is that something you or your sons can do?"

"Ah, no, sorry, Miss Aliya, but here." He pulls his wallet from his back trouser pocket, searches through it and hands her a business card. "I know this one since he was young boy. He's very good. See, look right on the card. It says 'expert'."

"Well, thank you for your recommendation, Mister Jio. I'll be giving this person a call. You'll be working at my place this coming Wednesday, right?"

"Oh, sure, sure." He bows his head twice and gives a sincere and cheerful smile this time as Aliya studies the card and walks away.

DOMINIQUE'S TREE AND LANDSCAPE
EXPERT TREE TRIM & ROOTING

It gave a cell phone number and a P.O. Box.

Troy arrived at the driveway of the orchard farm around six-thirty a.m. He brought his vehicle to a stop at a midway point and parked between a pair of palms. As he was unloading tools to prepare for the day's work, he noticed the main house was surrounded by a bevy of autos, so he reached for his field binoculars to get a better look when two uniformed officers strolled up on his rear, catching him completely unaware.

"Morning!" the seasoned veteran officer said in a loud voice.

Troy brought his arms down and turned to face the police. They were at least thirty to forty paces away. He couldn't respond right away, the words were caught up in his throat, so he harrumphed before speaking, "Good morning."

The officers kept their distance around twenty paces as though they were expecting Troy to do or say something else, but he didn't. He was very calm. He just looked back at them with his hands resting comfortably at his sides.

"I see you're getting an early start this morning," said the vet.

"Yes, I am," replied Troy, now taking a few steps toward them and displaying a row of even teeth. "I've got a full day ahead." He does a half turn to his left and points toward the gray overcast sky. "It just might rain, so I need to get started. I promised to trim at least six of these puppies today."

"Well, we don't want to hold you up, but first we need to ask a few questions," said the younger officer. "You won't mind answering a few questions?"

Troy frowned as soon as the youngster began his delivery. He was used to people acting differently towards him because of his speech impediment, but there was something about the young deputy's demeanor that Troy didn't like. He checked himself and slid back into character. He took a few casual steps forward and approached the pair with a smile and a swagger, "Oh, not at all. What would you like to know?"

In the veteran officer's opinion, Troy was a little too comfortable in his own skin. His gestures seemed slightly rehearsed, but more so, he seemed accustomed to being questioned in this manner many times before.

"You were working in this section yesterday, is that correct?" inquired the vet.

"Yes, I was. I got about four palms trimmed and called it a day."

"What time did you quit?"

"Let's see, somewhere between two and two-thirty."

"Did you notice anything unusual, like a suspicious vehicle or person wandering about?"

"No. My work takes a lot of focus and I work at a pretty steady pace. I get paid by the number of trees I cut, not by the hour."

The veteran officer paused and the young deputy was anxious to participate in the dialogue, so he slipped one in, "When you left yesterday afternoon, what route did you take?"

"I took Highway 140 west through Merced."

During the time it took to answer the question, the veteran officer removed a photo that was clipped to a board he was carrying. "Do you know this woman?"

"Why, yes. I've seen her drive through here, but I've never met her, if that's what you mean. Why do you ask, has something happened to her?"

The veteran officer removes his Smokey cap and runs his fingers through his hair but never takes his eyes off Troy. "Well, that's what we're trying to determine. She drove from here around the same time you did yesterday afternoon and we've found her auto parked off the roadway about six miles up from here."

"We're questioning every person who may have seen or spoken to her that day," added the youngster.

"Gee, I wish I could be of more help to you, although I do remember a couple days ago she tooted her horn before passing me by, but we never spoke."

"Where were you when that happened?"

"Ahh, I was cleaning my tools up and putting them away," Troy turns to his left and points. "Oh, I'd say I was parked just a couple palms down that way."

"Well sir, thanks for giving us your time and we'll let you get started. You've been very helpful."

Troy extended his right hand and the veteran was first to shake it, followed by the deputy. The troopers turned away and the deputy commented that he hoped they'd be finished before it starts to rain. The troopers walked back toward the main house and Troy got back to the work he'd come to do. He'd promised to try and complete six tree trims for twice the salary. It was already seven a.m. and he wanted to be finished by no later than four o'clock. The trooper's questioning never fazed him and before they could begin their next farmhand interview, Troy had climbed a thirty footer and was into his first palm.

There were two other troopers doing interviews on the farm that day. By nine a.m. they'd spoken to eleven employees and five family members. Before leaving the farm, the four troopers reconvened in the garage where the missing girl's Ford Mustang had been parked.

"Okay," said the veteran officer, glancing at his notes from a clipboard. "Let's make sure we're all on the same page before we turn in reports. Right here is where the leak got started," he said, pointing at a damp area on the dirt flooring. "The dampness and depth of the water saturation has remained because it's cool in here. The girl's father informed us that her car had been serviced several days ago at a local garage, a garage that's been doing auto repair for all the farm vehicles for several years. So we'll need to get down there and check all those employees out.

"Presently, the only farm employee of interest to us should be the tree trimmer. He's been working at this location for the least amount of time. I believe he's been on site for the past three days. He's been observed by other laborers scoping out areas that have nothing to do with trees. And he was seen leaving the farm just minutes after our missing girl drove off the premises. Yet, our background check shows he's clean. He has no criminal record whatsoever. No unpaid traffic citations, no warrants. Nothing. The farmer says his skill comes at a high price, but his work performance and references are stellar."

"Sir, shouldn't we have asked to search his vehicle?" asked the young trooper.

"If he's got something to do with the disappearance of the girl in any way or just made some contact with her, well, at this stage I don't want to spook him. There's not enough probable cause for a search warrant. No judge would allow that based on a hunch. And even though it's a remote possibility, the girl may have been picked up by a friend."

"I doubt it!" voices another officer.

"Let's see," says the veteran officer, glancing at his clipboard once again. "The Highway Patrolman that found the location of the girl's car reported no sign of foul play, other than the tow driver noticing that the petcock on the radiator was wide open."

"So, the engine must have overheated," said another officer.

"That's right. There had to be smoke and steam, but evidently she still had enough wherewithal to steer the car off the roadway."

"Or she may have been pushed," volunteered another officer.

"Well, that's a possibility, but it had to be by hand and foot because there were no indentations or markings on her bumper to indicate metal to metal grind, although the Highway Patrol has put out a bulletin inquiring about any motorist who may have travelled that route at that hour and seen what had taken place. Ah, one more thing. We've got a team that's fingerprinting and combing the entire vehicle, so we should know more on that by this afternoon.

Now, getting back to the tree trimmer, Mister Dominique. Don't be misled by his speech impediment. This guy is smart. If he does have anything to do with this girl's disappearance, he's the type that would meticulously cover and dispose of any trace."

"You got a good feeling about this one, don't you?" hedged another officer.

"Oh yeah, I most certainly do."

At ten a.m. three patrol cars rolled down the driveway and paraded past the palms. When they reached the wood chipper and hearse, they slowed their pace, gawked for a moment, then increased their speed. As they drove away a drizzle of steady rain was falling and Troy was finishing his third palm. If he worked through lunch he'd be finished by one o'clock.

Esquire Karrene Bonesteel and her twin brother Malik owned a hacienda style home in the city of Cupertino, which was once a suburb of San Jose. Malik was a natural early riser, especially on a Sunday, because he did volunteer work at a Montgomery Street homeless shelter near downtown San Jose.

Karrene got up around nine. She made a big pot of coffee and made herself a cup of tea. Next, she shoved a half dozen day old cinnamon rolls in a microwave, which was her typical style of breakfast. She was a fairly decent cook, but she didn't like to.

Fifteen minutes later, Niecee and Tahoe wandered into the kitchen wearing a pair of Karrene's terrycloth pajamas with hoodies, one pink and the other lavender. They resembled Teletubbie Babies, characters from a children's PBS feature. The girls weren't hungry. They'd eaten a grand slam breakfast at a Denny's restaurant around two in the morning. They sat on kitchen counter stools, poured their coffees, and Tahoe asked if she could smoke.

"Sure, go ahead," said Karrene. "Let me get you an ashtray." She flipped a ceiling fan on and removed a wooden Corona cigar box and an ashtray from a cabinet drawer. Tahoe lit her cigarette and Karrene opened the box and rolled a couple joints of weed.

"Uh-huh, sho' you right, girlfriend," chimed Niecee. The whites of her eyes were pink but her irises were twinkling.

There was no comment from Tahoe. She sat looking sheepish and demure. She was rubbing the inside of her left forearm.

Karrene passed the joint and everyone took a toke. Next, Karrene went back in the cigar box and came up with a stick of incense, then lit it. The fragrance was watermelon.

"Ooo-wow, now that is nice," said Niecee.

Karrene smiled. She reached under the counter and flicked another switch. Soft music rebounded from a hallway speaker. It was a Jordon Sparks rendition of *"The Best is Yet to Come,"* originally a Grover Washington Jr. tune that vas sung by Patti Labelle.

Karrene was a keen observer. In her line of business she learned to pay close attention to detail. Tahoe's arm itch did not go unnoticed. Every second Saturday of the month, Karrene spent a couple hours donating her time at a legal aid center in East Palo Alto. It was next to a methadone clinic. Her new clients, Tahoe and Niecee, had a drug possession charge on their juvenile record. Apparently, they claimed they were holding a quarter pound of weed for one of their boyfriends, but didn't want to give him up. They were charged with sales, but since it was their first offense, they got it plea bargained to a misdemeanor. They ended up getting community service.

The manner in which Tahoe continued fidgeting with her arm led Karrene to believe that perhaps both of the girls might be using some hard core drugs. Recreational drug use was not uncommon among most of Karrene's family members or friends, but when it came to hard drugs, in her opinion, it was too easy to slip from social use to destructive abuse. Karrene decided to talk to Brenda about it before she would consider tampering with the subject.

The herb helped. Tahoe and Niecee had a lot to contend with, and Karrene made the girls feel right at home. The house decor was predominately done in blues. The furnishings were not expensive. Nothing was overly precious and untouchable, but there was a sense of order. Karrene had a lot of paintings. They belonged to her brother, Malik. A few were hung, but most were leaning against the walls. In one corner was an shrine, a limestone Buddha sculpture, some pink rose decals, a couple unlit candles, and a tiny silver bell.

Tahoe's curiosity got the best of her. The weed had her feeling giddy, but she didn't want to make a joke about something that obviously was serious, so she asked.

"Oh, that?" chuckles Karrene. "That's my Buddha. And yes, I'm a practicing Buddhist. I'm an enlightened person," again she smiles. "The faith teaches you that you already have everything you need to have in the life you want. Every person can realize their full potential, and knowing that brings one peace."

"Do you chant?"

"Ah, sometimes, and other times I just play something soft and instrumental from my stereo."

"What's the bell for?" asked Niecee.

"It's a meditation tool. Before I begin and after I'm finished praying, I ring it gently. It's a ritual, but it also lets Malik know not to interrupt me until after the second bell is rung, AND TO BE QUIET!" she screamed, causing the girls to flinch. The shout broke their trance-like expressions and everyone laughed. The girls liked her. They sensed she was an easy going and fun person to be around.

Karrene continued, "I don't know what kind of life you've had, but I grew up in Richmond and it was a pretty tough neighborhood to grow up in. I learned early in life that I had to live by some kind of principles, and once I figured out what those principles were, my life went a lot smoother, even during troubled times or the worst of circumstances. And of course, my faith helps me stay on track."

Karrene was twenty-nine, not much older than Tahoe or Niecee, but she sensed the girls were searching for something, a role model perhaps, and she knew having a strong woman in their life would help them figure it all out, although she was a bit relieved when Brenda called and said she was on her way over to take the girls out to do some afternoon shopping.

Brenda's arrival was loud and audacious. The whole neighborhood was looking because she was driving her husband's car, Johnnie Ray's supersized Hummer, a gold metal flake body and sparkling jeweled hubs. She pulled up in the driveway and honked several times. If you'd just met Brenda, you'd think she was drunk, but it was just Brenda's country girl ways.

All three women ran out of the house to greet her. They hugged, they dapped, bumped elbows, hips and high-fived. After completing the exhausting ritual, they went inside the home. The women got dressed, then all four put their heads together and made out a quick plan. The nearest shopping mall was Valco on Wolf Road, so that would be their first stop.

They zipped from one boutique to another like they were pulling a series of armored car heists. Tahoe was not a browser. She knew exactly what she wanted and what she liked. Jersey dresses, pleated knits, cocktail skirts, booties, leggings, tall boots, ankle strap shoes, blouses with deep vee's, floppy felt hats, clutch purses, satchel purses, Chanel shades and scarves.

Niecee was a little more meticulous. She was into designer labels. She started out by getting Gucci shades, belts, bags, shoes and jackets. Next it was Tommy Hilfiger belted coats, velvet gloves, sandals, mini heels, heeled loafers, cocktail dresses, cropped jackets, fringed boleros, blazers, smart bags, paisley head bands, and denim everything. And both girls bought jewelry, watches, and perfumes.

At two forty-five, Brenda tweeted Aliya and told her to meet them at Buy the Bucket, an Italian family restaurant and bar on Stevens Creek Boulevard. It was in the heart of auto row, where car dealerships were lined up on both sides of the street for a three mile stretch. By the time Aliya arrived, the girls had ordered takeout: spicy meatball on French, eggplant parmesan, and deep dish lasagna. Aliya had eaten at church and she was anxious to start the car search because she'd sold homes to many of the salesman at dealerships on auto row.

BMW was their first of three stops. Tahoe showed interest in a silver-gray 328i eight speed automatic, but she didn't want to make a decision until she saw what the other lots had to offer.

The second stop was Toyota, where Niecee fell in love with a Prius, mainly because it was equipped with a built-in smart phone and a color monitor called an infotainment system. The gas mileage average is what sealed the sale, fifty-three city and forty-six highway. Her practical choice took everyone by surprise and Aliya was the happiest for her because she knew the Ghia was no match for a brand new car.

The final stop was the Mercedes dealership and Tahoe chose a Benz C250. Mercedes has a reputation for craftsmanship excellence and durability, a better drive than most any car on the market. This one featured satellite and radio navigation and a seven speed automatic. It was priced twice the value of the Prius.

Based on Aliya's advice to think of each purchase as an investment, both girls' picks were reasonably priced. Niecee wanted hers in magenta and Tahoe chose coral, a yellowish-red color. The model colors had to be special ordered. Delivery would come in a couple days.

The shopping spree ended at eight-thirty that evening. Everyone was mentally drained, although their adrenaline was still running a little high. At Karrene's place, Brenda helped with unloading their purchases. She promised to give the girls a buzz on Monday and off she went. Karrene's living room was spacious and sparsely furnished. There was plenty of room to stack the bags and boxes of garments, shoes, and hats.

It was understood that the girls would be staying with her until their new home was ready. She expected their court arraignment to be scheduled for Tuesday, and that they would both be present to make an appearance before a judge. On Monday, she planned to get a copy of the police report, Adam's statement, and talk to the assigned prosecutor to get a better feel of what course of action he was planning to take against her clients. While lying on her bed and thinking through the next day's strategy, Niecee's tap on her doorframe interrupted her train of thought.

"Hey, Karrene, you got a minute?"

"Sure, hon, what is it?"

"I know our cottage rental is temporarily sealed, but can I pick up the Karman Ghia tomorrow? I need to do some running around."

"Oh, snap!" cries Karrene, "I completely forgot about your car. We should have picked it up this morning. Okay, let me handle this right now."

Niecee didn't know landlady Wisekoff's number, so Karrene had to look it up in a phone directory and she made the call.

"Hello."

"Miss Wisekoff?"

"Yes, who is this?" said a weary and inquisitive voice.

"Karrene Bonesteel, I'm the attorney representing the tenants who were living in your cottage rental."

"Ooh! What do you want?"

"I just wanted to inform you that someone would be stopping off tomorrow morning to pick up their auto."

"Their auto? I didn't know they owned a car."

"I'm referring to the Volkswagen sports car that should be parked in front of your home."

"Oh, that. I had the tow company pick it up this morning because none of my neighbors knew who it belonged to."

Karrene cringed, "I see. Do you recall what tow company removed the vehicle?"

"Yes, they left me a card. Give me a moment and I'll get it."

During the pause for a search, Karrene looked over at Niecee, who was trying to listen in. "She had it towed," whispered Karrene.

"Oh no!" gasped Niecee. Her bleach blond eyebrow arched way past normal.

The landlady came back on the line, "Okay, I've got it. Bob's Towing and Salvage Yard, Old Oakland Road, San Jose." She recited the phone number. "And I have a question before you hang up. You say you're an attorney?"

"Yes."

"Well, how long before they'll be getting their things out of my cottage?"

Karrene hadn't a clue as to what the girls' lease agreement was about and she figured it wasn't a good time to press the issue of rental rights and eviction standard thirty-day notice. "Miss Wisekoff, it should be no more than a couple days, but I promise to give you a call as soon as I know something."

"Well, that would be helpful. Good night."

"Good night, ma'am," said Karrene. She powered off and looked up at Niecee, who was still standing over her with hands on both hips and her mouth flung open. Her shaggy blond natural was glowing under the bedroom's overhead lamp. Karrene dare not laugh, but Niecee's posture resembled Sesame Street's Big Bird.

"That dirty bitch!" screeched Niecee.

Karrene couldn't hold back. She grabbed her sides because it hurt to laugh so hard. "What did you expect, Niecee? Don't worry, honey. Malik will drive you down to Bob's Towing in the morning. As for me, I'm going to get ready for bed. I've got to get an early start tomorrow."

"Thanks for everything, Karrene. Me and Tahoe really appreciate all that you've done for us."

Karrene raises a palm and waves the air. "The two of you have thanked me enough already. Someday I may need a favor and I trust you're someone I can count on."

"Ya damn skippy," said Niecee with glee. They exchanged high-fives and Niecee retreated to the guest bedroom. She found Tahoe lying on top of the bed's comforter, snoring like it was the thing to do. Niecee tiptoed to the bathroom and was about to hop into the shower when her cell phone vibrated. She answered and gave a soft audible hello. Suddenly her eyes turned into half moon shapes and her thick pink lips stretched into a smile. Frank Dean was on the line.

"Hey, my little Princess. Did you miss me, because I surely missed you," he said in a cool husky voice.

"Oh, daddy, you sound so good. I'm sorry for not calling you back, but you wouldn't believe all that's happened to me," she said in rapid fire speech without hardly taking a breath.

"Oh. Well, tell me about it, loved one. I've got plenty of time. I'm all yours, sweetheart."

"Okay, but first I'm about to get in this shower. I promise to call you back as soon as I'm done, okay?"

Hearing the sweetness in Niecee's voice was like music to Frank Dean's ears. It shook him out of the funk that was fogging his brain. The last thing be remembered was standing over the Cinnabar jukebox. He'd loaded it with coins, made his selections and downed a fiery drink. At five o'clock Sunday afternoon he'd awakened on the floor of his motel kitchenette.

His moccasins were muddy. His clothes were sweaty and there were blotches of blood on his Panama brim and the front of his shirt. He knew the Chinese laundry lady would be pissed and he could hear her scolding him, "What you do, Mister George? I do the best I can, but this will not come clean, so sorry."

He knew that he must have used his gun for some reason, because his six shot revolver was missing three rounds. The paint job on the Dodge truck he borrowed from the tow yard was ruined. The scratches on the cab meant he'd scraped against a highway cliff railing or maybe the side of a stone bridge. Although it really didn't matter, he could always buy new clothes and the tow yard had plenty of trucks. He'd have the guys at the maintenance shack patch this one up. Frank Dean abandoned his private consternation when Niecee returned his call. She brought him up to speed on the highlights of the past two days.

"So, my brothers towed your car?"

"What are you talkin' about?"

"I'm serious, Princess. My brothers towed your car because we own the company."

"You're the owner of Bob's Towing?"

"That's right. My Brother, Bob Wayne, runs it and me and Billy Bear help him out from time to time. So don't worry because it's not gonna cost you a penny to get your car back, but now that you're a rich girl," he teased, "maybe I should charge you."

"I'm feeling so much like Shocka Zulu," cried Niecee, making a comeback with a ridiculous late night TV comedy line. She lost Frank, but he chuckled anyway. "Anyway, so what time did you say you were gonna pick me up?"

"I can pick you up at seven, if you wanna go to breakfast with me, but if that's too early..."

"No, no. That will be fine. Here's my address. I'll be waiting out front so you won't have to get out of your RV, I guess."

"No, I'll be driving just a plain old truck, Princess. I know the area, but if I get lost I'll call you."

"Okay, that sounds cool." She puckered her lips and gave him three kisses over the phone. He said goodbye and powered off.

Rob and Sunny's afternoon was rough going at first, but it ended on a positive note. The Sunseri family lived in an affluent neighborhood and Terry Sunseri was under the impression that Sunset Investigations had come highly recommended because they were an old establishment.

"Harry Newman failed to mention that you're relatively new to the investigation business, Mister Bonesteel?"

"In some ways, yes, and in other ways, no, Mister Sunseri. And do call me Rob, I'd prefer that," said Rob using his best representation of what he hoped would come off as charm. "I was a member of the Marine Corps, Platoon 3072, 3rd Battalion, 3rd Division's Reconnaissance Team. Possibly the best investigative techniques used in the entire world." It was a stretch from the truth, but Terry Sunseri, never being in any branch of the military service, accepted Rob's pitch. Sunny held a perpetual smile because she knew it was Rob's bullshit line 101.

Then Sunny was caught completely off her guard when Sunseri gave her a dose of his scrupulous scrutiny. "And what are your qualifications, Miss Jordon?"

Sunny rebounded quickly, "I'm in charge of stats and logistics. I have a photographic memory," she replied without blinking.

"I see," said Sunseri.

Rob upped the tempo and retook control of the business at hand. "We understand there's been a death in your family, a murder, yes?"

"Yes, that's right, and I don't trust the local police to do a thorough enough job. I need someone I can count on to find this murderous swine. I take it you haven't visited the crime scene?"

"No, we haven't, but we're hoping you could answer some questions before we notify the local police about our presence and intentions."

"Well, I can assure you that my father has no enemies whatsoever. He was a bit of a people pleaser and did every project to perfection and on time. His expertise in the residential housing development field was unmatched. My father was not selfish. He often subcontracted to many of the minority companies. Near the end of most projects he would camp out on the site until the last nail was driven or the last appliance installed. I can assure you that whoever killed him was somebody he was trying to help."

"What makes you say that?" blurted Sunny. Rob glanced over at Sunny. He felt the timing of her question sucked, but it was too late.

"I say that, Miss Jordon, because my father would help anybody at any time, day or night, even a complete stranger, if he thought that person needed him."

"Did your father own any guns or carry one on him?" injected Rob.

"Yes, he owned a couple hunting rifles, but he owned no handguns that I know of and it wasn't like him to carry one."

Sunny bogarted her way back into the conversation. She felt she had to make up for her near blunder. "Mister Sunseri, we'd be glad to take this case under certain conditions."

"And what are they?"

Sunny glances at Rob to make sure that she's not overstepping his boundaries. Rob picks up on it and once again takes control. "One, we'd like to set up an outpost in one of the tract homes nearest the murder site."

"An outpost?"

"Yes, we'll have to do some canvassing. We'll be interviewing people in the general area for at least a week and it would be easier to stay on site twenty-four-seven, rather than work from a hotel."

"Fine. What else?"

"We'll be expecting you to finance all our expenses while working the case," added Sunny.

"Whatever you'll be needing just refer the billings in whatever establishment you desire to do business with."

"You mean charge accounts?"

"Yes, that's what I just said, Miss Jordon. Charge them in my name."

With that said, the couple excused themselves. They drove to the city of Manteca and made a pit stop at the crime scene. The yellow taped police line was tied from one lamp post to a fire hydrant, to another lamp post, and finally a tree. The stretch of tape covered the span of six homes on one side of the street. The outline of the deceased was marked in florescent orange spray paint. There was a dried blood pool in the neck and head area of the outline, and there were traces of white clay where the police had lifted some tire impressions. Sunny used a digital camera and took a series of pictures from several angles. They had to assume that the house that was furthest away and at the tape's ending was the home from which Joe Sunseri had emerged, so they took pictures of it and every house in between. It was getting late so they called it a day. Their plan was to return bright and early the next morning around five. They wanted to interview some of the early risers before they left for work.

MANTECA
Monday, April 18th
Cupertino, CA

NIECEE COULDN'T SLEEP, and when she did it was only for a couple hours. She was up at five and ready to roll at six-thirty. Karrene and Malik were early risers as well. The house held two and a half baths, so no one was in the other's way. Niecee gave Karrene an update on Bob's Towing and shared her plans about having breakfast with the owner. Karrene was surprised, yet glad that Niecee was showing some initiative and independence.

They let Tahoe sleep in, but agreed to leave her a note so she wouldn't feel abandoned. Malik and Karrene left for the office before Frank Dean's arrival. He was driving another black pickup, a Chevy Silverado. He wore khaki work clothes, everything was starched and pressed. His work boots were suede, including a tailor made fedora.

Niecee dressed smart but casual for the occasion. She had a lot of new stuff to choose from so she wasted a good hour's sleep trying to figure it out. The weather man's forecast was for blue skies, cool low fifties and a high of seventy. She figured she'd be hiking through Frank's salvage yard and perhaps there would be a lot of dust, so she chose a denim outfit, sea green generic tennis shoes, a fringed turquoise bolero with head band, hooped earrings and a clutch purse to match.

Frank Dean took Niecee to a restaurant. He opened the door for her at least three times in less than half of an hour, getting in the truck, out of the truck and into the restaurant. Niecee wasn't used to that, and each time he touched her hips or placed his arm around her waist, she trembled. She couldn't quite figure it out, but it's just how her body reacted to his touch. He asked her about it. She lied and said she was cold.

The restaurant was Angelo's on Santa Clara Street in downtown San Jose. Not a big place. It was tucked between a bakery and an old hotel. It had a nostalgic feel. The flooring was linoleum, large black and white squares. The floor's center was filled with round short tables and white vinyl chairs. Each table was covered in red and white checkered cloths, arranged to seat one, two or three. Hugging the walls were square tables and each one had a mini-jukebox on it. Of course, that had to be Frank Dean's choice.

He introduced Niecee as his girl to a waitress with a name tag that said her name was Nadine. She wore a pristine white uniform, blouse, skirt and white shoes. Even the fry cook wore a white short-sleeved shirt, apron and a pillbox shaped hat. The restaurant only served breakfast and lunch. The breakfast was served on huge platters with double portions of everything at more than a reasonable price. Frank let Niecee choose the music. The juke was stocked with old school forty-fives, so she took a chance and picked something she'd remembered from a movie she'd seen on late night television.

"...*Mister Sandman, Bring me a dream...bum, bum, bum, bum...*"

Niecee was tickled pink. She rose from her chair and did a solo samba. Frank Dean got a kick out of watching her mischievous ways. The other patrons didn't mind, because when she twirled they all applauded. Before they left, Nadine and the fry cook beckoned Frank to bring Niecee back, because her fun and frolic brightened the start of their day.

By the time Frank Dean and Niecee set foot on the salvage yard, Karrene had opened her office, gone over the day's agenda with Malik and left him in charge. Her next stop was the superior court building on First and Saint James Streets. From the lobby she took an elevator to the third floor. It was courtroom eight, Judge Marilyn Chacon. Her calendar of arraignments were already posted in the hallway lobby six feet from the courtroom's door. Karrene let her fingers do the walking and, just as she suspected, Edwards, Holloway and Anderson were given the same docket number, but what she didn't expect was their arraignment was scheduled for one-thirty in the afternoon. Without a moment to waste, Karrene called the District Attorney's Office and asked for Gloria Nino, the prosecutor assigned.

Nino was on a tight schedule. She said she could meet her for ten minutes at the Levi Building at nine forty-five. The Levi Building was only three short blocks away. Karrene's car was parked in an underground parking lot which only charged five dollars for all day, so she elected to walk.

The courthouse building was once owned by the company, Levi Strauss. It was their warehouse for rolled lots of denim material, and for a while it was where they stocked their 501 line. Then the economy slowed and the building was finally closed. Around the same period, the California judicial system invoked a Three Strikes Law. Any criminal convicted in three separate felony cases was given a sentence of twenty-five years to life. There were guidelines and certain criteria that had to be met, but most career criminals knew the courts would go back into their history as far as they wanted to. Courtroom calendars were flooded. Cases were piling up like a Rwandan genocide. Every case was tried by jury and in most instances sentenced by one.

The county annexed the Levi Building. It was only ten blocks from the county jail and the municipal court building. The two lawyers, Bonesteel and Nino, held a meeting in an empty holding cell in the back hallway of a courtroom dungeon. They couldn't come to a reasonable agreement, so they tweeted Judge Chacon. She agreed to meet with them in her chambers, but urged them they must be prompt, because she had a lunch date at eleven forty-five.

When the attorneys arrived, the silver haired fifty-year-old excused her clerk, removed her robe and lit a smoke.

"Okay ladies, I've gone over the case, so what are the issues at stake? Miss Bonesteel, you first, and keep it concise."

Karrene was wearing a tailored gray and white plaid business suit with a lavender blouse. Her ears were adorned with pearl white post earrings and her hair was styled in short black ringlets that clung to her neckline and dangled past her cheeks.

"Your Honor, the police seized evidence in plain view and charged it to my clients, which is a violation of the invasion of privacy statute. There was no issue of a warrant on the occupants of the household. It was an intruder that was caught and placed under arrest for burglary. And the defendant, Adam Anderson, has an arrest history which shows drug possession and burglary as his modus operandi, as well as being an admitted heroin user."

"Okay. District Attorney Nino, let's have it, short and sweet." Judge Chacon smiles. The D.A. returns the smile and Karrene, being bisexual, realizes there's something brewing between the two women.

District Attorney Nino was five-foot-three, thick, not an ounce of fat. She had rose colored cheeks and wore very little make-up because she didn't need to. Her hair was black and coarse, parted in the middle and hung past her shoulders. She used a hair tie and wore it in a pony. She was dressed in a gray tweed business suit with a jeweled broach on the left lapel.

"Your Honor, yes, the seizure was warrantless, but the evidence was of incriminatory character and it was lawful for the officers to access it. The occupants, Miss Edwards and Miss Holloway, both have a juvenile file for drug possession, which warrants probable cause against them. I believe they've been rightfully charged."

Suddenly, the D.A.'s cell phone ring-toned. "Excuse me your Honor. This one's important. May I?"

The judge flicks her cigarette ash and glances at her Rolex. "I'll allow sixty seconds."

Both women had been standing. The judge waves at Karrene and motions for her to take a chair as the D.A. retreats to a corner to get a measure of privacy. Forty seconds later, she snaps the phone casing shut and rolls her eyes at Karrene. Karrene bounces up from her chair and the Judge and Karrene are waiting for the D.A. to say something.

"Your Honor..."

"Well?" urges the judge as she takes her last puff and crushes the filter.

The D.A. pauses to clear her throat. "That was Detective Sergeant Styles. Mister Anderson has just signed an admission statement of guilt. He's claiming the drugs and syringes are his and that he'd hidden drugs and paraphernalia in Edwards and Holloway's attic without their knowledge. The detective expects he's telling the truth because he gave up a credible source as his supplier."

"Oh ho!" chuckles the judge. "Well, Miss Bonesteel, looks like it's your lucky day. The judge glances over at Nino. "You are dropping the case against Holloway and Edwards, aren't you?"

"Yes, your Honor, I am."

"Good for you, ladies," declares the judge while opening a drawer and sliding a .380 automatic into her purse. "Counselor Bonesteel, need I remind you that although the felony counts against your clients have been dismissed, they will be ticketed and fined for destruction of county property, and if they make full payment by no later than five p.m. tomorrow, I'll see to it that the D.A. drops the obstruction charges as well." The judge winks at District Attorney Nino. "Now, are we all clear on that?"

The lawyers nod their heads in agreement and Judge Chacon continues rattling off a dialogue. "Now, in regards to the jog Miss Edwards took around the neighborhood, and because all charges are dropped, she cannot sue the Sheriff's Department for being tased. Is that clear?"

"Yes, your Honor, I'm perfectly clear on that, and thank you," chirps Karrene, trying her best to rein in her enthusiasm as D.A. Nino grimaces in defeat.

For Sunny and Rob, the four a.m. Monday morning trek from Los Gatos to Manteca was ambitious and a little more fun. Sunny did the driving. She borrowed her dad's Isuzu Trooper, an off-road high performance blazer which is a lot more durable than an on-road SUV. They packed it with a couple suitcases, sleeping bags, and an assortment of odds and ends that could be useful at their temporary outpost on the slopes of Manteca. Terry Sunseri gave them the keys to a modest one-year-old two bedroom on Hastings Drive, three blocks away from the crime scene.

At six a.m. they started at the top of a hill and worked their way down. Sunny was on one side of the street and Rob worked the other. They were surprised how many homes were still unoccupied, but Rob got lucky when he ran into a trucker who was pulling in a driveway.

"Howdy," said Rob with a smile as he walked toward the man and tipped the brim of his five gallon western hat.

"Good morning," said the trucker, "is there something I can do for you?"

The trucker was six-two, a couple inches taller than Rob. He was barrel chested, about two-fifty in weight, black natty beard but friendly brown eyes.

"Well, maybe you can," said Rob. He handed the man his business card and gave him a moment to examine it.

"Why, you're quite a few miles from home, Mister Bonesteel."

"Indeed I am, sir."

The trucker was looking past Rob because Sunny was coming their way.

"Good morning," said Sunny cheerfully as she lined up next to Rob's left shoulder.

The trucker nodded politely and returned his attention back to Rob. The trucker's surname was Alvarez. He was single. He'd been living in his new tract home for barely two weeks. He said he was out on the road the majority of the time doing deliveries for a variety of produce farmers on various routes. He said he'd noticed the police's yellow taped line down at the lower end of the street and he wondered what it was all about. Rob and Sunny filled him in.

"Oh, Sunday morning you say? Hmm..." He was scratching his bearded face with his left hand and squinting his brown eyes as though he were conjuring up an image of some kind. Then suddenly, he jerked his hand away from his beard and snapped his fingers. "That's it!" he said so loud that it startled Sunny.

"What's it?" said Rob, now wide-eyed with anticipation.

"Yeah, I was home Saturday night. I'd been drinking and was dozing in my Lazyboy chair. As you can see," he turns and points to his tract home, "I haven't put up any curtains yet, so around midnight I get this panoramic view of a star studded sky. Really a beauty, you know."

Rob and Sunny both nod their heads, anxious for Alvarez to get on with his story.

"Anyway, something wakes me from my doze and it's headlights. Truck headlights coming from the big willow tree on the other side of the street, right up that hill. And whoever is parked there leaves the lights on for a good ten minutes while I'm trying to see, but it's the high beams that are making me squint. So, I back my Lazyboy away from the window just a few feet and next thing I know the headlights go out. I take a second look but it's pitch black. Then, an interior light comes on. I see a silhouette of somebody wearing a hat. Then the interior light goes out and it's pitch black under the willow again. I get back in my chair and wait for what must have been a while, 'cause I dozed off. When my alarm clock sounded it was three a.m. I got up and headed out for a trailer pick-up in Stockton. I had to be at my assignment by four."

"You didn't happen to see the truck on your way out?" asked Rob.

"No, there was nothing parked on the other side of the road when I left, but that's typical since I moved here. I guess when more home owners arrive and all the street lights are working, they'll be parked cars all along this street."

Sunny and Rob could barely contain their excitement. They thanked the trucker, made an about face and walked back up the hill. When they got even with the willow tree they stopped but didn't cross the street. The lots were empty. There were no homes in that section on either side.

"Why are we just standing here, Robbie?"

"Give we a minute, pumpkin. You know we're both new at this, so we don't want to make any mistakes. Let me think it through."

"Okay," she replied, her mind spinning and her eyes moving over the terrain from left to right. She dug in her shoulder bag and pulled out a handful of zip-lock sandwich bags. Rob's still contemplating silently. His arms are folded across his chest and Sunny's fidgeting is messing with his train of thought. He glances over to see what she's doing.

"What's that for?"

"They're evidence bags, in case we find something," she says with glee. She looks cute, like a fresh faced teenager. She's wearing a navy blue peacoat and a canary yellow watch cap. Her blond curls are bouncing every time she swivels her head.

"Hey, good idea," replies Rob. "Let me have a couple. What else did you bring?"

"Just tell me what you need. I probably got it in here somewhere."

They cross the street and Rob stops about four feet from the curb. He shoots out a stiff arm to keep Sunny back. She wonders what's up but doesn't say anything.

"Do you smell that?"

"Pew! It stinks!" cries Sunny pinching her nostrils. "What is it?"

"It's urine."

"Are you sure?"

"Yep, and the gutter's bone dry, so it must be coming from the base of that willow tree."

Rob takes a closer look and Sunny follows his lead. He squats down and takes another sniff. "It could be raccoon or some type of animal urine, but the ground's still damp, so whatever peed here, they emptied their bladder by a whole lot. See how it's turned the grass yellow."

Sunny reaches inside her purse and comes out with a garden trowel. Rob chops the earth and scoops some into a baggie. He scoops another sample from a slightly different location, then another. Then he seals each bag and hands it over to Sunny. She tucks them in her purse without really looking to see what she's doing because her eyes are roving over every twig and leaf.

"Ooo, Rob, lookie!" she points but he doesn't see. She snatches the spade from his hand and shoves it under some dirt that's stuck to some kind of flat stone. It's about the size of a quarter.

"Don't mess with it," orders Rob, "just scoop it into the bag."

"Okay, okay, I know!" replies Sunny, getting a little flustered. She's seen plenty of C.S.I. TV and she feels as though she knows what not to do. She holds the baggie up to the sunlight and they take a closer examination of what they've captured in it as though the inanimate object was actually alive. "Robbie, it's a broach!"

"Right, you are, pumpkin. It looks like a tie clamp but it doesn't look much like the kind you'd buy at a store."

"It's so pretty. Look at the designs in it. I think the stones are mother of pearl," proclaims Sunny.

"Yeah, it's probably handmade," affirms Rob. "The question is, how long has it been here?"

Before sealing the baggie, Sunny takes a whiff. "Yuk! It's got the same urine odor too."

"Let me see those dirt samples," says Rob. He lays the samples alongside the patches of earth he dug them from and lays the broach next to where it was found. "Give me the camera."

"Ohh!" Sunny goes back in her purse. They take a series of snapshots, willow tree, curb, ground and gutter. They even go back to the Alvarez place and take a half dozen snaps of his home's front window and the willow tree from the Alvarez home's perspective.

"Okay, let's give Newman a holler and let him know what we found," said Rob.

They text Newman and he wants them to come to the lab right away. They agree to met with him around three in the afternoon, but first they want to do more canvassing.

Aliya Bonesteel was the sole proprietor of Cashmere Properties, a highly successful realtor in the heart of Silicon Valley. After her husband's untimely death, Aliya was tasked with rebuilding the infrastructure and integrity of the firm. She turned down a buyout from a larger organization and declined a merger proposal from a popular franchise firm. The early years were a struggle, but she held on. Her networking skills are what got her on a fast track toward success. She recruited a pool of six career salesmen, two were life and health insurance specialists and another ran a highly successful home alarm and security systems business. They all utilized the 'word of mouth' method and repeat customers. They each brought a substantial cache of their own clientele.

Aliya took care of their advertisements, which helped keep out-of-pocket expenses low. Aliya relied heavily on foreclosure auctions and the forfeiture laws. She made a mint on real estate drug seizures. She also made use of a Quit Claim Sale when dealing with people who paid with cash yet had no record of how they earned it. She kept that sort of clientele down to a minimum, often reserved for family and special friends.

Even with Aliya's full range of activities, she still missed her son. Young Jake was starting the second semester of his freshman year at Atlanta, Georgia's Morehouse College. All the students at Morehouse were male, although the women attending Spellman College were directly across the road. Jake was a high school football standout and he'd gotten a sports scholarship offer from Cal Berkeley, Karrene's alma mater, but Aliya was adamant about having him attend a school in the South. In his last phone call, he boasted of scouts from Grambling College wanting him to play for their team in his sophomore year. Aliya didn't relent. Jake was ordered to complete his undergraduate studies and then he'd be allowed to transfer to the college of his choice. Making a pact with Aliya meant you bad to stick to the terms agreed upon. There was no backing out, no ifs, ands or buts. Nevertheless, Aliya was a fair mom and Jake was her heart, so instead of having him come home for Spring Break, she allowed him to travel to Africa's Ivory Coast with a student dance troop. She thought his request was peculiar at first, until she realized it had to be about some girl. Aliya was never one to get in the way of her son's romances, because she instilled in him good values, good judgment, and above all, common sense.

Aliya's itinerary was a busy one. She spent most of her morning at her computer and on the phone. Her major focus was the Hull Street house. She made contact with all the necessary personnel that it would take to complete the home repairs, but Aliya liked to meet with the people she hired face to face before a project was undertaken. A window installer, carpenters, and a roofing team agreed to meet with her at four-thirty that afternoon. The only holdout was the tree trimmer. He never returned her calls. Aliya trusted Mr. Jio's recommendations, so she left Mr. Dominique a text to meet her at 515 Hull Street at no later than five p.m.

At one o'clock, her top salesman dropped by. He needed her signature on several documents. He'd returned from a long vacation and in the past ten days he'd sold two office buildings, a condo and an apartment complex. Midway through their transactions, Karrene gave Aliya a call.

"What up, sis?"

"Guess!" responded Karrene.

"Don't make me guess 'cause I'm not any good at it," said Aliya teasing right back.

"I got 'em off!"

"Off?"

"Yeah, scott free."

"Wait a minute, back up. Who, what and how?"

"No, it's how, when and where, silly."

"Excuse me, but it's my expression, not yours."

"Oh, so here we go again. I'm wrong for correcting you."

"Alright already, let's not go there," said Aliya, getting a little impatient with her kid sister. "Who are we talking about?"

"Tahoe and Niecee!"

"For reals?"

"Yes, that's what I've been trying to tell you."

"Okay, so what happened and how did you do it?"

Karrene brings Aliya up to speed on the morning's events and then they argue for another five minutes about who gets to pass the good news on to Brenda, who was out of town on business and couldn't be reached.

It was a blue Monday for Troy. Even with only six palm trees remaining, about five hour's work, he really didn't feel much like working. His grandmother had taken ill overnight. She'd raised him, and if there was any trace of emotion left in him, it was tied to her. His father was aging as well and Troy had no interest in following in his father's footsteps. He wanted no part of the mortuary business.

After his mother died when he was six, there was no love gained or lost between him and his father. The mortuary sat on thirty acres of forest and woods, and if there was anything Troy actually cared about, it was having full ownership of his father's land. Yet Troy had more looming concerns. When he left the Merced farm that Sunday afternoon, he had the notion that he was being followed. He didn't locate any police chatter coming over his scanner and he wasn't the type to be paranoid, but for caution sake, he still took the long way home.

Using a dry dock along the backside of his home's crematorium, he disassembled his wood chipper. He cleaned, sanitized and polished almost every part, a task more daunting than he had expected. It took him half the night, but it was easier putting it back together. He went through all his tools and sanitized and cleaned them as well. He vacuumed the hearse front to back. He removed fibers and debris from his tire treads, and he sandblasted the undercarriage and steam cleaned the grill.

It was plainclothes detectives that showed up on the Merced farm on Monday. They made it easy for Troy to detect them. They wore J.C. Penny suits and clunky cordovan shoes. Troy was up on most electronic gadgetry. He knew about tracer and tracking devices that resembled confetti, but no one made an attempt to come near his vehicle.

He discovered Aliya's text when he opened up his cargo box. He had just removed his climbing harness and was taking inventory of his clamps. He was accustomed to getting referrals for new jobs and Aliya was not the first customer that Mr. Jio had come to recommend. Los Gatos was a hop from Boulder Creek, almost like being in his own backyard, a perfect new beginning for a not so terrific yesterday.

It was the last week in April and rain had not been forecast for the evening, but it came. The workers showed up and Aliya was genuinely pleased after talking with everyone and going over her plan. They agreed to begin work on Wednesday. Aliya had locked everything up and was headed for her BMW when she noticed the hearse parked across the street. Troy had no signs posted on his vehicle, so she had no idea of who he was. Although he looked odd just sitting there like some kind of mannequin behind the steering column. Whomever he was, she didn't recognize him as someone from the neighborhood, because Aliya owned two homes on Hull Street and two more one street over. Out of sheer curiosity, she marched over to see if the driver was lost or needed some kind of help. When she reached the passenger side window she used her car keys to tap on it.

Troy's bald head swiveled to his right in a robotic like fashion and his green eyes were fixed on her as though he were in some kind of trance. He pushed a power button and the window came down, and Aliya got a powerful speaker blast of music from a New Wave group called Enya. Troy turned down the volume.

"Excuse me," said Aliya, "are you looking for someone?"

Troy held his gaze. He hardly even blinked. "Are you Miss Bonesteel, the realtor?"

"Yes, I am."

"Here." Troy reached into his coverall's breast pocket and handed her his business card, which she read.

"Oh yes, Mister Dominique. Well, come on," she waves her hand like a wand. "I've got just enough time to show you what I need done. Besides, it might rain so we should hurry."

"I'm sorry," said Troy slamming the auto's door shut and taking long strides to keep up with her. They detoured through a side gate. The backyard was a hundred and twenty feet wide but three quarters of an acre deep. It bordered a creek and the rocky side of a steep hill. Troy didn't slow his pace. He trampled around the perimeter and made a shortcut through the interior as he rambled and poked at brush. When he finished his tour, he found Aliya standing on the home's back porch top step. He remained ground level and spoke.

"I counted thirty-one trees and twelve stumps. Fifteen are mature. The rest are saplings."

Aliya was staring at his physique. His coveralls were sleeveless and she was admiring his massive arms. Then she searched for words in an effort to regain her focus for the business at hand. "Whoa! That many. What kind of trees are they?"

"They're called Tree of Heaven. They don't take much water and they'll grow just about anywhere. The roots are very shallow and they grow parallel to the earth, not downward."

"Oh, really?"

"Yes, and the roots will sprout everywhere, as you can see. That's why you've got so many of them in this one area. They feed off each other."

"Hmm, that's interesting." Aliya was intrigued with how he shortened certain words. She liked his manner of speech. Troy had a near perfectly shaped bald head. He looked youthful and virile. Aliya's libido was up. Her hormones were in concert. She pulls a cigarette case from her jacket pocket and offers Troy a smoke.

"No thanks," he waves his hand and smiles, "I don't smoke." Then he makes a quarter turn towards the backyard's miniature forest. "In case you didn't know, there's a couple hundred pieces of cut logs and fallen trees in that rubble. You can't see it because the foliage has camouflaged it. If we stack it, it will make a good source of firewood, although it's a little green."

At first, the rain was a drizzle, but now it started to pour. Aliya keys the back door to the enclosed porch area, "Mister Dominique."

"Troy. You can call me, Troy."

"Ah, okay. So, let's go inside and you can show me from the porch window." She holds the screen door open for him as he climbs up the steps. She is blocking half of the doorway and he can't slide through without brushing up against her bosom. She doesn't move so he places his hand on her hip and gently squeezes past her and smiles.

Troy is not the least bit aroused by Aliya's attractive figure nor her flirtatious behavior. She wouldn't be the first female client who tried to tempt him with an invitation for a fling. Troy remained calm and continued to chatter about trees and gave an estimate of how long and how much it would probably cost to do the job.

Aliya lit another cigarette and listened. She was the kind of woman that was particular about the men she allowed to get close to her. She knew her type and there was something about Troy's aloof manner that turned her on. Aliya was a Cougar and liked her men young.

They were seated on the porch swing when the cigarette ash fell. It rolled off Aliya's wrist and tumbled onto Troy's trousers. Aliya was aiming for his crotch but it landed on his thigh. She took a hurried swipe and brushed his groin.

"Oops! I'm sorry. I didn't burn you, did I?"

Troy quickly raised his buttocks from his seat and settled back down. He laughed and so did Aliya. It wasn't the fear of getting burned that made him jerk. It was Aliya's heavy caress that startled him as his penis began to swell.

Aliya's eyes were riveted to his crotch. She was estimating its length. Her free hand came down on his growth. Aliya stroked and Troy sat frozen while she searched for his zipper. She tried kissing him in the mouth. Troy didn't turn away but he didn't kiss her back. It didn't matter. Aliya was at a point of no return. Finally, she found the hidden trouser's flap, a short row of nickel plated buttons. She loosed them and freed his long one. It was thick and black. It felt hot in her hand. She massaged him tenderly until it got hard and almost perpendicular.

She worked him like she was licking sauce off a slab of spicy beef ribs. She slurped on his large one like a pro. It didn't matter to her if he climaxed. Ten minutes later his dick looked swollen. The tip was brick red, but he was unable to cum.

Aliya stopped and looked up into the gleam of his glossy green pupils. She was confident she could control this youngster. She was having him exactly as she wanted. She stood and turned her back to him. She let him struggle with getting his engorged member back inside his trousers. Then she walked him to his car in silence.

"I want you to start on Wednesday."

"How's six o'clock sound?"

"No," said Aliya smiling, "I don't want to upset my neighbors. How about eight o'clock?"

Troy agreed and they got into their vehicles and drove away. Aliya took the bridge over the Nimitz, and Troy exited onto the freeway at a maximum speed of fifty-five.

Troy was disturbed and a little confused. He had mixed feelings about what Aliya did to him. She was in control and that upset him. He was not accustomed to that. He killed the only woman who ever made him feel vulnerable. Yes, it was an accident and he was only a boy, but he'd forgotten how much he despised that woman. Aliya forced him to relive the feeling all over again. He was disgusted by her. She made his penis grow hard. There was something wrong with him. He could get hard. Yet, even during his adolescence he never experienced a wet dream. He didn't know what it meant to ejaculate. Troy imagined himself chasing her. Hunting her down, just like the girl from the farm. He lived for the hunt. The hunt was his climax. It made his whole body shutter. It always happened right before a kill.

The Thunderbird Lounge was a relatively new business in the heart of Scotts Valley. It was built on a bluff near Mount Madonna Road. It advertised cold beer, wine, mesquite wood barbeque and pool tables. The majority of its patrons were locals, a few out of town truckers, lumberjacks and a bikers' club.

Troy pulled into a parking lot that was almost empty, except for a dozen choppers two rows deep on one side of the entrance walkway. There was a spacious front sundeck with a green and white awning and several redwood picnic tables neatly aligned. Thursday through Saturday nights brought in the crowds, mainly due to the wet t-shirt competitions. The first place prize was two-hundred and fifty dollars.

On Sundays the lounge was closed and Monday through Wednesday it was generally quiet, business was slow.

This was Troy's first visit to the Thunderbird Lounge. He'd eaten very little that day, so he was quite famished. The green and blue neon sign that read 'Bar-B-Que' is what lured him in. Cold Play's *'Charlie Brown'* was the groove being played on the juke. There were four patrons seated at tables. The remainder were milling around a couple pool tables in the rear. They were shrouded in cigar smoke and the charred smell of chicken, steak and ribs. The sixteen barstools were vacant, so Troy had a choice. He decided on the number four stool. It was closer to the entrance and away from the crowd.

At first, there was no waiter or bartender in sight. After a couple minutes wait, both bartender and waitress bustled through the kitchen's curtained doorway. The waitress looked like a biker chick, a baking powdered face with bright red lipstick and a ponytail. She wore a skintight black t-shirt with a Coors Beer logo printed in white lettered script, Wrangler cut-offs, and cowboy boots. The bartender was stocky and short, about five foot-six. He wore a white long-sleeved dress shirt, a brown waist high apron over black jeans and a green shoestring bow tie. He had short coarse black hair, a neatly trimmed handlebar mustache and dark slits for eyes. He gave troy a worried stare and took his order, a slab of beef ribs, potato skins, coleslaw, two cherry turnovers and three ginger ales. The ginger ale arrived first, then minutes later, a platter of food. Troy quickly guzzled two bottles of ale and ordered another.

When the fourth ale arrived it was delivered by a Gypsy King, one of the biker club members. He sauntered through the kitchen's curtained doorway and pushed his beer belly up to the counter. His six foot-four inch frame was looming over Troy's plate of food. He smelled like a brewery. He had a dirty blond beard and burly sunburnt tattooed arms. The juke was still playing but all the gaming and conversations had ceased. Every patron in the lounge was looking over at the biker and Troy. Knowing he had an audience, the biker glanced over at the pool table area before he spoke.

"How you like them ribs?" he said louder than necessary but so everyone could hear.

"They're fine," replied Troy, still chewing but never taking his eyes from his meal. He scarfed on another rib bone and raised his head only to finish off his third bottle of ale. He set the bottle down hard on the counter, burped and reached for the other, but the burly biker was still holding on to it.

"You need to get finished and be out here before Sonny gets back," the biker said with a half grin, showing severely tobacco stained teeth.

Troy looked back at him, his green eyes gleaming as though he were thinking about returning the fake smile. "Who's Sonny?"

"Sonny is the president of this club and it's best for you to 'vamoose' like now, 'cause there's gonna be trouble if he finds you here."

Troy nods his head a few times, grabs a napkin and dabs barbeque sauce from his mouth. "Okay, right after I finish this last bottle of ale."

Once again, the biker grins. He's got an attentive audience, so he rolls his eyes and smacks the bar with an open palm and yells, "Barkeep, we'll need one more banana for the monkey!"

Troy didn't blink or flinch. Like a cobra's lightning strike, he snatched the biker by his collar and slammed his forehead into the counter before the man had time to inhale. The burley biker winced and moaned as blood gushed from his nose. On pure instinct, he swung wildly at Troy's bald head as though he couldn't see. Troy braced the counter like he was about to dismount from a pummel horse routine. His legs scissored and his left knee caught the biker flush under his chin. The biker flew backward about four feet and crashed into a half dozen kegs and several cases of beer.

Spinning back onto his heels, a cue ball whisked past Troy's head just as two more bikers rushed him. One dove for his legs. Troy skipped away, but the second hit him with a shoulder to the chest with the force of a pro linebacker. The blow didn't faze Troy. He grabbed the dude by his shoulders like he was bear hugging a tree, kneed him in the groin and slammed him into his partner, who was still trying to recover from his tumble.

"Hold it right there!" shouted the bartender, pointing a twelve gauge shotgun at the back of Troy's skull, then tapping him on the shoulder with the barrel as Troy turned around. "Get the hell out of my lounge, Mister! RIGHT NOW!"

Troy stared back at him and everybody else remained perfectly still. Troy groped for his wallet, but the bartender said he didn't want his money. He just wanted him to leave or he'd call the police.

Troy walked out and the crowd followed from a safe distance and watched him from the sundeck as he strolled toward his hearse.

Someone threw an overly ripe tomato in his direction and missed. The ponytailed waitress screamed nasty expletives at him, but Troy didn't respond.   And just as he was climbing into the front seat of his vehicle, the irate waitress slipped from the porch, bounced off the first bike that was parked, and the rest went crashing like dominoes. Someone used a cell phone camera and put it on the Web. The next day the Web cam went viral. It got over three thousand hits.

MOONSTRUCK
Tuesday, April 19th Thru
Saturday the 23rd

THREE MILES OUTSIDE of the city of Merced, Chief Detective Dan Valdez had just finished drinking his second cup of coffee when his pet rooster crowed. He hadn't gotten much sleep, because he'd been out late last night celebrating his tenth wedding anniversary. It was his second try at marriage and his new wife, Lydia, fifteen years his junior, seemed to be working out much better than his first. Yet, by most people's standards the arrangement was a little kinky. They first met when he was working on the vice squad. Lydia ran an outcall escort service and two of her girls were arrested for offering after dinner sex to a client that was a cop. The basic escort service fee was fifteen hundred dollars, but the girls offered sex for a thousand dollars more, which caused Lydia to lose her business license.

Detective Dan and his wife shared their anniversary at one of Ramada's finest inns. They'd reserved a honeymoon suite and their rendezvous began in a bar's lounge. They'd pretended to be strangers. Lydia was draped in a provocative black laced evening gown. She wore vibrating panties. Dan carried the remote control in his vest suit pocket, which only worked within twelve to fifteen feet. Twenty minutes before the charade began, Dan had to make a restroom call and spray his penis with a product that would keep him hard for at least three hours. His performance was superb and Lydia's romantic anniversary wishes were fulfilled. Detective Dan was reminiscing over the highlights of the event when his cell phone vibrated. He checked the Caller ID window on the back and flipped the phone open.

"Morning, Dan. Guess what?"

"Okay Marcus, what is it this time?"

"Our boy went viral. Check him out, he's on YouTube."

"Oh, really."

"Yeah. Apparently, he pissed some biker club members off down in Scotts Valley."

"Okay, let me take a look."

The chief detective gets on YouTube and forty seconds later he checks back with Detective Marcus.

"Gee, I sure would like to have seen what he did to piss them off," he stated with a chuckle. "What else you got?"

"Hold on to your skivvies, chief. Remember the picture we took of the hearse and wood chipper?"

"Sure do."

"Well, we hit pay dirt. The Highway Patrol found us an eyewitness that recalls seeing our boy's contraption parked behind a red car on Highway 140 last Saturday afternoon. And check this out. I've got his statement which says he left the farm between two and two-thirty, right?"

"Right."

"Well, they picked him up on a traffic cam over in downtown Merced. He ran a yellow light and halfway through the intersection it turned red. So the cam takes a picture and sends him a ticket."

"Yeah, I know all about those," agrees Detective Valdez. "The traffic court mails you a picture of yourself behind the wheel, license plate number, etcetera. But what you haven't told me is how does that fit into our investigation?"

"It's the timing issue. The pic was taken on Saturday at five-thirty p.m. It's only an eight mile drive from the farm to the city of Merced, twenty minutes tops. So what's our boy doing between three o'clock and five-thirty?

"Hmmm, that's not exactly enough for a warrant, but we could bring him in for questioning."

"How do you want to proceed, sir?"

"Let me think on it. I'll see you in the office in about an hour."

"Okey doke, later."

The month of April was ending with summer-like weather. Tree blossoms had morphed into raw fruit. Spring gardens were flourishing.   Petunias and primroses were in full bloom.   The reconstruction of Aliya's 515 Hull Street home was off to a great start. The roofing crew began work on Wednesday and by Thursday afternoon they were nearly halfway done.   The glass repair and plumbing jobs were minor and the painters were working inside and out.   They were a tandem of four that were set on milking the job. Aliya had to get after them for taking too many breaks.   Tree trimmer Troy Dominique was a one man army.   Strong as a Clydesdale work horse and energetic as a beaver.   He was cordial when he needed to be but basically kept to himself.   It made the other workers wonder...was the tree trimmer on something or just addicted to his work?

"Slow down, Troy!" the lead roofer would yell at him.   "If you die from overexertion, you'll never get paid.   Besides, you're making us all look bad!" he'd blab.

Troy would smile to himself and wave, but it didn't matter what anybody said.   He kept doing his thing.   He had to disassemble a fence so he could park and have access to his wood chipper.   On Thursday he showed up driving a flatbed truck with side panels.   He loaded it with garbage and backyard trash.   It took him three trips to the city dump to get rid of it all.   On Friday he began buzz sawing logs and stacked green cords of firewood.   For Saturday he'd planned the more difficult task of uprooting stumps.   Even though the roots were shallow, he still would need to rent a truck with a winch.

Aliya showed up like clockwork twice daily around ten and later in the afternoon.   She never came empty handed, coffee and donuts or pizza and cold drinks.   The workers had high praise for her.   She didn't mind grabbing a broom and helping out, but sometimes she annoyed them whenever she got in their way.   She was quite gorgeous and she wore her denim slacks extra tight. She didn't mind the guys staring at her slim goodies or her bodacious buns.

Aliya gave Troy special attention, and everyone noticed. Whether it was a cool drink or a slice of pizza, she always streaked to the backyard and served him first.   He was the first employee to arrive and last one to leave.   She tried to hang out with him but he would always run her off.   Troy was a hard case, but Aliya didn't relent.   She was confident her experience and charm would subdue him.   She played him like a spider toying with an insect that was trapped in her web.   Everything was going her way until Tahoe and Niecee showed up.

They pulled into the driveway in Tahoe's new Mercedes Benz.

They were loud and bombastic. It was evident to Aliya the girls were both high. Their uproar got everyone's attention. All the workers stopped and stared, a few even whistled. The girls were high-fiving and doing a shimmy out on a patch of front lawn. They were celebrating their new home, gloss white with gray trim, twin bay windows, and walnut double doors. The entrance porch was a ten by forty foot deck. A cobblestone walkway and desert like plants thrived in a predominately sandy front yard.

Tahoe was sipping on a cold margarita in a can and holding a slim brown cigarette in her left. She was wearing a summer green flop hat, a striped pullover with a plunging neckline. Her waist was tapered with a hip-hugging mini, and white spike-heeled booties adorned her feet. She was fashionably cute but gangly. She was laced in ten layers of gold chains. There were three around her wrist and seven worn loosely around her neck.

Niecee was sporting a fresh curlicue pixie-cut. She wore designer sunglasses. A multicolored bandage covered most of the plastic surgery that was done on her new nose. She wore a backless apple green jersey dress with white ankle strapped sandals. Her triple pierced ear lobes were adorned with double hooped earrings. A jeweled platinum Rolex was strapped to her left wrist.

"Hello girls," said Aliya approaching them with open arms. They each gave an embrace and pecked her on the cheek.

"Hey, Sugar Momma," replied Tahoe, tipping her drink with the right hand and holding on to her flop hat with the other.

"How you doin', Miss Aliya?" echoed Niecee, switching her big hips as though it was impossible for her to remain still.

"How does it look, girls?" asked Aliya as they marched up the walkway.

"Now that it's all spruced up, it looks huge!" exclaimed Tahoe.

Niecee was suddenly being quiet and coy because the painters were gawking at her thick bronzed legs. She had painted glitter highlights on them.

They toured every room in the house. Most of the flooring was still bare. The carpet layers were scheduled to begin work on Monday. All the bedrooms had been freshly painted shades of yellow, beige, and creams. New gold plated plumbing fixtures replaced chipped and tarnished chrome. The kitchen cabinets and the bathroom shower tiles were in excellent condition but still needed scrubbing before the workers could paint. Aliya coaxed the girls into making a commitment to help out on Saturday.

"Have you given any thought to the kind of furniture you're going to buy?" asked Aliya hoping they were going to take her advice and furnish it with antiques.

"We're going modern," replied Tahoe. "We found a store in Monterey that's got furniture to die for."

"Sounds like Fiesta Furnishings, over in Cannery Row."

"Wow," said Niecee, "you got ESP skills, Miss Aliya. How did you know?"

"I may be older than you two, but I still get around."

"You're not old, Miss Aliya. "You still got it, girl."

"Thanks, honey. Let's go outside. I want you to meet someone."

When they reached the back porch steps, Troy was using a chain saw to carve up a fallen tree. As soon as he shut off the machine the three women walked over.

"Troy!" shouted Aliya, not giving him a chance to restart his saw, "I want you to meet the owners."

Troy didn't camouflage his surprise. He'd assumed Aliya was the property owner. The girls appeared to be close to his own age. He was polite and shook their hands. He was wearing his usual sleeveless coveralls. The girls ogled over his muscular frame. Their mouths fell open but no words came out. Troy was used to it. He looked past them and spoke to Aliya.

"I'll be quitting early today. I've got some business to take care of. Do you have my check?"

"Oh, of course. Let me get it. It's in my briefcase. I'll be right back, girls. You can keep Troy company while I'm gone," she said with cheerfulness.

When Aliya left, Niecee and Tahoe continued to stare at Troy as though he were some kind of alien from another planet. They were making him a little uncomfortable. He sensed they were doing it intentionally. Niecee boldly took a step forward and tweaked his bicep.

"Humph, where did you get arms like that?" she prodded with a giggle.

Tahoe was still puffing on a brown one and Troy kept blinking because the smoke was getting in his eyes. "I used to wrestle," he said.

"Where?"

"In high school."

"I bet you were good. Did you win any trophies?"

"No, I quit."

"How come?"

"I didn't like it. I was just doing it because the coaches kept bugging me to try out for sports."

"I played basketball in high school," announced Niecee."

"Oh yeah. Were you any good?"

"I was all right, but Tahoe was better. She was the point guard."

They glanced at Tahoe, but Tahoe knew Niecee was trying to hit on Troy, so she elected to stay out of her best friend's way. But if Niecee struck out, then Tahoe wouldn't hesitate to see how far she could get. It was a game they'd been playing with boys and later men for as long as they both could remember. They knew what one would say before the other could finish the sentence.

"So what position did you play?" continued Troy, now finding Niecee a little more interesting.

"I was the center."

"Let me see your hand."

"My hand?"

"Yeah," said Troy, and for the first time smiling, "hold it out like this."

Troy holds his hand like a fan and they press palms. Niecee's fingers are almost as long as Troy's, only shorter by a centimeter. They hold the position for a moment and smile at one another.

"Hey, I saw that!" alludes Aliya, returning with Troy's paycheck in her hand. She's jealous but knows it's not a good time to show it. Troy takes the check, says thanks, and picks up his chain saw.

"Get his card, Niecee," urges Tahoe.

"Huh?"

"Ask him for his business card, because after we move in we may need to hire him to do our yard work."

"Ah, he's a tree expert," volunteers Aliya, "he doesn't do yard work. Am I right, Troy?"

"Yes and no," replies Troy as he attempts to answer the question with fairness to both sides. He knows it's time to make his exit before the claws come out. He likes Niecee. He intuitively knew that she'd make a good friend. He felt Aliya was a little overly assertive, but his hormones responded to her like nothing he'd ever thought he was capable of or had ever experienced before. He didn't know exactly what it was, but he knew his life's viewpoint was changing. For most people real change doesn't happen overnight. It usually takes one drastic event or a series of small and uncomfortable ones to get a person to change. The change for Troy was maturity, but he didn't have a grasp on that concept yet.

"If you need gardening or general upkeep of your yard," said Troy looking directly at Tahoe, "I know a few excellent gardeners."

Tahoe was determined not to let him off the hook. She still wanted his business card. Troy fished through his pockets and handed her one. Aliya lit a cigarette and tried to pretend like everything was fine.

Suddenly, the ringtone on Niecee's cell went off. *"Mister Sandman, bring me a dream."* Niecee walked away from the group so she could talk to the caller in private.

"Hello, pinky-dew!"

"Hello, Princess. Did you miss me?"

"Of course I miss you, daddy."

"Are we still on for dinner tonight?"

"Ya damn skippy! We're going to Frisco tonight?"

"It's San Francisco, baby, not Frisco."

"Sorry, my bad. Hey, can Tahoe come?"

"Well of course she can come, Princess. Two pretty ladybugs is always better than one."

"Alright, daddy, we'll be at your place around seven and I promise no later than seven-thirty."

"Now that's my girl. See you at seven, Princess."

Troy packed up and drove his rig from the backyard and into the street. He drove past Tahoe and Niecee, who were sitting in the Mercedes blasting Nicki Minaj's Starships CD. When Troy reached the freeway's on-ramp, Tahoe pulled her Mercedes up behind him.

"You're taking the wrong exit," proclaimed Niecee.

"No, I'm not."

"Yes, you are. Karrene's place is in the opposite direction."

"That's because we're not going there just yet."

"So where are we going?"

"We're going on a mission."

"Oh, so we're stalking Troy. Is that what you're trying to say?"

"That's right, and don't tell me you're not diggin' his vibes 'cause I'll be glad to take him off your hands."

"No way! I put all the work in so let me roll with him for a while."

"I'm cool with that. So let's do some sneakin' and peekin' and find out where he lives."

"Yeah, and who he lives with," adds Niecee as she snaps her fingers to the auto's stereo vibe.

Troy's freeway drive wasn't long and the girls kept a safe distance, three car lengths behind. He breezed by the Summit Lake exit and took a dirt road, a rear entrance up to Boulder Creek. After traveling for a mile, he turned left into Maple Hill Cemetery Park.

"What's the matter?" cried Niecee, "why are we stopping?" She hadn't been paying attention during the drive. The Mercedes was so quiet and smooth that Niecee had dozed off.

"Troy just turned into that cemetery park."

"A cemetery park?" mocked Niecee yawning and readjusting the recline button on her seat. "What's up with that?"

"Remember, he told Aliya he had to take care of some business."

"Hmm, so what should we do now?"

"Heck if know, but I guess he's visiting a family member's gravestone."

The Highway 9 traffic was picking up. The girls decided not to wait around. Tahoe turned left into the cemetery park. She was planning on making a turnabout and getting back on the highway.

"Wait a minute!" barked Niecee while grabbing Tahoe's right wrist to prevent her from turning the steering wheel. "Isn't that Troy spread over the hood of that police car?"

"It looks sort of like him," replied Tahoe squinting as though that would improve her vision.

There were two county sheriff cars that were blocking Troy's vehicle. Four men were in trooper uniforms and three men wore suits. The men in suits were standing beside Troy and one of the suits was handcuffing him. He was led to an unmarked car and shoved into the back seat. An elderly black man walked up to the auto's window, spoke to Troy, and returned to the walkway which led to the Maple Hill Cemetery office.

Tahoe and Niecee had parked alongside the driveway's entrance and waited until the convoy of police vehicles paraded by. The girls saw Troy leaning forward in his seat. He was frowning and looked worse than just uncomfortable. The squad car's back seat design allowed for little or no leg room. The girls made their turnabout and followed for a short distance behind. Finally, after getting back on the main Highway, the lead car picked up its pace and used a carpool lane to escape the rush hour traffic.

Niecee and Tahoe pulled up in the Bell Motel's parking lot, space seventeen, at fifteen minutes after seven. Frank Dean was warming his RV's engine. He was seated in the cab and waiting for their arrival. When he saw them pull up, he backed the RV out of his private carport and let Tahoe back the Mercedes into the vacant slot. Once they were on board, Frank took the Nimitz Freeway northbound for thirty miles to the first Hayward City exit. The girls had never ridden BART (Bay Area Rapid Transit), so Frank parked at the station and purchased tickets for everyone.

After BART crossed the bay by way of underwater tunnel, they got off at the Civic Center Station and hailed a cab to San Francisco's North Beach. They made a pit stop at Big Al's, a bar and strip joint which often featured two or three of the hottest porn stars on the circuit. The trio had a grand time watching the strippers compete for the money that customers were waving and tossing at their favorite dancers. The DJ was spinning vibes from the Foo Fighters and Bruno Mars latest hits. Niecee jumped up on one of the mini-stages and joined another dancer. She lifted her suede skirt to her thighs, exposing her bodacious buttocks, and the audience went berserk. They threw a slush of dollar bills at her feet.

Tahoe rushed over and coaxed her down before the bouncers got to her. Frank Dean was laughing so hard he almost fell off his stool. He couldn't believe how much fun he was having without taking a drink of hard liquor. He was ordering tall glasses of Seven-Up with a lime twist. The club's quota was five dollars per drink, and they delivered each customer a fresh one every fifteen minutes. You had to pay the cost or you'd be asked to leave. They stayed for forty minutes. The drinks increased their appetites, so they made a beeline for the Hof brau that was directly across the street.

The Hof brau was a smorgasbord type restaurant, a perfect place for everyone's palate. Frank Dean could no longer hold out; he ordered mugs of cold German beer for everyone. Niecee loaded her tray with mashed potatoes, a turkey drumstick, a thick slice of baked ham, corn on the cob, and two jumbo dill pickles. Tahoe chose fried liver smothered in onions, cornbread stuffing, a cucumber, lettuce and tomato salad, a half loaf of sourdough bread, and carrot cake. Frank Dean had the traditional German sausage links, sourkraut, two large pretzels with mustard and a pitcher of beer.

By ten o'clock everyone's belly was satisfactorily full. Frank Dean used an American Express card and charged everything on it. The girls took care of the busboy's tip in cash. Tahoe snatched a couple dozen after dinner mints from the cashier's counter and gave the lady a five dollar tip.

Once they gathered outside, the chill off the bay had dropped the temperature by fifteen degrees and a thick fog had drifted in. Frank had warned the girls about the climate's severe changes at a moment's notice, and everyone had brought along an overcoat.

They recrossed California Street and got at the tail end of a block-long line. It was a twenty minute wait before they walked into the parlor of Basin Street West, where Wynton Marsalis was about to start his second show. Although the club was packed, they were able to get a table right up front when a party of two decided to leave. Frank Dean tipped another waiter and within seconds a third chair was delivered. Wynton and his musician's first set ran for forty minutes. They took a fifteen-minute break and the second set was performed at a feverish pitch for almost an hour. The audience gave them several standing ovations and they finished with a double encore.

After the show, Frank Dean hailed another cab and they were driven to a coffee shop-bookstore directly across from the Civic Center BART Station. Tahoe struck up a conversation with some guy who looked like a twin of Kanye West. She invited herself over to his nook, which allowed Frank Dean and Niecee a chance to be alone.

"A penny for your thoughts, Princess," said Frank while browsing through a coffee table magazine that featured classic cars. "Did you enjoy yourself tonight?"

"Oh yes, I had a ball! I loved every minute. It was really wild, but I was just thinking about my new home, ya know," replied Niecee, just brimming with enthusiasm. "I'll be so glad when it's ready for moving in."

"That's gonna be soon, I hope?"

"For sure, Aliya says it should be ready by the middle of next week."

"Sounds marvelous, Princess. You and Tahoe have done a wise thing with your money. You can never go wrong by investing in real estate. So, what is left to do?"

"Oh, a little more painting, and carpets need to be laid. And tomorrow this landscaper is gonna pull up these stumps in our backyard."

"Landscaper?"

"Yeah, and oh-wow, daddy, I almost forgot. I think he got arrested today. Oops, I mean yesterday."

"Arrested?"

"Yeah, it was at the cemetery. Maple Hill Cemetery Park, right off" --

"Highway 9. I know that park. It's next to my property. The owner was a good friend of my father's. So, start from the beginning and explain how all this came about."

"Aliya introduced us and he gave me his business card. When he left work early, Tahoe was curious so she followed him, and that's when the cops got him. It was kind of like they were expecting him or something."

"Well, that's understandable because he lives there."

"For real?"

"Yes, for real. His father is a mortician. He runs the cemetery and owns most of the property that surrounds it."

"Oh, I see, but it doesn't explain what the police want with him. I sure hope he's all right."

"Oh, don't worry yourself over it, princess. It's probably a business matter. Do you have his card with you?"

"Yeah, daddy, it's in my purse."

"Let me take a look at it."

Niecee digs inside her Gucci bag, removes a clutch purse and pulls out a small stack of business cards and hands them to Frank, then quickly excuses herself and scurries off to the restroom. Frank shuffles through the cards until he comes across Troy's. He pauses, thoughtfully stirring his coffee.

DOMINIQUE'S TREE AND LANDSCAPE
EXPERT TREE TRIM & ROOTING

Reading the name on the business card opened up a logjam of memories for Frank Dean. He could still remember the first day he met the big toothed kid with the ridiculous grin. He was one of several kids hired to pick fruit in his father's orchards during the summer. Troy was the kid who was always snooping around places he shouldn't be.

The first summer he worked, he was fired for using the

refrigeration unit as his personal club house. It was Billy Bear, Frank Dean's youngest brother, who found the deer's head. Apparently, Troy had killed it, not for food, but for some kind of experiment. The animal's skull was soaking in a metallic tub of vinegar. It was a God awful stench.

The next year, Frank Dean's father gave Troy another chance and hired him back. Before the summer's crop was picked they had to fire him again, but this time they took their complaints to Troy's father. Troy had turned the well into a spawning tank for a poisonous breed of puffer fish, which contaminated the farm's drinking water and a portion of the lake. It killed dozens of fresh water fish.

Frank Dean remembered that Troy was a hard worker, but when things were going good he'd find a way to screw things up. After Frank Dean's father passed away and Frank took ownership of the land, he'd occasionally run into Troy on jobsites or see him in his hunting gear, usually taking a shortcut through the George's property. It had been almost a week since Frank Dean had visited Summit Lake, but suddenly everything was starting to make sense. The dead fish he'd discovered and the restart of the warehouse generator was probably not a fluke. Someone had tampered with the settings, and that someone had to be Troy.

Frank Dean made a mental note to himself to drive up to the lake at the crack of dawn and check things out.

The detective's interrogation of Troy began on Friday in a Scotts Valley Sheriff's conference room at six p.m. By one a.m. Saturday, the interrogation ended and a deputy escorted Troy back to his home. The interrogation was not legal. The detectives were working outside of their jurisdiction, but it was a courtesy that was allowed by the Scotts Valley Sheriff. He had hoped that the Merced detective's suspicions were more concrete and could somehow link Troy to the poisoned female cadaver they discovered in a forest near Ben Lomond Creek.

For the first hour, they left him alone in the locked conference room and observed him through a video cam. Troy was extremely calm. He even took a nap. Detectives Valdez and Marcus took turns interviewing him. They tried a good cop/bad cop routine, which was a waste of time. Troy seemed to be a step or two ahead of them. He gave a precise and formidable explanation for every question asked. He had an established bank account at the Citi Bank of Merced, and he'd picked up a take-out at a nearby diner. He carried a bank deposit receipt that was electronically dated and teller signed, and he had the cash register receipt from the diner. "No," was his answer about parking along the roadside behind a red vehicle.

The detectives were not baffled by Troy's answers, but they felt a little frustrated. They sensed something was amiss. The time clock on the receipts still left a one-hour window during which Troy claimed he spent parked and resting under a chestnut tree right outside Merced's Central Park. The answer required more canvassing by the police. Still, the recurring question...was Troy telling them the truth or sending them out on a goose chase? Yet, after six hours of continual questioning, Troy's story never faltered nor changed. Finally, the Scotts Valley Sheriff made a half-hearted apology, and the Merced detectives tried to disclaim any further interest in him. They offered him another business card and asked Troy to contact them if he recalled anything that might help find the missing girl.

Troy never allowed himself to get rattled by the officer's obvious bold faced lie. He returned a polite smile and stated that no offense was taken. He said he knew they were just doing their job. Troy knew he left the detectives feeling a little embarrassed and perturbed. He knew the interview was done too soon and the Merced police didn't have the manpower to follow him, but he wasn't certain it would be the last time he'd see them.

From Chief Detective Valdez's perspective, the interview went just as he expected. Detective Marcus wasn't in agreement, but it didn't matter. Valdez had more experience at this cat-and-mouse game, although Troy was not only good at it, but seemed to relish answering every question asked. Valdez believed that sooner rather than later Troy was about to make a mistake, and they would be on him like a heat seeking missile when it happened. Troy's outdated CB radio and police scanner were no longer useful tools to avoid police scrutiny. Valdez believed Troy was damned lucky and the type who thought he could get away with anything and never be caught. Valdez was confident that he would be the one to catch him and put him away for life.

It was one-thirty in the morning when Troy was dropped off at Maple Hill Park. The interview had not tired him, but the snacks they'd offered him were unsatisfactory and he had refused to eat, so he was now famished. His father had someone move his truck from the front of the office. Troy took a walk down a narrow roadway for an eighth of a mile. When he reached the dock outside the crematorium, he removed a set of keys from a hook near the doorway. The keys were for a Jeep Wrangler Rubicon, an army green off-road vehicle. Troy grabbed a toolbox and walked over to the main house, grabbed a quart of orange juice and guzzled it down. Next, he took a quick shower, changed into fresh work clothes and loaded up the truck.

Troy traveled the Nimitz Freeway, got off at the Bascom Street exit and rolled into a fast-food restaurant on the west side of San Jose. He ordered three fish fillets, two jumbo fries, and two pints of fruit juice, then pulled his Jeep into the rear entrance of a self service gas station. He went inside the restroom to wash his hands. He parked the Jeep Rubicon in the corner lot and dug in. Five minutes into his meal, a tan Dodge Charger pulled up next to him. The Jeep's chassis sat much higher than the Charger's. Troy instantly knew the auto was parked too close.

Suddenly, someone opened the Charger's driver's side door and bashed the Jeep's siding, not once but several times. Troy immediately got out to see what the problem was. It was a blond female, obviously drunk, who was either in a blackout or just a belligerent human being. Troy shouted at her and she immediately began cursing at him as though it was his fault that his Jeep wouldn't allow her to get out of her own car. She shut the door, restarted the engine, and proceeded to back out. Troy raked his knuckles against the Charger's driver's side window. The driver pushed the power button and the window came partway down.

"WHAT?" she screamed scrunching her face like a Miss Piggy doll.

"Turn your headlights on!"

"Fuck you, nigger!" She shifted into drive and tires squealed as she raced out of the parking lot with the rear bumper scraping pavement. She missed the driveway and ran over the sidewalk. Then she zigzagged for almost a block down a street that fortunately had no other traffic at the moment.

Troy wasn't certain, but he thought he recognized the woman as the same waitress who worked at the Thunderbird Lounge. He climbed back into his Jeep and took off after her. At the third signal light traveling north on Curtner Avenue, Troy caught up to the woman. He pulled up next to the Charger but he couldn't see inside because the windows were tinted. Then someone turned on the overhead interior light. Troy spied three other male passengers. He recognized them as the trio he'd had a wrestling match with at the bar. They were all too drunk to sit up straight, but the waitress' reckless driving must have wakened them. When the light changed, Troy continued his pursuit. He kept a distance of about three hundred feet. The drive was about fifteen minutes long, and they ended up in San Jose's Almaden Hills.

The blond pulled into the driveway of a three-acre mini-ranch. There were several of them side by side. This one contained a main house, a guest home, trailer home, barn and a stable. The Almaden Creek separated the ranch home from a section of moderately priced residential homes.

Troy made a U-turn and parked alongside the creek. He traversed a slope, crossed the creek and ended up behind the barn. There were two horses in the stable. Troy let the horses out and led them to a pasture on a neighboring ranch. He had to kick down a portion of a rickety wooden fence. The racket woke two sleeping Dobermans. They raced across the pasture barking as though they were planning to attack, but once Troy pushed the horses through, the dogs retreated. Next, he pried open a shed and removed a five gallon can filled with gasoline.

He sloshed some on several bales of hay and emptied the can in a pit of fresh mesquite wood. Then he walked up the driveway where several motorcycles were parked and picked up a hefty rock. His initial plan was to toss it through the house's large front window, but a baby's cry startled him. A light from inside the trailer came on and Troy moved back into the shadows of the barn. He stood perfectly still in the dark. His heart was not beating any faster, but a bizarre kind of calmness came over him. It was as though he were holding his breath under water.

Troy reflected on the time he lit the camper's sleeping bag afire, a childhood prank that turned deadly and killed a man. Troy had long ago excused it away. It was a mistake. He was only a boy. But what about now? Troy didn't bother searching his mind for an answer. He didn't know the answer. He did know he wasn't angry or lonely anymore. For the first time in his short life, he realized he was acting on impulse, out of habit. He was still thinking as though he were a kid, when he was doing things for kicks out of boredom and seeking excitement. Even when his idea of excitement was grossly sick and disturbing.

Troy released his grip on the rock and it fell to the ground. He slid back down the slope and recrossed the creek. He needed to get at least a couple hours of sleep. Saturday morning had already arrived. He had a truck and winch to rent and twelve stumps to pull.

At seven-thirty a.m. Aliya expected to be the first to arrive at 515 Hull Street, but Tahoe and Niecee pulled up just a few seconds behind her. The painters were union men, so they wouldn't be working on the weekend. The roofers said they would be arriving around eight-thirty. They didn't want their pounding to upset the neighbors.

Tahoe and Niecee were dressed for grunge work. Aliya was glad to see them so bright and energetic. She brought a few extra mops, pails and general cleaning supplies. As soon as her auto's trunk was unloaded, work began. When the roofers finally arrived, the girls were finished with the bathrooms, and they all took a break before they began work in the kitchen.

"Hey, Troy!" yelled the roofing foreman, "I see you've already got five stumps pulled. What did ya do, spend the night?"

"Aliya and the girls were astonished by what they just heard. They never thought to check the backyard. All the roofers were laughing, but Troy had gotten used to getting razzed by the foreman so he laughed right along with them. The girls abandoned their work and went outside to greet him.

"Wow, talk about the early bird gets the worm," said Aliya, grabbing his right bicep and nudging up against him. Troy smiled and waved at Niecee and Tahoe, who were just catching up.

"Hi, Troy," said Niecee, "you sure are up early. Is everything all right?"

Troy returned a broad smile but wasn't quite sure what Niecee meant. He said everything was fine, then he spoke directly to Aliya, "The way it looks, I'll have these stumps pulled in no time at all. Will you be needing the wood or do you want me to get rid of it?"

"I think the girls have enough firewood to last them through a couple of winters, but it's their call," said Aliya.

Tahoe looked over at three cords which were stacked against the back side of the garage. "That pile looks like more than enough to me."

"Me too," agreed Niecee.

"Well, that settles it," said Aliya. "Troy, you can chop it up if you'd like. I've got clients who'll buy it so you can make yourself some extra money."

"All right," says Troy, "I'll chop it and divide it into smaller bundles. It will make it easier to deliver."

"Sounds great!" said Aliya. "Girls, I've got to make a quick check on another property down the street. I shouldn't be away very long. Do you think you can handle the kitchen work by yourselves?"

"Oh, for sure, Miss Aliya," replied Niecee. "We're working girls. We'll have it spotless and sparkling in no time at all."

"Ya damn skippy!" echoes Tahoe as the girls exchange a high-five.

By ten-thirty the girls were done with the kitchen. They were admiring their handiwork when Troy stepped inside.

"Excuse me, anybody using the bathroom?"

"Nobody's here except for us," answered Tahoe. "It's the first door on your left," she said, pointing down the hallway. Then she winked at Niecee, grabbed her by the arm and dragged her onto the back porch area.

"Now's your chance, Niecee," she whispered.

"What?"

"You know. Troy. Ask him out. Talk to him. Do something," she said with a frantic look in her eyes.

"I don't know, I like him, but..."

"But what?"

"I don't want to hurt Mista' George."

"That man's old, Niecee. And you don't need his money 'cause you got money. Troy likes you. Haven't you been noticing?"

"Yeah, I think he does, but he's so fine. He's probably got a dozen other girls waiting in line for him."

"Boo-who, so what if he does. Besides, if he had a girlfriend, why would he let Aliya rub up against him? I'm tellin' you, Niecee, it's open season on him and you're first in line today, so go for it, girl. Aliya won't be back for a while. I'm gonna make a store run. You need somethin'?"

"Yeah, bring me a wine cooler."

"What flavor?"

"Plumb or peach."

"Alright, I'm outta here." Before Tahoe leaves she bangs on the bathroom door, "Troy, it's Tahoe. You need anything from the store?"

He opens the door, "Yeah, could you get me three quarts of orange juice and a bag of ice? Here." He digs in his pockets and hands Tahoe a twenty. She pushes his fist of money away.

"Oh no, I got it. See you in a minute!" she shouts as she dashes through the hallway and out the front door.

Troy had to pass through the porchway to get to the backyard. When he enters, Niecee stops him, "Troy you got a minute?"

He turns to look at her and smiles, "What?"

Niecee is sitting on the porch swing. The same couch where Aliya seduced him a few days ago. Niecee pats the seat, indicating she wants him to sit down with her, and he does.

"Um, Tahoe and I are going to a fair in Vallejo tomorrow and we'd like you to come with us. That's if you're not planning on working tomorrow."

"Hmm, a fair. You mean like a county fair with pigs, sheep and cows that smell up the whole neighborhood?" he teases.

Niecee giggles, "Yeah, and you know, fun stuff."

"Will they have one of those games where you can shoot a basketball through a hoop?"

"I don't know. Maybe and maybe not. We'll just have to see. So that means you're going with us?"

"Yeah, why not? I haven't got anything planned for Sunday. So what time we leaving?"

They arrange a meeting time and place. They rise from their seats and Niecee grabs him by his hand, gets up on her tiptoes to kiss him on the cheek, but she stops when she hears voices coming from the kitchen. Niecee peers over Troy's shoulder and sees Aliya prancing down the hallway, and Frank Dean is with her.

"Look who I ran into!" preens Aliya while trying to catch her breath.

"Hi, Princess!" chirped Frank Dean, his gaze fixed on Troy.

"Well, hello," replies Niecee, trying to force some excitement into her voice.

"It's about time you took a break, Troy," asserts Aliya, moving in closer to lean against him.

Troy doesn't reply right away because he and Frank Dean are feeling each other out. There's ice in the room. Suddenly, Tahoe comes barging in, "Hey, ya'll! What's this, a party? Excuse me. Give me some room so I can set this bag on something."

She sets the bag onto a steamer trunk and empties out the contents. "Troy, here's your juice and ice. And look at these pastries, they're hot and fresh from the bakery." She opens up two pastry boxes. The sweet aroma pervades the room.

"I know you bought coffee," presumed Aliya.

"Wouldn't cha' know?" teases Tahoe, reaching inside the bag and removing Styrofoam cups, a hot pot, and an eight ounce jar of instant coffee. Tahoe's calamity took the men's focus off each other. Troy said thanks, grabbed his orange juice, slipped out the back door and retreated to the backyard. Tahoe got the water boiling. Aliya unraveled the cups and plastic utensils and set everything up on a fold-out card table. Then she hollered at the roofers to come on down. Frank Dean and Niecee escaped to the living room.

"What's the matter, Princess, aren't you glad to see me?" said Frank, searching for the twinkle in Niecee's big gray eyes.

"Of course I'm glad to see you."

"Well, what were you doing with that guy?"

"His name is Troy, daddy. And I thought you two knew each other?"

"Yeah, we do."

"So why didn't ya'll speak?"

"It's a man thing, Princess. You wouldn't understand even if I tried to explain it to you," said Frank Dean, realizing that he shouldn't have brought up a subject he wasn't yet ready to explain.

Niecee rolled her eyes and pouted her thick lips. "Well, we were just talking, daddy."

"I'm sorry, Princess. I didn't mean to pry. Besides, I'll talk to Troy in a little while. How about us doing something together tonight?"

"Ah, I can't daddy. I sort of made a promise to Tahoe to do a girls night out with her and Brenda, 'cause last time we tried to get together with her we ended up in jail."

"That, I can understand. The three of you making up for lost time," said Frank, smiling.

"Uh-huh, sort of like that."

"Okay then, what about tomorrow?"

"Ah, tomorrow..." Niecee pauses. She's doesn't want to be dishonest, but she doesn't want to hurt Frank's feelings. "I was going to a fair tomorrow."

"Oh, that sounds adventurous. What time do you want me to pick ya'll up?"

Niecee paused again. She was desperately searching for the right phrasing, but there were none. "Well, Troy is taking us...umm, me and

Tahoe. We're going to the county fair in Vallejo." Frank Dean's smile drifted. The crease between his curved mouth became a straight line.

"How about Sunday evening, daddy?" said Niecee, toying with the buttons on his leather vest. Frank Dean doesn't hear her, because his mind just went somewhere else.

COTTLE ROAD
Saturday, April 23rd
And Sunday, the 24th

FRANK DEAN WAS in turmoil. For most people it was a simple matter of the heart, an older man being infatuated with a woman young enough to be his daughter, but for Frank Dean it was much more serious. Frank had never been married. In the romance category he'd practiced being the first to cut off a relationship just to avoid the possibility of being hurt. He never could handle rejection. At least, he couldn't handle his interpretation of rejection, although it was simply an insecurity within himself. He warned himself about girls like Niecee. He hadn't intended to allow her to penetrate his heart, but it was too late. When Niecee told him about her date with Troy, Frank Dean went comatose and everything around him went pitch black.

When Frank Dean awakened from his stupor, he was sitting behind the wheel of a black Ford Bronco and traveling east down McKee Road. He pulled into a nondescript parking lot and moments later he was turning the door knob to Dr. Denardo's office.

"Good afternoon, Mister George. Glad you could make it," said the doctor, shaking his hand with her right and crushing the butt of a cigarette into an ashtray with her left. She blew a plume of smoke and turned on the desk fan.

Frank Dean sat motionless in a straight-back wooden chair. He was dressed in a combination of grays and blacks. Black shirt and jeans, gray moccasins and vest, string leather tie with a broach-like clamp, and a gray felt fedora which he placed on his lap and held with both hands. His silence made the doctor a little uncomfortable. He was two hours late for his appointment. The blond receptionist had already left. The waiting room was empty of patients. The doctor was planning on leaving as soon as she'd finished going over her notes and tidying up some files.

"Mister George, I've received your blood analysis. You know, the lab tests you took on Thursday."

Frank Dean doesn't respond. Dr. Denardo hands him a sheet of paper. "This is a printout of all the chemical elements contained in your body. Too little or too much of any chemical listed will create a dysfunction in your physiology, or simply stated, take you out of balance. Now, you've only been taking the lithium for a short time, so it's not going to show up in this test, but if you take it three times daily as I've prescribed, you will build a reservoir of lithium in your system."

Frank Dean is staring at the printout but saying nothing. Dr. Denardo doesn't interfere with his somber mood. She makes a mental note of it, but her goal is to get him to take his medication. The test clearly shows that he hasn't, but the doctor decides to save that battle for another day.

"Well, Mister George, if you don't have any questions, I'll mark you down for an appointment next Saturday at one-thirty, okay?" She smiles broadly. "May I suggest a walk in the park. It's been a beautiful day and there's a nice park with a fountain near here. I often take my lunches there."

Frank Dean still doesn't say anything. He opens the office door and walks out. Although Frank Dean chose not to dialogue with the doctor, he still took her advice. He walked over to the park and found himself an isolated bench under a shady elm tree. It was almost four-thirty. He texted Niecee, but she didn't respond. He waited fifteen minutes and texted again, but didn't wait for an answer. He powered off and walked over to his truck.

PRINCESS

DID I FORGET 2 TEL U HOW MUCH I LOVE U

THAT YOUR NAME BEGINS AND ENDS EVERY PRAYER

DID I TEL U THAT LOVING U IS EASIER THAN BREATHING

THAT 2 LET SOMEONE ELSE SHARE YOU IS SOMETHING I CANNOT BEAR

A DARK CLOUD HAS COME OVER ME

MY HEART IS NOT MADE OF STONE

When Frank Dean walked into the Cinnabar it was seven p.m.

He'd made a stop at the Bell Motel to shower, shave and change into a fresh set of clothes. Jim the bartender was washing out shot glasses. He used the bar room mirror to keep watch and he spotted Frank the moment he poked his head through the doorway.

"Hello, Frank. How the hell are ya?"

"Oh, I've seen better days, Jim. How are you?"

"Hardly working, but busy," he kidded.

Frank Dean walked over to his favorite table and began dropping quarters in the jukebox. Then he stepped up to the bar.

Jim finished with his small chores and set a clean glass on the bar and poured Frank a tall twelve ounce of light beer. Frank stood with his hands outstretched and bracing the bar's countertop as he observed Jim go through the ritual. The beer foam came over the sides of the frosty glass. Jim was about to mop it up, but Frank Dean pushed his hand away before Jim could get started. Frank snatched the glass and downed the beer in four gulps, five seconds flat. Then he slammed the empty glass on the counter. Jim was waiting for him. He held the tap ready to pour another. After the fourth refill, Frank Dean let loose a modest belch and took a barstool seat.

"I'm kinda' hungry, Jim. What kind of sandwiches have you got?"

Jim named four and Frank Dean chose a meatball on sourdough. Jim reached into a cooler and placed the sandwich on a platter and slid it into the microwave.

"Let me have a couple bags of those chips," said Frank pointing to a rack, "and a pickle. You still got those dill pickles?" he said with a slight slur to his words.

"Sure do, Frank."

The microwave beeps. Jim slides the sandwich, chips, and pickles onto a round plastic tray and Frank Dean takes it over to a lone table. The juke is blaring a selection of sad songs. Freddy Fender's *"I'll be There Until the Last Teardrop Falls"* was everybody's favorite. After his second bite of sandwich and a mouth filled with chips, his cell phone vibrates. He's got it tucked in his cummerbund under his shirt. He unsnaps two buttons on his Western style shirt and digs out the cell. He checks the Caller ID and flips the phone open.

"Hello, Keith."

"Yeah, Frank, it's me."

"Where are you?"

"I'm at the corner drug store on Market and Post."

"You been going to meetings?"

"Of course, Frank. That's what you're paying me for."

"So, why are you calling me?"

"I need a fresh meeting card for Monday. Damn, Frank, you should know the routine by now."

"Look, Keith, I ain't in the mood for no bull Those signatures are legitimate, right?"

"Yeah, Frank, of course. Listen, in the gardening business we go to different locations almost every day. My dad has a regular list of clientele to cater to, and he assigns me and my brother to a variety of places throughout the Bay Area. I keep an AA manual with me that lists all the meeting places and times for Santa Clara, Alameda, and Santa Cruz Counties."

"Okay, that's fine. I'll meet you at the Greyhound bus terminal in half an hour. Is that cool?"

"Yeah, see you then."

Frank Dean never rushed to do anything. He made sure he completed thirty-two chews with each bite of his meal. He was hoping the call would have been Niecee, but it didn't surprise him that it wasn't. When he arrived at Greyhound, Keith was smoking a cigarette and pacing the sidewalk in front of a hotel building next-door. He saw Frank Dean pull up, so he jogged over and hopped in the passenger seat. Frank had left the motor running and veered back into traffic.

Keith Jio was an Asian youngster who grew up in Boulder Creek until his family moved to San Jose. His Father ran a gardening and landscape business for over thirty years. The entire Jio family was involved in the nursery business. Keith was one of the kids who during the summer helped out at Mr. George's orchard farm. Keith was presently Mr. Jio's right hand man, but Keith was also a heroin addict who maintained an outward appearance that was civil and very clean.

Frank Dean had money to burn and Keith's income was modest. He had to earn extra dough just to facilitate his habit. The men traded AA cards, one with signatures for a blank one. Then Frank passed Keith an envelope with cash.

Keith whistled, "Nice! Very nice."

"We wade a deal, Keith, and as long as you keep your end of the bargain, then I don't mind payin'."

Keith had temporarily lost his driver's license for getting one too many speeding tickets. He liked driving sports cars and he couldn't resist the temptation of getting behind the wheel of one. Around town he used the transit system to avoid the risk of being pulled over. "Say,

Frank, there's a couple chicks I know that invited me over for a little get-together. You wanna come?"

"They hookers?"

"No way," answered Keith laughing loudly. "They're straight but I'm in tight with them. They're nurses."

"How old?"

"Ah, late twenties, early thirties, I guess."

"Where you meeting them and at what time?"

"Oh, around eleven. They got a place off Cottle Road."

"IBM area?"

"Yeah, that's right. You know 'em?"

"Naw, but that's quite a while from now. What are you going to be doing in the meantime?"

"Well, if you don't mind, you can drop me off on Eleventh Street so I can pick up a package."

"Is this gonna take long 'cause I got some unfinished business waiting for me at the Cinnabar?"

"No need to wait, Frank. Just drop me off and I'll give you a holler later, around ten o'clock."

"Okay, good deal, but I'm shutting my phone down at ten-thirty."

"Oh, don't worry, I'll call you, with plenty of time to spare."

Frank Dean made his trek back to the Cinnabar. He returned to the same table and jukebox and everything other than the music being played was left untouched. He ordered a couple more beers and even mingled with the crowd at the pool table and played a couple games. The loser of each game had to down three tequila poppers. Frank Dean lost two games. He downed five poppers and blacked out.

The songs coming from the jukebox remained sad and bluesy. Frank heard the songs but he couldn't remember them. He enjoyed the mood as well as everyone else. It soothed the soul. It made everyone's troubles and woes a little more bearable, a common thread of life experience that no one could avoid or predict. For every patron, drinking alcohol was the shellacking, the veneer finish that coats the hurt and the pain. For Frank Dean it was a last ditch attempt to cap his volcano of hurt from erupting. The tequila had taken full effect. For the next eight hours, every action, deed or thought that was recorded in Frank Dean's mind was instantly erased, like a computer virus destroying a program code. All there was left for Frank Dean to do was pretend to be a fun drunk like everyone else.

The girls on Cottle Road were professional nurses, Anna Bradford and Wilma Davis. They were also ex-felons and had both spent time in prison. Anna was five-nine, thirty-two, all ass and legs. She had a smooth black coffee complexion, high cheek bones and a smile that made everyone seeing her want to smile right along with her. She was articulate and well read, had a warm personality and was easy to get along with.

Wilma was thirty, short, sassy and cute. In prison her handle was Hot Stuff. Crème de cocoa complexion, thick nappy hair which reached the middle of her spine. When she wasn't working at the Santa Theresa Convalescent Hospital, she was shopping at a mall or getting her nails or hair done at some health spa or beauty salon. Wilma was a smooth operator; every other sentence she uttered was a lie. Her prison stint was for keeping one of her boyfriend's cars a lot longer than she was supposed to. He just happened to be old enough to be Wilma's grandpa. She left him without a car for a week, a car that she was supposed to return to him within a few hours. She'd done it before, but this time grandpa got tired of her games. He reported the car stolen.

Anna once worked in the county hospital, but she lost the position when she was charged with prescription drug theft, her first offense. The only reason she got prison time is because she was supplying drugs to an out-of-state criminal ring which she didn't realize was under police surveillance. She lost her nurse's license but was still able to work in the capacity of home care. Despite the girls' checkered histories, neither girl was an addict, but they kept a stash of cocaine around for parties and occasional use. Both were bisexual and they loved to drink.

Frank Dean and Keith showed up a little past eleven. The girls had everything set up and waiting for them. Keith gave them a heads-up on everything his friend liked and didn't like.

The home was a deluxe model. Built in the nineties, a combination of Dutch and German architecture, a brick and mortar two storey structure with twin turrets and a steepled roofline. Four bedrooms, two full baths and a huge round fireplace centered on the living room's calico carpeted floor. High beamed ceilings and a full mahogany bar with brandy, scotch blends, bourbon and a few specialty wines, chardonnay, cabernet sauvignon and a petit chenin blanc.

Frank Dean and Anna Bradford hit it off right from the start. They dabbled in one subject after the other from what type of fish could be found in the Caribbean to Hindi and Pakistani cuisine. They sipped on wine and played spades while Wilma prepped everyone's brand of cigarette with a cocktail laced with cocaine. The nurses made Frank Dean feel like an embassy prince. The cocaine and wine mix served as a nice aphrodisiac, a tantalizing sensation that Frank Dean was not accustomed to. Usually, the amount of booze he drank numbed his nature and he had difficulty getting a rise, but tonight was different. The nurses had him sandwiched between them. They were taking turns feeling him up by teasing his loins.

At one in the morning Keith got a call from a friend who needed to purchase a couple grams of coke. He said he was throwing a party and had run out. Keith wasn't the type to stay in one place for very long. He was used to being in the nurse's company and found himself a little bored. Since he didn't have his car, he asked his friend to send someone to pick him up. Twenty minutes later, a car horn's honk was Keith's signal that his escort had arrived.

"Sorry girls, but I've gotta run."

"You coming back?" asked Wilma.

"No can do. Unlike you, I work on Sundays," he said with a smile. "Enjoy yourself, Frank. I'll be giving you a call around Thursday or Friday."

"Okay, Keith. Catch you later, man."

The girls gave Keith a hug and told him to be careful.

Now the gathering had gotten a little more cozy, so the girls went into action. Wilma decided she needed freshening up, so she headed to the bathroom to take a shower.

"Frank, let's move over to the couch where it's a little more comfortable," Anna cooed in his ear.

"Why not," answered Frank, smiling.

They got situated on the couch. Anna crossed her leg over his and played with the broach that was clamped to his leather string tie.

"You mind?" she said as she reached for the frame of his glasses. She didn't give him a chance to answer. She laid the thick bifocals on a coffee table, stroked his right cheek and pressed her warm lips over his mouth. Her succulent kiss lingered. Then she repositioned herself so she could straddle his thighs. Frank's breathing picked up. He braced himself with both palms pressing against the seat of the couch.

Anna was five-nine. Her elongated fingers stroked the bulge that hugged Frank Dean's thigh. The anticipation was too much for her. She looked up into his eyes just to make certain that what she was about to do was something that he was ready for. She gently pulled down on his trouser zipper and opened his fly. His shank had stiffened, so he had to rise up slightly to allow Anna to pull him out.

"Ooou, Frankie, look at the size of you!" she murmured before taking the head of his prick into her mouth.

Frank's eyelids were at half mast, but the name Frankie caught him by surprise. He and Niecee had kissed and cuddled. They never had sex. Frank looked back at Anna as she fondled his tool. She was very good.

Frank moaned, "Stop, baby."

Anna looked up with a frown, the whites of her eyes widening. "What's the matter, honey, am I hurting you?"

"No, no, not at all. I...I don't want to come just yet."

"Oh, is that it? Hold on for one minute," she said, smiling. Anna left the room and returned only seconds later with two fat rubberbands. She looped one band around the base of his shaft and double looped the other around his scrotum.

"Aye! That's too tight," protested Frank grimacing, and opening his legs much wider.

"Relax, honey. I assure you, you'll get used to it. Look how pretty your dick looks. See how it swelled."

Frank looked and continued to grimace until Anna ran her tongue up and down the length of his penis, then massaged his balls by slurping them into her mouth.

Frank shivered, then moaned. He was now focused on her mouth and not the pain.

"These will keep you hard for a long time. It's gonna hold back your climax. Watch."

Frank leaned his head back and closed his eyes. Anna was wearing a pair of black spandex and a turquoise miniskirt. By the time Frank Dean opened his eyes again, he was looking at a salacious pair of naked hips and thighs. A thick mat of black hair was in between them. Anna straddled him. She worked his shaft inside her as though it were a surgical instrument. Her cadence was gentle, rhythmic, and smooth. She made him spread his legs wider. Once she warmed up, she pushed his legs together, then rode him until her climax erupted. She went buck wild.

Frank gritted his teeth and grabbed Anna by her love handles to steady her gyrations. She slapped his hands away and they lost their balance and tumbled from the couch. Frank's shaft was still deep inside her womb.

"Hold up a minute, honey," she managed to say in a breathless husky voice. "Let me use the couch for support."

Frank pulled out from her loins and Anna placed her knees on the couch seat and latched on to the headrest. Frank didn't need a handwritten script, he knew what she wanted him to do.

As the sexual frenzy accelerated into warp drive, Wilma returned from a fresh bath. Her body had the fragrance of Jean Nate'. She wore a gold satin negligee that clung to her curvaceous body like cane syrup on French toast. She flopped into a Lazyboy and watched the lovers perform.

Anna and Frank Dean were wreaking havoc upon one another. From Wilma's viewpoint, it looked like a fuck contest. Finally, the grunts and the glistening skin slapping subsided. Unlike the motion in the ocean, everything came to an abrupt finish.

"Oooh, shit!" screeched Anna Bradford as she slopped a wet kiss on Frank Dean's face, then pranced off half naked to the bathroom shower.

Frank Dean was still seated on the couch but without his magnifying specs. His bleary eyes appeared extraordinarily large and black. Wilma was seated directly in front of him, crossed legged and dolled up like she was waiting to do a centerfold photo shoot. She didn't have to guess as to whether Frank was into her because his dick was still rock hard and he was holding on to it as though he were getting ready to masturbate.

Although the cocaine was still doing its magic, Frank Dean's mind was somewhere else. Wilma decided to mix him a stiff drink, and that's when the scenario changed. Frank downed two tall glasses of JB, a scotch blend, in succession. "Say, Miss Wilma," he slurred, "forget about the friggin' mix. Just bring me the damn bottle," he commanded.

Wilma followed his lead. She liked her foreplay rough, so she was anxious to find a way to get him angry and mean. She tried to coax him into taking off his trousers, but he wouldn't go for it. Finally, she abandoned that idea. She laced the helmet of his dick with cocaine, twisted his balls then snapped the big rubberband that was wrapped around his prick. Frank Dean yelped. He shoved Wilma off him and she thumped her head on the carpet floor.

Wilma bounced up and made love to Frank's pole, but with a lot more tenderness this time. She doused it with sloppy wet kisses. "I'm sorry, daddy," she murmured, "I'll make it all better."

Frank just stared back at her and took another swig from the liquor bottle. Suddenly, he snatched Wilma by the hair and yanked her off the couch. "Where's your bedroom, woman?" he gruffed.

"Oooh, oh, right through that hallway, honey," she rejoiced. She knew if she got him inside her parlor she'd have to role play and hopefully keep him under her domain for the remainder of the night. But before leaving for the bedroom, Frank drug her over to the bar and grabbed himself a quart of Johnny Walker Red.

No more than ten minutes into intercourse, Frank Dean passed out. Wilma was pissed. She began pounding on his torso in anger, but it didn't do any good. She couldn't even muster a murmur out of him. Thoroughly frustrated, she left the room to get Anna's help.

"Look Anna, I checked his vitals, so he is still alive, but he's out cold."

"Huh, what did you do to him, Wilma?" chuckles Anna.

"Me? Hell, what did you do?" she shouted back, laughing along.

"I must have zapped the zing right out of him," replies Anna.

"Well, he was fun while he lasted. Let's get him undressed and put him to bed."

"Wait a minute," said Anna. "Didn't Keith mention he was rich? I wonder how much cash he's carrying on him?" Anna looked at Wilma as though she wanted her support. Her brown sparkled irises looked huge.

"You're not thinking about shaggin' him, are you?"

"No way, silly. I'd be damn foolish to do a thing like that. Abuse a potential meal ticket?"

"Oh, frigit. Help me turn him on his side so I can get to his pockets."

The nurses searched him and found nothing.

"Maybe he hides his cash in the truck," deduced Wilma.

"That's a possibility. Why don't you check it out and I'll stay with him in case he wakes up."

While Wilma was out on a mission, Anna noticed a lump near Frank Dean's ribcage. She copped a feel and slipped her hand inside his western shirt and pulled out two thick wads of cash. She took it over to Wilma's mirrored dresser and removed the money clips. The bills unraveled like an accordion. Some fell on the floor and Anna was trying to scoop them up when Wilma returned, panting and shivering.

"I couldn't find nothin' and it's damn cold out there. I should have worn a..." She froze in mid-sentence. Her gray eyes bulged when she saw the huge amount of cash.

"You can close your mouth now, Wilma," jibbed Anna.

"Eeee! There must be at least twenty grand right there!"

"Shhh! Wilma, you're gonna wake him." Anna tosses her a fist of cash. "Here, count this."

The conscious mind shuts down and the subconscious continues to record, but in Frank Dean's case, the alcohol coats the brain and, through time, the electrons that fire throughout the brain's pathways are slowed. Memories become obscure. Frank Dean's brain had a lot of blind spots. The alcohol gene was still a mystery to science. Even the oldest living AA member had no real clue on how to figure it out, other than to just stop drinking.

Frank Dean was still asleep, but Frank George awakened. He saw a blur in a mirror, and the blur was something unrecognizable. He was in an unfamiliar room, with unfamiliar smells. The girls were too absorbed in their count to notice him. He rose from Wilma's queen sized bed like Michael Myers, the creep in *Halloween*. He receded into the shadows of a walk-in closet. There was no escaping the shape-shifters that deceived Frank George's comatose vision. There was no escaping the macabre. He slid the .22 revolver from the bindings of his cummerbund. He took dead aim and fired without warning.

The first bullet hit the third lumbar in the tallest girl's spine. The short girl ran. Fifties and hundred dollar bills flew from her hands as the second bullet splintered her upturned nose.

The shooter stepped forward and the kill shots were taken no more than a foot from each target. The tall girl was down on one knee. She was clinging to the dresser. A single shot to her right temple left blood splatter on the dresser mirror and Frank Dean's western shirt.

The short girl tried to escape by crawling under her queen sized bed. It was too late. A bullet ripped through the aorta. Blood gushed from her mouth. The final shot zigzagged through her torso and shattered her lungs.

Moments later, Frank Dean drove away like he was leaving a crime scene. He was lucky.

Nobody noticed.

Rob and Sunny were jogging the Santa Cruz Seascape Trail when

Newman voicemailed them. The morning had begun on a foggy note, but the fog went inland by eight-fifteen. The air was a cool fifty degrees. The ocean was calm; patches of aqua green and cobalt blue. The freshman P.I.'s finished their jog and boarded the Isuzu Trooper. Ten minutes later they were pulling up in a parking lot a block from the boardwalk.

Newman had arrived early. He was sitting in the window booth at a Starbuck's cafe. The trio did their ritual greetings. Rob gave Newman a fist pump and Sunny got a bear hug and a peck on the cheek. Then Newman ordered a round of coffee, juice, milk, and a tray of hot apple strudel. The joggers have an appetite and Newman is continually stuffing his face, but nobody's talking until they're satisfactorily full.

"Okay, here's the latest scuttlebutt," said Newman, his coarse black eyebrows meeting as he licks his thumb and forefinger. "I got some lab work back on your case, as well as a couple cases I've been working on the side."

Rob pulls off his Nike sweatband. He's sporting a shaved head again. His gold trimmed front teeth are sparkling and his chinstrap goatee is glistening with sweat. Sunny is wearing a pink beanie and a baby blue running suit. She's anxious to get on with whatever Newman's about to say so she can go outside for a cigarette break.

"Remember, we started with two female corpses. My initial lab stated that both died of poisoning, one arsenic and the other was antifreeze, right?"

"Right," answered Rob in agreement.

Sunny bobs her head, but the frown on her face indicates that she's puzzled because she's hearing the details of the girls' deaths for the first time.

"Well, the FBI lab tests have proved me only half right," said Newman with a sigh. "They found another element of death that was common to both."

"Okay, and what was that?" interrupts Rob hoping Newman would get to the point.

"Puffer fish."

"Puffer fish?"

"The vics were killed with poison found in puffer fish."

"Are you saying they both ate the fish and..."

"No Sunny, I'm saying someone extracted the poison from the fish and used it on the vics."

"Wait a minute," said Rob, "are you talking about an ocean fish that makes itself look bigger than it really is so it can ward off predators?"

"Exactly, but hold up a minute and I'll explain." Newman is holding up his left index finger and pauses to take a swig of coffee. "There are over a hundred varieties of puffer fish. Most live in warm oceans and few are found in rivers and fresh water. Sunny, you're right. Some puffers can be eaten, but most are poisonous. And yes, they can greatly expand their stomachs to take a shape of a ball by rapidly swallowing water or air. Like you said, Rob, it's a protection device used to ward off enemies. Oh, and one more tidbit. Some puffers do well in home aquariums, but you have to keep other species of fish in separate tanks because the puffers have strong upper teeth. They'll crush and eat defenseless and smaller fish, and their skin and sexual organs contain a poisonous nerve that causes paralysis."

"Okay, Harry, stop right there," said Rob throwing up the palm of his hand as though he were a traffic cop. "If you're saying they didn't eat the fish, then how did the poison get into their system?"

"Zombie powder," replied Newman.

Sunny giggles, "What the hey?"

Rob has got a scowl on his face. He's Looking back at Newman as though he's just been insulted.

"I know it sounds ridiculous," said Newman, combing his fingers through his curly black hair. "It's a theory, but it's got legs. You see, the Zombie Powder is a Haitian concoction that's applied to the subject being healed or exorcised during a voodoo ritual. The potion is a combination of plants, some chemicals, and the main ingredient is the liver of the puffer fish."

"Why the liver?" asked Sunny.

"Because it's the filter and the most toxic organ."

"Oh, I see. So they drink the poison and it kills them. It's a spiritual sacrifice or something."

"Well, you're close," rallied Newman, "but that's not it. First of all, voodoo, or voodun as it should be pronounced, is the natural and supernatural worship of ancestors. It gave the black slaves in Haiti during the Slave Trade a form of cultural expression and a rallying point for protest against their oppressors. Now, what the Zombie Powder does is it shuts down the heart rate and breathing and all muscles become paralyzed."

"Even the throat muscles? " blurts Rob.

"Right, especially that, but the first stage before paralysis takes over is...uh, let's see..." Newman is staring at the plate where the apple strudel was, but now it's all gone, so he finishes drinking his coffee.

Rob glances at Sunny and Sunny tries to help Newman get back on subject, "So what happens first, Harry?"

"Ah, there's tremors and vomiting, then paralysis. The victim can see and hear but can't do anything. It's like being in suspended animation. Next, a funeral is performed. The subject is placed in a tomb and within twelve hours he or she is revived by using ammonia camphor."

"Oh, I know!" screeches Sunny, "just like in the movies, the person is dead but they come back to life!"

"Well, I don't know about that, but in this case the person is still alive but has to be revived or eventually die."

"Okay, I get it," adds Rob, "the voodoo doctor performs the ritual and after everyone's out of sight, he comes back and revives the corpse, which makes the voodoo doctor look powerful."

"That's the ideal scenario, but it's not an exact science. More often than not, the person really does die, which is probably the case in point with Guadalupe Creek and the Scotts Valley females. Somebody is playing a deadly game and placing the subjects on ice.

"Ice?" questions Sunny.

"Yeah, ice or some type of cold storage. They're keeping them for several months, then dumping the bodies. In that way the discovery is of a fresh cadaver, which makes it almost impossible to predict an exact time of death. And in these cases, it makes it difficult to tell what actually killed them."

"So, we're looking for a Haitian?" deduced Rob.

"No, not necessarily. Even if you're a novice, info about zombies and voodoo practices can be found on the Internet."

"Gee," announces Sunny, looking a little hopeless, "how in the world do we figure out who's doing this to people?"

"All we need is a little luck," declares Newman, "and I may have something. I did some checking with the Fish and Game Department and BINGO!" Last month a Mister George reported a discovery of thirty dead fish floating in his lake."

"What lake?" probed Rob.

"Summit Lake. It's on private property and it runs into the Lexington Reservoir."

"Stop. You said the man's last name was George?"

"Yeah, you know him?"

"Maybe. Did you get his first name?"

"Let's see..." Newman goes to his cell and zips through a file. "Got it! Frank Dean George."

"Robbie, we know him," chirps Sunny. "He and his brothers are the owners of Bob's Towing and Salvage yard."

"No Kidding," said Newman. "What else do you know about him?"

"Actually, not very much," adds Rob, glancing over at Sunny as though she can remind him of something he's forgotten.

"Harry, you say he turned the fish over to the game warden. Is that right?" inquired Sunny.

"That's right."

"So that eliminates him as a suspect, right?"

"Well, if I had a suspect list, he wouldn't be on it, if it weren't for this." Newman reaches inside his sweatshirt pocket and removes a folded sheet of paper and hands it over to Rob. "What you're looking at is a copy of the lab report from the Sunseri case. Your case."

"Oh, goody!" yelps Sunny, clapping her hands.

Rob scans over it, frowns, then passes it over to Sunny.

"The urine sample is a positive match," said Newman. "It's Frank Dean George's urine. The crime lab in San Jose had it filed in their computer. Apparently, Mister George has a history of driving under the influence. As of last March he's still fighting a felony charge for a vehicle collision plus private property damages. It's his third arrest."

"What about the broach?" inquired Sunny.

"You mean the tie clip?"

"Whatever, if that's what they're calling it."

"Ah, I guess it was too small to pick up any prints or DNA particles, but here, look at this photo blowup on my cell." Newman hands Sunny the phone. "The pattern on the surface is an American Indian design. I've been told it could be one of several tribes, Seminoles, Crowe or Cherokee are just some of the possibilities."

Rob was looking back at Newman with an incredulous stare. It's as though something is lodged in his windpipe and he's incapable of clearing his throat.

"Robbie! Are you all right?" cried Sunny tugging his left forearm.

"Yeah, yeah, I'm cool. Look, Newman, we need to holler at Uncle Floyd. He knows the George family."

"Okay, but you and Sunny are on your own 'cause I got some

duties to look after this morning and I'll be checking into the office a little early this afternoon. Text me as soon as you get something solid."

"Will do," affirms Rob.

MANNEQUINS
Monday, April 25th

AT TEN A.M., the house off Cottle Road was seized by an army of police detectives, forensic specialists, emergency medical technicians, a television crew and a coroner. The Monday morning cleaning lady discovered the bodies. She dialed 911 a little after eight.

The house was warm. Everyone held a handkerchief over their mouth and nose to fend off the putrid odor of corpses just beginning to decay. For some, the stench was unbearable and they had to periodically leave the room to catch a breath of clean air.

The hazel brown bodies resembled storefront mannequins after dark. The rigor mortis cycle had begun. The bodies were swollen. The tall girl was lying on her side in a fetal position. The short girl was lying prone. Her head and shoulders were lodged under the foot of the bed. There were pinpoint hemorrhages to the eyes and bruises on the face and neck. The bodies were littered with everything that had fallen or was pulled down from the dresser. Bath powder, perfume, combs, lipstick, bobby pins and jewelry. Twenties, fifties and hundred dollar bills were in all parts of the master sized bedroom. It was as though the currency were searching for an escape route, attaching itself to a heater vent, window panes, curtains, a bedspread and closet door.

A couple detectives checked every room in the house, walking about and filling out forms that would outline compartments and elements of the murders. The coroner examined the hands of the corpses. He then tied plastic bags around them to protect the fingernails for further examination of blood and DNA traces.

He made a simple incision in the rib cage area. It was there he inserted a large thermometer. Based on a formula of liver and room temperature, an approximate time of death was determined to be between thirty to forty hours.

The techs placed the pair in body bags and carted them off to the county morgue for autopsy.

The bedroom was cleared and sealed. The forensics team sprayed the chemical ninhydrate on the floor and walls. The fumes would expose any fingerprints. Photographs had been taken before and after the bodies were removed. The majority of the stills showed pools of blood and traces of splatter. There was another team outside the house inspecting the grounds and canvassing the neighborhood. The San Jose PD was ranked as one of the best trained units in the nation. The police science department at the city university was renowned for its state of the art technology.

The Manteca murder of Joe Sunseri was on every county sheriff's radar. The search for a killer had become more than just a community effort. The San Jose detectives were privy to a network with an FBI database. Matching a .22 caliber bullet to one suspect without shell casings or gun was a challenge for the detectives, and it was an undertaking they were determined to achieve. The double murders near Cottle Road had become their rallying cry to their fellow officers to help them catch a cold blooded killer.

In the city of Los Gatos the 515 Hull Street work crew got an early start, cool blue skies, a sunny sixty-three. Troy arrived at eight. The roof job was complete. All that remained was discarded shingles and debris. A trio of painters were finished with the bathrooms and by ten they were working in the kitchen. A team of six carpet layers arrived at eight-thirty. They worked on three areas in teams of two and sometimes three. They carpeted the living room, den and three bedrooms. They were getting paid by the job rather than an hourly rate. The furniture movers were scheduled to arrive at one. The foreman of the carpet team promised Aliya his crew would be finished before noon.

Aliya showed up at nine o'clock sharp. She brought with her two dozen pastries, éclairs, bear claws and glazed donuts. She was making her rounds to each work crew when Niecee pulled up in her brand new Prius. Niecee honked and Aliya came running as Niecee parked her auto on sidewalk and lawn.

"Hey, girl," said Aliya with cheer, "your car is the bomb!"

Niecee was grinning from ear to ear, "I know, I know. It's cute, ain't it?"

"Yeah, girl, and I love the color you chose. I don't recall ever seeing a car painted magenta."

"Where's Troy? Did he make it to work?"

"Oh here, honey. As usual, he was the first to arrive. He's loading up some cords of wood onto his truck. We're about to leave and make a few deliveries.

"Gee, you think he can spare a minute to holler?"

"Why yes, of course. Go right ahead, honey. By the way, how was the fair?"

Niecee's face was a question mark.

"Brenda told me," chuckled Aliya.

"Ah, it was cool. The three of us had a really good time."

"So what have the three of you, excuse me, you and Tahoe got planned for the day?" said Aliya feigning a grin.

"Today is the day the furniture is supposed to get delivered."

"Oh, what time?" quizzed Aliya, even though she already knew.

"I called them twenty minutes ago. The delivery should arrive between one o'clock and one-thirty, is what the desk lady said."

"Excellent!" said Aliya. "That's perfect, because the carpet layers have got another customer lined up for this afternoon, so they promised they'd be finished by noon. I'm going to leave you so you can holler at Troy. Besides, I have to go check on the painters. They should be just about done with the kitchen."

They turned away from each other and Niecee called her back, "Miss Aliya, I almost forgot. Tahoe and I are having a house warming party on Friday. It's a come as you are party. Brenda and your Aunt Liz have promised to come, and of course you must come," offered Niecee. "We'll have an open house around four in the afternoon."

"Oh, for sure, honey. You can count on me being present. How about I invite some of the neighborhood bitches so ya'll can get to know who's who and who ain't?" teased Aliya.

"Huh?"

"I'm just kidding," rebounded Aliya with a laugh. "The women I invite, you will definitely like, and they will come bearing gifts as well."

"Cool," replied Niecee as she spun away, skipping through a pathway that led to the backyard. She found Troy arranging cords of wood on a flatbed truck. Niecee crouched behind a stack of chopped wood. She waited patiently until Troy jumped down from the truck, then she ambushed him by leaping onto his back.

"DOKE!" he hollers foolishly, pretending to be surprised. His peripheral vision was very keen.

Niecee had her thighs clenched around his waist and her right forearm clamped around his neck. Troy spun around in a circle. On the third spin, he finally stopped when he realized Niecee wasn't about to get dizzy or let go of her grip. Troy, trying to outwit her, faked a cough, "You're choking me!" he crowed.

"No, I'm not!" she giggled as she tries to cover his eyes with her free hand. "Guess who?" she teases.

"Ah, Freddie Kruger!"

"No, no!" said Niecee laughing, "Try again."

"Uhh...Aliya!"

With that remark, Niecee instantly released her grip, slid from his back and kneed him in the buttocks. Troy turns. He has an exaggerated look of surprise. "Oops! My bad."

Niecee isn't finished with him. She shoots a straight jab to his rib cage and is about to strike with her right.

"Okay, okay, I'm sorry, I give!" he yelped, trying not to laugh. "You're a wild child Niecee. You play rough, girl."

"You ain't the first Ninja that's tried to bust my peanuts, Mister Troy Dominique, but it ain't happening." she admonished.

"Peanuts? What the heck is that supposed to mean?"

Niecee is only teasing. She doesn't want to spar with him. She pulls. him by the neck and gives him a kiss. He can't get away this time so he kisses her back.

"I'm ready when you are, Troy!" yells Aliya from the back porch screen door.

"Okay, just a sec!" answers Troy, breaking Niecee's hold, "I'll be ready to roll in five!" he yells back.

"She so nosey."

"She's the boss, Niecee, and she pays me good."

"She's trying to do more than just pay," snaps Niecee. "I got money and I can pay, if you want me to."

"Niecee, cut it out, girl. It's going to be a beautiful day, so take a breath and think positive."

"Positive? Yeah, I'm cool with that, Sir Troy Dominique. But if you expectin' me to be your bottom bitch, well, I got a surprise for you, mister." Niecee is up in Troy's face and bumping her chest against his.

Troy rolls his eyes like the comic Bernie Mack. He pecks her on the cheek and scoots past her, then turns quickly to face her again. "By the way, Miss Niecee, I got a new tree trimming contract. I'll be starting next week and the assignment is just two blocks away. So you'd best be cool 'cause I'll be watching." He smiles and tries to walk away.

Niecee is not finished. She picks up a dirt clod then slings it sideways, hitting Troy square in his back. He just laughs, throws his hands up in the air, but never turns around.

Niecee and Aliya's pursuit for Troy's attention has kept him preoccupied with trying to keep each girl content. The girls have influenced his thinking in a way he hadn't quite figured out. All he knew for certain was his passion for hunting was dwindling. The climax of the kill was no longer the primary thought that propelled him through each day. Troy was a beast, but his attitude was changing because he was beginning to find a measure of resolve to his turmoil and gain a little inner peace. He really didn't want to continue killing. And for the first time in his life it really mattered how he lived or died.

At the Bell Motel, Frank Dean awakened not recognizing his surroundings. His motel cottage was in complete disarray. He rose from his bed and staggered into the bathroom. Someone had pulled down the shower curtain rod. There were wet clothes in a bathtub half filled with water. He looked into a shattered mirror that hung over the wash basin. On the floor was an empty plastic receptacle which once held thirty tabs of lithium, his prescription medication. He picked it up and examined the label as if he were reading it for the first time. Frank Dean looked back into the mirror and realized that shards of glass had fallen into the face bowl. His eyes were jaundiced. His throat was desert dry. His lips were parched. Frank ran his fingers through his graying kinked hair. He was dizzy. He was seeing two and three of everything. His breath was shallow. He needed fresh air. Using a narrow hallway for support, he left the bathroom.

Entering the kitchen, he placed a kettle of water on the stove and removed a half dozen brown eggs from the fridge. He warmed a small black skillet with oil, made toast and buttered it. He took two bites and his stomach lurched.

He opened the front door. The sun blinded him. He reached down and scooped up two rolled up newspapers at the foot of his doorway.

He closed the door and unraveled both. One was dated Sunday, April 24th, the other was Monday, April 25th. Where did all the time go? He couldn't remember. He ate, cleaned up the bathroom and the rest of the cottage. He needed to make a trip to Kim's Cleaners. He opened a canister marked 'Flour'. He reached in. There was nothing inside it. He opened another canister marked 'Cookies', that was empty as well. Frank wobbled over to a closet. From a top shelf he pulls down a shoe box and checks inside a brand new pair of moccasins. Nothing.

He goes outside barefoot, still dressed in his pajama bottoms but without a top. The hotel manager's wife is watering planter boxes that front each motel window. She sees him and waves. In the carport, parked next to the RV is a red Ford pickup. Frank Dean is puzzled. He detests the color red. He searches the cab, then the truck's bed. Once again he finds nothing except a single key in the ignition. It's tagged and he realizes it's a tow. He'll have to call his brother to let him know he has it.

Frank finds his cell phone. The power is off, so he turns it on. There's no message on it. The bar code is down to one emblem, just enough juice for one or two calls, so he punches in a few digits.

"Hey, Mike."

"Yeah, this is Mike. Is that you, Frank?"

"Yep."

"Hey, buddy. How's it goin'?"

Frank Dean takes a moment to clear his throat. "Hell, I don't know. Could be better, I guess. I was--"

"I know, Frank. You were just checking in. I haven't seen you at any meetings lately."

"Ahh, probably not. I'm trying out some new places."

"Oh, it never hurts to venture out and meet new recovering alcoholics. Have you started writing on your Fourth Step?"

"Excuse me, Mike," said Frank Dean coughing, "be right back." Mike hears Frank coughing a little more, then throwing up. Forty seconds later he speaks through the phone. "Sorry for the wait. I had something caught in my throat."

Mike can clearly see through Frank Dean's line of B.S. He's been there and done that himself. "Recite me Steps One through Six, Frank."

"Now?"

"Yes, now, and don't use the Big Book or anything else."

"Okay, I can do that." Frank recited the first five of the Twelve

Steps and couldn't remember the sixth.

"Frank, the sixth step says you've gotta be ready to let go and let God do his work in you, but if you don't complete the fourth and talk it over with someone, your character defects will continue to be your nemesis."

"I feel you, Mike."

"I don't want you to feel me, Frank. I want you to work the Steps so you can get better at living life on life's terms." Frank Dean didn't have a response. His head was throbbing. He felt a nasty headache coming on. "Frank! Are you still there?"

"Yes."

"Look, the Men's Meeting is at eight o'clock tonight. I hope to see you there, buddy. Try and make it, alright?"

"Sure, Mike. I'll see you there."

Attending the Men's Monday Night Meeting was not the primary thought on Frank Dean's mind, because besides misplacing his money, he couldn't remember where he put his .22. But it wasn't that important. He owned several guns. Yet, the .22 was a gift. There were no papers on it. It belonged to his dad.

Frank Dean got dressed and stuffed his laundry into a pillowcase. He went to the closet and rolled out a steamer trunk. There was a padlock on it. He searched his ring for the key.

The trunk held a family album, a Dream Catcher and other hand crafted memorabilia. He found what he was looking for, his dad's money clip and a .25 automatic with a full nine bullet clip. He checked it, set the safety and stuffed it in his cummerbund at the small of his back. He thought about sending Niecee a text and a moment later changed his mind. He had what seemed like a million things to do, go to the cleaners, stop by the bank and drive down to the salvage yard. More importantly, he wanted to stop by the lake property and check out the warehouse refrigeration system.

When Sunny and Rob stepped through the sliding glass doors of Floyd Bonesteel's gazebo, they were flooded with surround sound from a Paul Hardcastle Jazzmaster CD. Sunny was light on her feet. She pranced, then shimmied her way into the spacious green room. Uncle Floyd and Aunt Elizabeth were playing a card game of Uno at the bar. They stopped to watch Sunny do her shing-a-ling as she circled Rob with a few hip hop moves she'd seen on video TV.

"You go girl!" said Elizabeth, cheering her on, as Floyd snapped the fingers of both hands like he was at the jazz club on Cannery Row.

The gazebo was a frosted glass enclosure that separated the mansion from a six car garage. Aunt Elizabeth was an award winning interior designer and she had recently refurbished the room. She replaced the wall to wall Persian rug with a smaller version and utilized the three foot marble border with an assortment of tropical plants. Floyd built an aluminum trellis that could be raised or lowered from the ceiling. It was adorned with ivory and purple flowering scaevolas which could clamber or hang. Elizabeth swapped Floyd's lambskin three-piece couch for rattan furniture and several stained glass lamps and a coffee table.

Floyd wasn't too pleased with the new decor, but he allowed his wife of thirty-plus years to do her thing. He knew that within eight to ten months she'd come up with an entirely new scheme, so he'd wait patiently until then to make a bid to get his couch back.

When the music stopped, so did Sunny's rumba. Floyd got up from his seat to install a new CD.

"Okay, you two gumshoes," teased Elizabeth, "what kind of suspense and intrigue are you going to share with us today? Have you solved the Sunseri murder yet?"

"We haven't solved anything yet, Aunt Liz. We've got a few pieces of the puzzle, but there's still a whole lot missing. We're here to find out what Uncle Floyd can tell us about the George family," explained Rob.

"Indian George?" said Floyd.

"Yeah, that's right, I guess."

"Well, I knew the father and he's deceased, but his sons have inherited all of his investments and properties."

"Yeah, I know about all of them, Uncle Floyd, but what can you tell me about Frank Dean?"

"Frank Dean is the eldest son and the brains of the family. He's detail oriented and he's got a shrewd business mind. He inherited the sole interest in a couple properties, one being the Summit Lake estate, and he also owns the Bell Motel over on Alameda Boulevard down in Saint Joe.

"You mean, San Jose," clarified Sunny.

"That's right, honey, it means the same thing."

"Is Frank Dean in trouble, Rob?" asked Elizabeth.

"We're not for sure, Aunt Liz. It's just that we need to inspect his property, but we can't let him know he's being investigated yet."

"You're working out a theory, is that right?" alleged Floyd.

"Actually, we're not sure if it's a theory or just a hunch, Uncle Floyd," offered Sunny.

"Which place do you plan to inspect?"

"Summit Lake."

"When?"

"Today. Is there a back entrance to the property so we can avoid going through the front gate?"

Floyd pauses for a moment. "Yes, there should be a fire trail that runs parallel or above the neighboring property."

"What's the neighboring property?" asked Sunny.

"Maple Hill Park."

"You mean the cemetery?"

"Yep," said Floyd with a smile, because Sunny was looking back at him with bugged eyed blues, "it's the Dominique property."

"Dominique? What kind of name is that?"

"It's French," chuckled Floyd as he rises from his seat. "Let's take a stroll to my office. I believe we can pinpoint a fire trail on my computer."

They rose from their seats and followed Floyd's lead, Rob, Sunny and Elizabeth trailing. They took a short stairway up the landing of the mansion's kitchen and stepped down into the living room. Another right down a hallway and a quick left placed them in Floyd's library office. Floyd took a seat at computer number one and everyone huddled over his shoulder.

He logged into Google Earth and then focused on the city of Los Gatos. He hit the zoom button twice. The map showed some major streets and highways. He moved the mouse a fraction and clicked. Lexington Reservoir and Summit Lake came into view. Floyd pointed at red squiggly lines.

"Those lines are fire trails. This one to the left runs off Highway 9. Its entrance is a little past the cemetery boundary, here, and it dives down into..."

"That's a creek!" declared Rob.

"Right, but it's probably completely dry this time of year. It's in a hilly area, so it's probably a gulch or a small ravine. Hike through it and you come out on the north entrance of Summit Lake."

"Wow!" exclaimed Sunny. "How long do you think it will take to hike that trail?"

"Oh, no more than half an hour," assured Floyd, "but my advice to both of you is to stick to your protocol. Get in and get out before nightfall."

"Nightfall?" echoes Sunny, her big blue eyes widening again.

"Yes, and I mean that!" said Floyd, raising his voice. "There's been reports of mountain lion sightings in that area. Mountain lions are accustomed to hibernating by day and hunting after dark."

"Don't worry, Uncle Floyd," assured Rob, "we'll be in and out of that property without haste, and my three-eighty goes wherever I go."

"Okay, lad. Do be careful and don't keep us in suspense. Give us a call as soon as you're out of there."

"Will do, Uncle Floyd. Will do."

It was an hour and fifteen minute drive from Monterey to Los Gatos. Rob Bonesteel and Sunny Jordon had to make a pit stop at their office to pick up a few things before making the journey to Summit Lake. Sunny texted her dad to let him know she'd be hanging on to the Isuzu for a couple more days.

By three-thirty they reached the end of the fire trail and found a clearing that was safe enough to park. They weren't in any rush. They'd planned to start the trek back around six. Sunny brought along a backpack filled with items she insisted they might need. Rob didn't want to argue so he let her have her way. The hike through the gulch was not hard, lots of oaks, tall grass and knotty pines. The gulch was steep and fairly wide, a feature the computerized map didn't clearly show.

At four o'clock they reached what they assumed was the interior of the George's property. Green and yellow sticker grass had infiltrated their clothing. Sunny's shoes and socks were covered with their pointy darts. She was forced to stop and pull some out.

"Wow, this place looks like a community dump site for machinery and appliances," said Rob.

Sunny hears him but what he's saying doesn't register. "I know I should have worn my boots instead of these tennis shoes. Then I wouldn't be having this problem," she whined.

"You'll be alright as soon as we get out of this tall grass," consoled Rob. "Let's check out that graystone building, then we'll go to the lake and work our way back."

They climbed the porch of the mansion and checked every room closet and cabinet. They reached the top terrace and Rob climbed up the roof.

"I can see the entire layout from here, Sunny!"

"Can you see the lake?"

"Yeah, and I also see four bungalows and couple storage shelters we need to check out."

Rob climbed down and they trampled the tiny trail that had been smothered by more of the prickly wild grass. Finally, they reached the short pier where a rowboat was moored to one side and an aluminum raft to the other. They walked a hundred yards up the lake's sandy shoreline.

"You see anything, Sunny?"

She was looking though a miniature set of field glasses. "I don't see any floating fish if that's what you mean. What's making that god awful noise?"

"It's a bull frog."

"A bull frog? He sounds like he's in some serious pain."

"It's probably a mating call."

"Well, if he's calling up his girlfriend, I wonder what she sounds like when she answers him back?"

Rob laughs, "You're crazy, woman. Let's get moving. I think there's nothing left to see here."

They rummaged through the bungalows and one of the warehouses. There wasn't anything to show for their efforts, but they were covered in dust. Sunny marched over to the well to refill her canteen and get the smut off her face. She fumbled through her backpack, pulled out a camper's flashlight, and as she peered down the well the warehouse generator clicked on.

The shrillness of fan belts whizzing over pulleys startled the pair. Rob spun around to see if anybody was approaching. His .380 was drawn. He kept it pointed downward and held it close to his side.

"Robbie, I think it's on a timer," said Sunny in a hoarse whisper. She was down on one knee and crouching beside the well.

Only one of the warehouses was equipped for refrigeration. If no leakage occurred, the constant cooling would last indefinitely, throughout the life of the system. Wooden planks fronted the building's entrance. The double doors were padlocked and the windows were only slats of wood that were installed for ventilation. The only possible entry was an air vent on the roof. While Sunny remained crouched by the well, Rob circled the building. A couple minutes later he returned.

"Is there any chance you packed a rope in that backpack?"

"I most certainly did!" replied Sunny cheerfully, eager to show Rob that she could be useful.

The yellow forty foot rope was actually a half-inch cord. Rob surmised it was strong enough to hold his weight. His plan was to drop through the vent and let Sunny in through the lone exit door from the building's rear.

Twenty minutes later, they rolled a hot water tank carcass against the building. Sunny hugged it steady and Rob climbed onto the roof. Luckily, after tying one end of the rope to a pipe, his descent was an easy one. Once he opened the back doorway and let Sunny through, he was left with no choice but to repeat the climb and retrieve the yellow hemp before he could proceed with the search. Sunny didn't wait for him. Using a hefty rock, she propped the door ajar and began the search with her flashlight. She located the electrical panel and by the time Rob entered, the building's overhead lamps were on and the generator had shut down.

The room was cold and damp. Condensation had rusted most of the metal and rotted some of the wood. The warehouse contained several rows of shelving. Each shelf was stacked with a variety of tin cans and Mason jars. They began their search. Sunny was reluctant to touch anything. Most everything was caked in frost. They searched for what seemed like a very long time when Sunny checked her watch.

"Robbie, it's five minutes to six. Shouldn't we be going now?"

"In a minute, babe." Rob was down on his knees. He was tugging at an oblong cardboard box that was stuffed under a bottom shelf. After becoming a little too impatient and applying more force than needed, the corrugated box ripped open and Rob held a corner piece in his hand.

"Bring me your flashlight, Sunny."

"You find something?"

"I don't know."

Sunny hustled over and squatted next to him so she could be eye level with what he was doing.

"Shine it right over my shoulder...WHOA!"

Rob jerked and Sunny shrieked. His momentum propelled her into another iron shelf. The flashlight was jarred from her left hand and skidded down the slick concrete floor where it ended up in a pool of water near a drain.

"What the hell was that?" cried Sunny, her light blues were now a jaded green.

Rob had to clamp his left hand over her mouth to shut her up. "Shh," he said raising his finger to his lips. "There's somebody out there. Just be still."

Sunny was holding her breath but she couldn't resist peering over his shoulder. Her mouth flew open but she maintained her poise and exhaled slowly. She was gawking at a pair of bare feet wrapped in thick plastic. The corpse must have been female because the toes had nail polish and a silver bracelet was strapped around the ankle.

"Get out, now! Hit the light switch. I'll meet you outside," instructed Rob.

As Rob fumbled to find his pocket knife, the lights were doused. He could hear the padlock and chain being untangled from the warehouse door. In one swift motion, Rob sliced the plastic, yanked the bracelet from the ankle, and bolted for the rear exit. When the front door opened, Rob was already outside. He grabbed hold of Sunny's hand as they hit the ground running. They raced to the front of the building and took cover behind the well.

"What are we doing?" said Sunny, her eyes widening again. "We're not gonna just sit here, are we?"

Rob didn't say anything for a few seconds. His heart was racing and he was short of breath. "We have to hold up for a while and make sure whoever is in there doesn't turn around and walk out. Do you still have that flashlight?"

"Huh? Oh no!"

"It's okay. Forget about it. We'll find our way out of here before dark, even if we have to crawl out on our bellies."

Frank Dean wasn't feeling much better in the afternoon than he did when he first woke up. He'd accomplished all the errands on his agenda by three p.m. There wasn't another black pickup he could borrow from the tow yard, so he chose one that was army green. He parked it at his motel carport and slid behind the wheel of his recreational vehicle.

The moment he arrived at his lake property, he sensed something was amiss. He noticed a footpath of trampled grass and broken twigs leading towards the lake. The warehouse generator was whining full bore when he first drove up and suddenly it shut off. Frank took precaution. He removed his father's .25 automatic from his waistband and shoved it in his jacket pocket. When he stepped onto the wooden planks at the warehouse entrance, a noise from inside halted his movement. He pressed his ear to the door before removing the lock and chain, then he stepped inside.

When he flicked the panel switch, the overhead lamps did little to illuminate the large and shadowy room. He glanced up at the rafters, as if doing so would make the lights become brighter. He noticed the screen on the vent that led to the roof was askew. Then he saw the flashlight. He picked it up and checked the batteries. They were still warm. He was about to check the back door when he noticed the ragged edge of a corrugated box that looked out of place. He didn't remember ever seeing it before. He muscled it out and drug it under an arc of light.

The female corpse didn't startle or astonish Frank Dean. He was a veteran of the Iraq War, Operation Desert Shield. He was accustomed to viewing the dead. The blond haired woman wore cutoff jeans and a halter top. She was tall, about five-eight or five-nine. Her ears and nose were pierced. Patches of her skin were ash gray and other areas were black. Her bodily fluids had pooled inside the plastic that contained her, but the room's frosty air had halted the decomposition process and kept her frozen. She was cold as ice.

Frank Dean stayed with the body for almost an hour. It was a little past seven. He knew he'd never make it in time to attend the Men's Meeting. He made a trip to the RV and returned to the warehouse with a hand truck and a navy blue plastic tarp. He carefully wrapped the body and bound it with neoprene tape. Then he strapped the corpse to the hand truck and pushed it to the entrance. After securing the warehouse, he took a shortcut through the woods. Thirty minutes later, he unloaded the hand truck and placed the corpse on the stairway of the crematory's dock. He wrote a note.

THIS BELONGS TO YOU.
IF IT OR ANYTHING LIKE IT
WINDS UP ON MY PROPERTY AGAIN
I WILL KILL YOU.

Frank Dean made a brief appearance at the Men's Meeting. He received a warm welcome, although he was forty-five minutes late. All that mattered to his sponsor was that Frank was clean and sober, and the only thing that mattered to Frank was that he remained a man of his word.

Crime gets prominent slots on the evening news. If it bleeds, it leads. The local TV stations advertised the Cottle Road murders as their top story. The newscaster analysts were already trying to tie the Joe Sunseri Manteca murder with the homicides in San Jose.

Down in the city of Merced, Detective Valdez was paying close attention to the broadcast. The murders done with a .22 caliber didn't fit the method that was a trademark of his prime suspect, unless Troy Dominique had changed his M.O.

When Aliya Bonesteel invited Troy inside her home for a drink and conversation, she was hoping she'd be able to coax him into staying overnight. Troy claimed he had some errands for his father to attend and the night was still young. He promised Aliya that once he took care of business he'd come back. Aliya did everything she could to get him to change his itinerary. She placed wet kisses that penetrated his clothing along his chest and neck, and she clung to his crotch like it was the Stanley Cup Trophy. Troy was restless and Aliya didn't want to anger him. Experience with men like him reminded her to let him do his thing and make him feel as though he was still in charge. Besides, she had recently booked him with another project and she hadn't told him that she owned the property. Aliya wasn't worried. She'd have Troy back in her lair before the week's end.

Troy was amused but not impressed by having two women vie for his affection. It was interesting but it wasn't the kind of excitement that would challenge him or bring his adrenaline to a boil. He missed the hunt, and like a jungle cat, the full moon gave him the impetus to kill. He had to be prepared if unsuspecting prey just happened across his path.

He rambled up the main driveway of Maple Hill Park. He parked the flatbed in front of the crematorium and took a shortcut to the rear of his father's home.

"Troy, come here and pay your respects!" squawked the accented voice.

"I'll be there in a minute!" replied Troy as he rummaged through a kitchen drawer in search of the hearse car keys. Not finding them, he slammed the drawer and invaded his father's bedroom.

"What is it? And did you borrow my keys? I..."

Mr. Dominique had already plucked the keys from a lamp table and tossed them to Troy. "Go to your cah. A package and note be waitin' for you."

"A package?"

"Yes."

"Is that all?"

Mr. Dominique did not answer his son. He went back to watching the game show on his television set. He was disappointed that he could not correct his son's treacherous nature when he was just a boy. The voodoo island doctor assured him that he was successful in casting out the dark spirits that were harboring his son's mind. He advised the Dominiques to leave the island. A change in geography would ensure the evil spirits would not return. The doctor was wrong.

Troy found a folded blue tarp on the front seat of his hearse. Yet even after reading the note he was still perplexed. When he parked the truck, he wondered why the crematorium's furnaces were lit at such a late hour. His father was required to follow strict city ordinances in regards to running the furnace. Any use after six p.m. was not permitted.

Troy hurdled over a stretch of lawn that contained a batch of cemetery plots. He raced up the crematorium's stairway and slid open the iron doors. Then he grabbed a pair of goggles and peered through the open slot just large enough for a pair of eyes. Within an instant, he backed away. The radiant heat was unbearable. The female corpse was just a fireball, unrecognizable to anyone unless you did a forensics on the dust.

DÉJÀ VU

Midnight Monday April 25th thru
Wednesday April 27th

A WARM BATH AND TV DINNER was the foremost thought on Rob and Sunny's minds.   Upon returning from their twilight reconnaissance, Aliya came rushing down to greet them at the front office door. She'd mistaken them for Troy. The pair knew something was up. They sensed Aliya's disappointment. After a shower and fresh set of clothes, they gathered in the kitchen while Aliya prepared them something to eat.

"What in the world have you two been up to?" quizzed Aliya.

"Ask me no questions and I'll tell you no lies," said Rob while removing the pickles from the submarine sandwich that Aliya had set in front of him.

"This is déjà vu all over again," said Aliya, looking back at them. "Are you two going to let me in on this secrecy crap or do I have to starve it out of you?"

Sunny giggled, "We found a body."

"You found a body!"

Rob continues chewing. Sunny is looking at him with wide eyes searching for her cue to continue with the tale.

"Don't you dare leave me in suspense!" cries Aliya. "Whose body was it? You're talking dead, right?"

"We don't know," said Rob, wiping mayonnaise from his mouth with one swipe of his fingers. "It's a she, and yes, she was dead. That's all we can discuss at this point."

Aliya ignored Rob's last comment. "Where's the body now?"

"We had to leave it," volunteered Sunny, "because we were being chased."

"Chased?"

"What she's trying to say," said Rob, cutting in, "is we had to leave the body there or get caught snooping on someone else's property. We didn't have a search warrant so we can't even file a report."

"Okay, so whose property was it?"

Rob sighs, "Frank George's."

"You mean Frank Dean George?"

"Hey, that's right," replied Sunny. "You know him?"

"Why yes, he's Niecee Edward's suitor. One of the girls who just bought a home from me. It's the house on Hull Street. Mister George came down to visit with her last Saturday."

"No kidding!" said Sunny.

"Okay, you two. Hold it right there!" howled Rob. "Newman will be here in less than an hour. I'm gonna leave it up to him if he wants to bring you up to speed, Aliya, but for now, you've already heard too much."

"Party pooper! My brother's a pooper," lamented Aliya.

After putting a damper on the conversation, Rob ate in silence and Aliya tidied up the kitchen. Then the women stepped out in the garden and had themselves a cigarette. It was half past midnight when Newman showed up. The trio never moved from the kitchen.

"Sorry guys, I didn't mean to keep everyone up," apologized Newman.

"Hi Harry," greeted Aliya, "You look a little beat. Would you like me to fix you a drink?"

"What have you got?" replied Newman, arching his jet black eyebrows and rubbing his palms together.

"You name it and I've probably got it."

"A Margarita!" shouts Newman.

"Margarita?"

"Why, sure."

"I don't know, I may not have all the right ingredients." Aliya opens up a cabinet filled with an assortment of liquor bottles.

"Oh, yes you do," squealed Sunny. "Here, let me help."

The girls made some salsa and Rob made a quick trip to an all-night market and returned with a couple jumbo bags of Nacho chips.

"Okay, Rob, I read your text," announces Newman. "So the body the two of you found is off limits until we figure a way to get a search warrant to check the lake or something like that."

"I don't know, Harry. He's bound to have moved the body by now, especially if he found the flashlight we left behind."

"Exactamundo, buddy, but didn't you see his face? It was Frank Dean, wasn't it?"

Rob looks over at Sunny and she looks back at him. "No, we didn't see his face, but he didn't see ours either!" blurted Sunny.

"Then how do you know for certain it wasn't some other shmuck?" Rob looked back at Newman like Homer Simpson stuck on stupid. It made Newman chuckle. "It's okay," consoled Newman. "Don't throw in the towel just yet. We still may have something. Did anyone happen to see the lead story on the evening news?"

"Oh, you're referring to the those Cottle Road murders down in San Jose," volunteered Aliya.

"That's right."

"What murders?" said Sunny.

"Two nurses were found shot dead at their home this morning," replied Newman.

"Yesterday morning," corrected Aliya.

"That's right, and they were killed with a twenty-two caliber, just like..."

"Joe Sunseri," said Rob, filling in.

"Will someone explain to me where does Frank Dean actually fit in all this?" said Aliya, looking worried.

"For one thing," said Newman, "the urine sample the two of you discovered is officially his, and the puffer fish poison extracted from those two female corpses have not been linked to the breed of fish found on the George property, but the frozen corpse you discovered fits in with my killer's modus operandi. Now, if perchance Frank Dean owns a twenty-two revolver, then we may have your killer."

"Don't forget the broach," added Sunny.

"Yeah, she's right," said Rob, "the tie clip we found. You said yourself that it's an American Indian design and Uncle Floyd told us that the George's mother was a black woman and their father was Cherokee."

"Hold on, you three!"

"What's the matter, Aliya? Did we miss something?" said Newman with a slight grin.

"Yeah, like motive. What's a man of Frank Dean's stature doing poisoning women and shooting people like a Fringe vigilante taking out shape-shifters from a parallel world?"

"She's right," agrees Sunny, "we haven't got a credible motive."

"We don't need one. We just turn the info over to the local police and let them decide," said Rob.

"Not so fast," counters Newman. "I got a text yesterday afternoon from a detective up in Merced. He said he was running a check on all neighboring counties for a female who came up missing a couple weeks ago. He said he got word that I autopsied the Scotts Valley girl and he wanted me to contact him if I ran across any new info or similar cases. When I talked to the Scotts Valley Sheriff, he told me that Merced's chief suspect was a Haitian named Troy Dominique. So I did some checking and--"

"The Dominiques run Maple Hill Cemetery Park," said Rob. "Right."

Suddenly, a chair crashed to the floor and a margarita drink went flying. Aliya had fainted. Sunny was the nearest. She immediately dropped to the floor to help revive Rob's sister.

Saratoga Heights was a senior citizen's complex in the city of Saratoga, another quaint villa just southwest of Los Gatos. It was best known for the Paul Masson Vineyards where summer jazz and rhythm and blues mini-concerts were held in their rustic outdoor pavilion.

Keith Jio and his brother Wilkie parked a Ford van and twin trailers loaded with lawnmowers, gardening supplies and other tools. They arrived at Saratoga Heights at six a.m., an hour earlier than they had planned because Keith couldn't sleep and he was in a foul mood. Their father had been taking care of the four acre complex for the past five years. It was one of the Jios preferred list of special clientele. On most projects, the brothers kept watch over one another by working as a team, but big brother Keith was throwing a tantrum because he wanted to shoot some heroin and he forgot to bring his rig.

"Come on Wilkie, just keep it simple, bro. Loan me your kit."

"It ain't happenin', bro. Pay me what you owe me and I'll think about it."

"Cut me some slack. You know payday is not until Friday."

"Why don't you just drive yourself back home and retrieve your own shit!" snarled Wilkie.

Keith cringed and banged his fist against the van's siding.

"I didn't think so, fool," continued Wilkie, "cause you know there's no way you can sneak past dad's watchful eye. And if he spots you, he's gonna dock you some serious pay. If you wasn't prepared, you shouldn't have rushed us out here so early."

"I know, I know already. Look," Keith kicks off his left shoe and pulls out his stash," I got more than enough smack for both of us. Besides, I won't be worth a shit to either of us if I don't get my bang."

Once again, Wilkie gave in to his older brother's fast talking charm.

By noon, the lawns were mowed and all that remained were some bush pruning for the afternoon. They bought lunch at Little Sicily, an Italian deli located in a strip mall nearby. Their orders were identical, sliced cappacola and salami with Monterey Jack cheese on sourdough, and a six pack of Heineken. They ate under a canopied table facing the parking lot that fronted the tiny store.

"You look like shit, bro. Didn't you get any sleep last night?"

"Fuck you, Wilkie. And you look like my left nut. Why do you ask me that anyway? You're not pop."

"And I ain't your enemy, dude, I'm your brother. You always be gettin' an attitude when you're high. But I know when something's eating at you. So, whuzup?"

Keith takes a swig from his beer bottle, then he scans the faces of the patrons sitting at tables nearby. He reaches inside his tan khaki coveralls and hands his brother the front page section of the Mercury News. "Read that," he barked.

"Oh, this, I..."

"Shh, shh, keep it down, bro."

"What are you...look, I already know about this. I caught it on the eleven o'clock news. So what about it?"

"I know those girls."

"The nurses?"

"Yeah."

"No shit," said Wilkie grinning.

Keith grabs him by the forearm, "I'm serious, bro. This ain't no joke. Eventually the police are gonna be looking for me."

"For you? For what?"

"Cause I was one of the last persons to see them alive and they may think that I did it."

"You're bullshitin' me, right?" Keith gave his brother a blank and hopeless expression. He didn't even blink. "Well, did you do it?"

"Fuck you, smart ass. Get real!"

"Alright, alright, calm down. I'm family, remember. I'm on your team. Sooo, who's the other person that seen 'em last?"

"Frank Dean."

"Yo! The cool-ass Poppa Smurf, the suave O.G.?"

"Yes, him. He gave me a ride to that Cottle Road house last Saturday Night. I'm the one who introduced him to the broads. They were hittin' it off pretty good, so I left them around an hour past midnight. Jerry was throwing a party and sent someone to pick me up because they ran out of coke."

"So, you're telling me you're gonna rat on this dude and you don't even know if he did it? Why the fuck would O.G. Frank do a thing like that? It makes no sense."

"I don't know. Maybe he got drunk and just tripped out. Or maybe the broads slipped him a Mickey and tried to roll him. Fuck, I don't know!"

"Just chill for a minute, bro. Have you talked to him yet?".

"No."

"Well, don't you think you ought to do that first?"

Keith didn't have an immediate reply, because he was more worried about himself than he was for Frank Dean. He knew his prints would eventually turn up in the police investigation, and due to his multiple speeding tickets, the Santa Clara County Sheriff's Office already had his mug shot and DNA on file.

Wilkie Jio had never seen his brother so rattled and out of character. He was usually the calm one in the family. But Wilkie could see that even another fix of heroin couldn't help his brother right now.

"Tell you what, bro. Let's give him a call. Better yet, we can go and see him down at the salvage yard."

"You're coming with me, right?"

"Of course, dumb ass, but let's call first."

When the Jios called Frank Dean, he was cruising down Highway 101. He wondered what was so urgent that Keith wanted to talk to him in person. He agreed to meet him at the salvage yard around three-thirty. The Jios finished work a little early so they could beat the rush hour freeway traffic. Bob's Towing and Salvage Yard was just a seven mile drive from where they were. Frank Dean was working the desk.

He recognized their white and green van as soon as they pulled though the driveway. He told his brother Billy Bear that he'd be taking a short break.

"What's up fellas?" said Frank, extending his right hand for an exchange of handshakes.

"You mind if we walk some?" said Keith.

"Sure, we can do that."

Frank Dean and Keith walked side by side and Wilkie trailed. He pretended to be checking out the huge stacks of fenders and Cadillac parts.

"Have you seen the newspapers yet?"

"The paper boy shoots me a daily, but I've been too busy. I haven't had a chance to check one out."

"What about TV?"

"Do I watch TV?"

"Yeah."

"I don't own one. I gave the boob tube up a long time ago." Frank stops walking. He rolls his eyes at Wilkie then back over to Keith. "Okay, so what gives? This obviously isn't about any of our usual business, so you can speak freely. Give it to me straight."

Keith throws a nervous glance in his brother's direction, then he clears a frog from his throat, "Somebody killed the nurses."

"Nurses?"

"Anna and Wilma, Frank. Last Saturday night. Cottle Road."

"Huh?" Frank Dean shrugs his shoulders.

Wilkie is still within earshot. He walks up and stands next to his brother so he can look Frank Dean straight in the eye, and Frank looks back at him with a bewildered glance.

"You've lost me, fellas. Who's Anna and Wilma? How do you expect me to remember someone I never met?"

"Frank, are you serious?" said Keith, raising his voice an octave, his complexion becoming flushed.

Frank Dean is extremely calm, because he really doesn't remember. "Ah, okay, am I supposed to know these girls?"

"Frank, last Saturday you met me in front of the Greyhound Bus station, remember? I gave you the list of meetings with the signatures and then you took me to a spot on Eleventh Street, and around ten you picked me up and we drove down to the nurses house on..."

"Yeah, I do remember dropping you off on Eleventh Street, but I don't recall ever meeting any girls. You got me there, pal. I'm stumped."

"Frank, you have to remember. What are you on, Dude, some kind of dry drunk?!"

Keith totally lost his cool and Frank Dean was becoming more than just a little disturbed by Keith insisting that he was somewhere he'd never been.

"Listen to me, Keith. Read my lips. I don't know what the fuck you're blabbing about and I don't really give a shit. For the last time, whatever it is you two have been smokin', well, ya'll need to quit. Now, get off my property or I'm calling the cops!"

Keith couldn't comprehend the unbelievable performance that Frank Dean had just laid on him. He leveled Frank with the look of a pitbull that was ready to rip him to pieces.

Frank Dean reached around his backside and pulled his .25 automatic from under his coat. He only brandished the weapon. He kept the muzzle pointed towards the ground. The brothers flinched, each taking a backstep away from the gun. Keith knew Frank wasn't faking and his brother Wilkie was terror stricken. Frank Dean's actions did not help his cause. It only solidified Keith's belief that this man was a psychopath who was in complete denial for something no one else could possibly have done.

The Jio brothers got on the turnpike and merged into the 280 Freeway traffic. Frank Dean followed them for more than a mile. He turned off on the Bird Street exit and pulled up at the Cinnabar on the west side of town.

Keith Jio was not the only person that wasn't able to get a good night's sleep. Aliya spent her entire day in the office and on the phone. She wanted to talk to Niecee but she and Tahoe weren't answering any of her texts. They had flown down to San Diego on an emergency because Tahoe's grandmother had become very ill. In the late afternoon, Karrene stopped by to talk shop with her sister and have a few drinks. They were sharing shots of Amaretto with lime twists when Mr. Jio called.

"Miss Aliya, hope I'm not disturb you at this hour. Are you having dinner now?"

"No, I'm not, Mister Jio. My sister and I have made plans to eat out this evening. What can I do for you?"

"Ahh, you once tell me about your sister, the lawyer."

"Yes."

"She family lawyer or criminal lawyer?"

"She's trained in both, Mister Jio."

"Oh, how so?"

"Mister Jio, would you like to speak to her? She's sitting here with me in my kitchen at this very moment."

"Oh yes, yes. Thank you."

The conversation lasted for almost thirty minutes. Aliya left at the start to allow her sister and Mr. Jio some privacy. She went to her bedroom, took a quick shower and got herself ready for the dinner outing. When she returned, Karrene was waiting in the parlor.

"I'm ready if you are," said Aliya, while searching through a shoulder bag for the house keys.

"Sis, I've got a situation and it's going to delay our dinner plans momentarily."

"Oh, rats! Is Mister Jio in some kind of trouble?"

"No, his son is. They're going to meet me down in San Jose at the police department. I need to be present to make certain there's no violations of his rights."

"Ooou, more excitement! Let's get going. You can tell me all about it on the way up."

The interview lasted three hours, much longer than Karrene was expecting or prepared for. She wasn't accustomed to police interrogation tactics. Right away, she could see they were prejudiced against her client and they practically accused him of doing the Cottle Road murders. They hadn't believed a word he said.

Karrene did her best to keep the cops from bullying Keith into a confession. She believed her client was only reporting what he knew and that he came forth because he was concerned and afraid. The interview was stopped once Karrene realized the detectives were determined to take the interview into the wee hours of the night. They were tenacious in their attempts to find holes in her client's story and weaken his resolve.

On Wednesday morning at ten o'clock, two plainclothes detectives swooped into the Bell Motel's driveway, showed the manager their official IDs and asked about unit eighteen. They were looking for Frank George. The manager explained to the officers that Mr. George was the owner of the motel and that he would be returning shortly.

He'd left the unit at a little before eight-thirty. He often walked to Denny's restaurant for breakfast. The detectives said they'd wait, and ten minutes later Frank Dean strolled up.

If he were surprised by the detective's visit, he didn't show it. He was very courteous and cooperative. The officers explained that they were looking into a citizen's complaint that was filed by Mr. Steven Jio, the father of Wilkie and Keith. Frank Dean invited the men into his home.

The detectives were Joe Tomaino and Fred Morillo. Both had begun their careers with the police department fresh out of high school. They were twenty year vets. Lieutenant Tomaino, tall, pale and slim, was in line for a captain's job. Morillo, short, heavy and balding, was a chief homicide detective. They took notice of the tiny apartment's cozy atmosphere. It was hospital clean. It held a pine tree fragrance.

"This is a nice place you have here, Mister George," stated the Lieutenant.

"Would you gentlemen like something to drink?" offered Frank Dean. "Coffee, tea? It would only take me a second to boil some water."

The lieutenant glances over at the sergeant. "Yeah, sure," said Morillo, "I'll have some tea if you don't mind."

"I'm fine," said the lieutenant.

Frank moves over to the kitchen space. Lt. Tomaino keeps the conversation fresh. "Is the Bell Motel a franchise ownership?"

"No way. My father purchased it back in the fifties. It's been in the family ever since."

"Is he still living?"

"No, he passed away in ninety-seven."

"So, your family owns Bob's Towing as well?" added the sergeant.

"Yes, my brothers and I share in that ownership."

"Now, that's a good business to have. What else you got?" continues Sergeant Morillo.

"Huh?"

"Does your family own any other properties?" replies the lieutenant, rephrasing the question.

"Oh." Frank Dean Chuckles and sets a tray on an antique walnut coffee table with an inlaid mosaic Indian pattern around the border. The tray contains two cups with tea bags, a bowl of sugar and a couple spoons. "My brothers own a hundred acres right outside of Morgan Hill, and I inherited the Summit Lake estate."

"No kidding," said the sergeant. "That's the lake that dumps right into Lexington Reservoir."

"Yeah, that's it," replied Frank Dean.

"How's the fishing up there?" asked the Lieutenant.

"Well, not nearly as good as it once was," replied Frank, "but I suppose it's okay. I haven't fished it in years."

"You are a gun owner, is that right?"

"Yes, I own several." Frank Dean stands and whips out the .25 automatic and gives it to the lieutenant, handle first. The officers were a little surprised by the agility and quickness displayed when taking the gun out. Frank Dean went to his closet and pulled the steamer trunk out and removed four cases and stacked them on the coffee table. Each case displayed a pistol, a nine millimeter Browning with a thirteen round magazine, a Smith & Wesson forty caliber revolver with eight rounds, a Colt .45 with eight rounds, and a .380 automatic with a ten round clip. All the guns were in pristine condition. None showed evidence of being recently fired. Ownership tags accompanied each weapon.

Frank Dean observed the officers' appreciation and the special care they took in handling and examining each weapon, but the officers were looking for something he didn't have.

He didn't know what that was but he picked up a hint of disappointment in their eyes. Sergeant Morillo seemed a little restless, as though he were anxious to leave. Lieutenant Tomaino was a lot harder to read. The hot water pot was hissing. Frank removed it from the stove and filled the two cups.

"Mister George, did you do any work down at the salvage yard last Saturday?"

"Saturday? Yes, all my Saturdays are spent at the yard. Then I have dinner at Palo's and then I polish off the evening at the Cinnabar for conversation and drinks."

"Is that what you did last Saturday?" reemphasizes the Sergeant.

"Oh, yeah," smiles Frank.

"What time did you get home?"

"The usual, between ten and eleven o'clock."

"Did you see or hear from Keith Jio on Saturday?"

"Matter of fact I did. He called me while I was at the Cinnabar and asked me to meet him at the bus station, which I did. Then he had me take him to a house on Eleventh Street."

"Did you wait for him?"

"No, I returned to the Cinnabar."

"So, you're saying, what?" said the sergeant, his interest being sparked. "He called you just to pick him up and take him to a house that was only a short distance from the Greyhound station, a distance he could have easily walked or taken a cab."

Frank Dean raises his mug of tea and takes a sip. "The reason I agreed to meet with him is because I owed him some money for work he'd done for me, and once I delivered it, he asked me to drop him off at Eleventh Street."

"Did he ask you to pick him up later?"

"Yes, as a matter of fact he did. He invited me to go to a party with him. He was supposed to call me back before ten-thirty, but I never got the call. I guess I had my power off."

"Why is that?" asked the sergeant.

"Because I always switch my power off at that time of night."

Frank Dean's reply to Sergeant Morillo's last question just seemed to suck the air out of their balloon. It was at that point the lieutenant was ready to get back to his office and try another interview with Keith Jio.

"Mister George, hope we haven't taken up too much of your time this morning."

"Oh, not at all gentleman, but please relay my apologies to the Jio family. I harbor no ill feelings toward them and I didn't mean to frighten the boys. Yes, I warned them I'd call the police, but drawing my weapon was certainly uncalled for and out of line."

"Next time there's a problem, call us," said the lieutenant smiling.

"Mister Gorge, thanks for the tea," said the sergeant as both men got in a green Ford Taurus and drove off.

After traveling past a couple blocks, the policemen pulled into a self-service gas station.

"What's the matter, Joe?"

The lieutenant sighed, "What did you think, Fred?"

"I think the guy's credible and the Jio story doesn't add up."

"Yeah, I know. Plus, the kid's a heroin addict, and the two vics are ex-felons. We need to interview Jio again."

"You think he's covering for somebody? Maybe he knows who the real killers are."

"You could be right," said the lieutenant. "He's the one crying wolf. I'll ask the captain if I can assign someone to keep an eye on him. In the meantime, we'll just hold up the next interview until the lab reports come in."

"What, the DNA and prints?"

"Yeah, which makes our job a little easier."

"How's that?"

"We got George's and Jio's DNA and prints already on file."

Sergeant Morillo nods his head in agreement. "Well, I'm gonna check those phone records to see if Mister George is correct about not receiving that call."

"Good idea, and while you're at it do a check on George's military records."

"What, you wanna know whether he's an expert marksman?"

"No, you don't have to be any of that to kill someone at close range. But I am interested in his conduct record."

"Oh, you mean like if he's a mental case."

"Exactly."

When Niecee and Tahoe's Jet Blue flight from San Diego touched down at San Jose International Airport, Aliya was waiting at the arrival gate. The girls were in a festive mood. Aliya was glad to see smiles on their faces. She gave each girl a big hug before walking over to baggage claims. They agreed to let Aliya buy them lunch. The girls followed in Tahoe's Mercedes as they caravanned down North First Street and pulled into the parking lot of Plateau Seven, a restaurant and bar on the seventh floor of a bank building. They rode the elevator up and were fortunate to get a table because they barely beat out the lunch crowd's arrival.

The patrons were mostly lawyer types and a few judges. The superior court building and city hall were all within walking distance, as well as a few dozen law firms. The girls agreed on a white table wine. They were eating a light lunch, each girl eyeballing the other's figure. Quiche Lorraine, cheese and crackers and apple slices. Niecee deferred. She chose a lone fruit salad. She had the largest set of hips amongst the trio.

"How's your grandmother?" asked Aliya.

"Oh, she's back to her old fat and jolly self," said Tahoe.

"Ooo, you wrong for saying it like that," cooed Niecee.

"No, I'm not. I'm just being truthful. I love her to death, but granny is a drama queen about anything and everything. That woman is healthy as an African elephant. She just craves attention."

"Are you saying her illness was not that grave?" inquires Aliya.

"Grave!" She betta' not catch you using a word like that around her, Aliya. That women is liable to cut your tongue out."

Aliya laughs, "Okay, I get it. Well, let me bring you girls up to speed. Since you've been gone some creepy things have occurred."

"Oh, yeah, like what?" said Niecee, her hazel eyes looming large.

"Well, first, there were these two nurses that were found murdered in their San Jose home."

"Murdered? How so?" said Niecee.

"Somebody shot 'em both and they think the killer is the same person who killed that big time contractor Joe Sunseri up in Manteca."

"Wow," said Niecee, "I'm so glad we live in Los Gatos, 'cause there's always dead bodies popping up in San Jose. Remember the dead body we ran into when we took that shortcut through Guadalupe Creek?"

"I'll never forget that," co-signed Tahoe. "That was gross. That lady looked frozen like somebody had put her on ice or something."

"You're kidding?" said Aliya, looking as though she'd just swallowed something whole and it was still lodged in her throat. "Well, what killed her? I mean how did she die?"

"I don't know," said Tahoe, "the police never said, because I guess they never figured it out."

"Oh, they probably know," said Niecee. They just want to keep it a secret just so the real killer doesn't have any idea of how close they are to catching him."

"Well, that's kind of why I need to share this information with you," said Aliya, looking directly at Niecee.

"What you talkin' about, Miss Aliya?" clowns Niecee.

"You girls ever heard of Sunset Investigations?"

"No, should we?" they said in unison.

"No, I guess not, but their office is in my building and it's my brother's and his girlfriend's business."

"Your brother? I thought your brother was married to our boss lady, Brenda?"

"No, that's Johnnie Ray. I've got four brothers. This is my younger brother, Rob. He's closer to your ages."

"I knew it," said Tahoe, "the be-atch been holdin' out on us. And you know I'm lookin' for a man! How come you never brought him around?"

Again, Aliya laughs, "As I was saying, he's got a business partner and she's his girlfriend," she reemphasized. "Her name is Sunny."

"Sunny? Oh, she's a white girl. Hey, I'm cool, that's all I need to know."

"What's that supposed to mean?"

"It means I don't know any sisters named Sunny, and as the song says, 'If You Have a Choice of Colors, Which One would you Choose, My Brother'."

Aliya giggles, "I know that song, but I think you got the lyrics twisted."

"No, I don't think so," rebounds Tahoe. The wine they've been drinking has got her running at the mouth, as Niecee sits back quietly just grinning and watching the two women go at it. She knows it's going to be hard for Aliya to get a word in edgewise once Tahoe gets juiced.

"Okay, time out!" Aliya makes a letter 'T' with her hands like some kind of football referee. "It's my turn, so let me finish."

The girls are getting loud, but no one pays any attention. The restaurant is packed. There's a line forming just to get drinks and squeeze in at the bar, and conversations at the lawyer tables were getting just as rowdy.

"Niecee, Frank George is in trouble."

"No way!"

"Yes, way in trouble. He threatened one of Karrene's clients down at the salvage yard. Plus, he's under investigation by the police."

"Hold up," said Niecee, "the threat I can understand."

"No you can't. He pulled a gun on this guy."

"Excuse me," said Niecee getting defensive, "Daddy Frank ain't no punk. And whoever this guy is, he probably deserves to be threatened!"

"Well, that may or may not be true, but listen. The frozen body the two of you found in that creek..."

"Okay, what about it?" erupts Tahoe, obviously anxious to side with Niecee.

"Rob and Sunny found one just like it on Frank George's property."

"Really?" replied Niecee.

"So what do the police have to say about the discovery?" asked Tahoe.

"Well, nothing yet because my brother hasn't reported it."

"But you just said he was under police investigation," reiterates Tahoe.

"I know it sounds confusing, but I'm only telling you what they allow me to know. Actually, I probably shouldn't be telling you this anyway."

"So, he's not in jail or anything, right?" cries Niecee.

"No, but there's something else that I should tell you."

Neither Tahoe or Niecee have anything to say. They're just staring back at Aliya as though she's the repo lady that's threatening to tow away their new cars.

"Troy is under police investigation as well."

"We already know," volunteers Tahoe, "cause we were there the day he was arrested at the cemetery."

"That's right," adds Niecee, "and he came to work the next day and said everything was fine."

"Okay, but did he tell you what he was arrested for?"

"Probably for taking up for his dad!" cries Niecee.

Suddenly, Aliya realizes she should have kept her mouth shut, because what she was about to convey just might put a huge wall in their relationship, but it was too late to retract any statement or even hold back. She just wanted to protect Niecee, just as she knew she needed to back out of her relationship with Troy because she had to protect herself. So Aliya hesitates.

"Well, we're waiting," demanded Tahoe. "Tell us why he was arrested, Aliya."

"He was taken in for questioning because he's the prime suspect in a missing persons case in the city of Merced."

"A missing person? What the fuck does that mean?" crowed Tahoe.

"I was told it was a girl. They haven't found her yet and I guess Troy was the last person to see her."

"Troy!" said Niecee with a sour look on her face. "We are talking about the same dude that we both like?"

"Yes, that's right," agreed Aliya, frowning as though she were about ready to burst into tears.

Niecee's facial expression changed from sour to someone who just got hit in the face with a couple of rotten tomatoes. She bounced out of her seat and rushed into the ladies room. Tahoe shot Aliya a nasty glare, then took off after Niecee.

Aliya waited almost twenty minutes for their return to the table. Neither girl came back. When Aliya mustered up enough courage to go check up on them, they were nowhere in sight. Aliya retreated to the restaurant's parking Jot. Tahoe's Mercedes was gone.

Aliya was devastated. An hour later, someone tapped the side of her auto's window. It was the parking lot attendant. He'd noticed her slumped behind her steering wheel. Although she thanked him for checking on her, she said she was okay, just resting. He could tell that she had been crying. Aliya finally got the car in gear. It was three in the afternoon by the time she merged into freeway traffic that would take her home.

MERCED
Thursday, April 28th Through
Saturday, May 30th

TROY COULDN'T SLEEP. He wasn't the tossing and turning type. When he played his relaxation music, he had no problem getting wherever he wanted it to take him. In this instance, he needed it to help him stay focused.

Niecee was continually texting him. She wouldn't say why it was so urgent. She just wanted to see him. He replied,

NOT RIGHT NOW, PEANUT.
HOW'S FRIDAY?

Niecee wouldn't relent and neither would Troy. Then he got an odd text from Aliya.

HEY STUD!
SORRY, BUT I'M GONNA
RENEGE ON OUR CONTRACT
HUGS AND KISS-KISS

It didn't matter about work. Troy could always get work. Besides, a little vacation time is exactly what he needed right now. Trying to please two women had thrown him off his center. It was fun while everything was fresh and in play, but now it was time to get back to what really mattered.

His pathways were narrowing. One of his victim's burial sites had been invaded. There was no room for forgiveness in Troy, nor did he ever forget. Once again, Mr. Frank Dean George had cost him. Troy didn't need the old man messing with his mojo again. It was Frank Dean George who got him fired twice back when he worked summers on the George's farm. And it was Frank Dean George and his brothers who bullied and teased him just because he had a speech impediment. Hiding dead bodies on their property was Troy's method of getting back at them. He had hoped that someone else would discover the frozen corpses. The thought of it made him smile. What would Mr. Frank Dean George say, "Oh, it's not mine. It belongs to my neighbor's son."

Of course, Troy knew that if his own father was not so strict about following city ordinances, he would have had access to the crematorium's incinerator and rid himself of the bodies he was now stuck with. But there was something that intrigued Troy when it came to moving dead bodies from one site to another, it had something to do with the type of psychopath Troy truly was. He was impulsive but organized. Hunting and then killing was a ritual. His dump sites were not random locations. His wood chipper was spared for special occasions and a specific corpse. Because of Frank Dean George's threat, Troy had to remove two bodies from the stream directly under his neighbor's well.

At three-thirty a.m. on Thursday, Troy's silver-gray hearse Cadillac and wood chipper hit the pavement on Highway 9. About fifteen minutes into his drive, he zipped past the City of Santa Cruz and switched over to Highway 1. By four-thirty, he was headed north on Highway 152 when he noticed a blue Chevy Suburban was following him. He had no doubt it was the same car and driver he'd spotted twenty minutes ago as he crossed the highway's bridged on-ramp that led to the route he was presently on. The orange florescent decal that was glued to the passenger side windshield was what gave the Suburban away. Troy was headed to his favorite dump site, Yosemite National Park, but now he couldn't do that. He had to change his plan. Once again, the fog and cover of darkness was his ally.

After traveling past the city of Merced by a couple of miles, he waited until the last possible second before switching lanes and taking a freeway off-ramp. He hoped he'd catch the Suburban's driver asleep at the wheel, and it worked. It gave Troy the extra seconds he needed to evade his pursuer and dash into the woods.

The Suburban pulled off the freeway. It was equipped with a heavy duty drive train and four thirty-eight inch tires that could climb mountains and plow through mud and various types of slush. Troy may have gained a few seconds, but he was not going to escape. Detective Marcus knew from experience that most killers are caught because they get too comfortable in their routines. He and Sergeant Valdez were keen on that, but in this instance, Detective Marcus was just lucky, because he almost never hit the road at this time of the morning, and Troy Dominique was the furthest thought from his mind.

The detective lived on a farm in Los Banos. He purchased the place fifteen years ago. The real estate wasn't so pricy then, and the hour long commute to his Merced office was something he looked forward to. Perhaps it was just a fluke or maybe Dominique was on his way to a jobsite. The detective had only planned to follow him for a few more miles, because he was on his way to the town of Mariposa to pick up some parts for his farm tractor's engine. When the hearse took a sudden exit, the detective's suspicions were aroused, so now he was in pursuit.

After making the sudden detour, Troy barreled down the same dusty road he used on the day he kidnapped the farmer's daughter. He drove deeper into the abandoned orchard. The fog was much thicker there. Without a breeze, it would keep the area blanketed for another two to three hours. Troy parked, climbed over the front seat, and rummaged through his tool box. He passed through the side panel door and climbed the nearest oak and waited.

Detective Marcus knew the fog was his nemesis, so he had to react quickly enough to see what course the Cadillac took. He picked up the wood chipper's brake lights. He thought about calling in his location for backup, but realized there was no reason because he had no proof as to whether a crime had actually been committed. The detective was a smart veteran cop, but sometimes even a vet is subject to taking unnecessary risk. He was caught up in the moment and the excitement of the chase.

Rambling over rough terrain, he used his right hand to open his glove box and remove a flashlight and a .357 Magnum. He checked the chamber. It contained a full six rounds. He flipped the safety and continued driving over damp clumps of dirt for four hundred feet. He stopped a few yards from the wood chipper's rear and flicked his high beams several times. He got no response, so he exited his vehicle and walked up to the driver's side window.

The window was down. The hearse was vacant. The fog had crept its way inside the cab. The raw stench of fresh cow manure invaded his nostrils. His eyes watered. He gagged, then coughed. With his flashlight, he scanned the auto's interior. Two gray burlap sacks were piled atop each other and tethered to the side door. A platoon of tiny red bugs were escaping from a tear in one of them. As the detective pulled on the door handle, a twig's snap distracted him. He glanced over the Cadillac's rooftop and noticed leaves falling from a giant oak. He surveyed the ground for footprints. There were none. He walked under the oak and a falling leaf brushed his shoulder and made him look up.

The last thing Detective Marcus would remember was not the thirteen inch steel boots that kicked him in the face and busted his nose. He wouldn't remember the single shot that missed its mark and ricocheted off the hood of his Suburban. He wouldn't remember the Marine Corp chokehold that cut the oxygen to his brain and caused him to pass out. What he would remember was waking up with his feet and his hands tied to the grill of his Suburban.

Suddenly, everything went completely red. The ground. The sky. And the leaves on the tree. A flash of yellow, a tinge of blue, then black. His left eyeball went east and clots of blood from his mouth and nose flew west. The second blow from a sledge hammer crushed his mandible, split his jawbone, and shattered teeth. The final blow turned his brain into hash.

Even a killer listens to his gut occasionally. Troy wasn't angry, but for the first time he didn't feel the adrenaline rush. There was no gratifying satisfaction for what he was doing anymore. He squatted by the detective's remains. He had no power to undo what he'd just done even if he wanted to. For the first time in his life, he wished he hadn't killed, and he didn't understand why. For an instant, he considered getting in the hearse and just driving away as far as his vehicle would take him. No. He couldn't do that. The detective might be discovered too quickly. Besides, he had to find a burial site for the bodies he still had.

Further in the woods, he found an old abandoned farmhouse and barn. The barn was small but the Suburban was a perfect fit. Detective Marcus was dumped down one of the farmhouse wells, and the twin cold corpses were thrown into the sewage of a contaminated canal.

By eight-thirty Thursday morning, the temperature had soared past sixty degrees. The inhabitants of Silicon Valley welcomed the warm weather. The Summer Solstice was near. At 515 Hull Street, Tahoe was backing her Mercedes out of the driveway when Troy pulled up in a brand new Lexus. He got out of the vehicle and was walking up the home's pathway when Tahoe gave him a blast from her auto's horn.

Troy stopped.

"Can't you speak? Is yo' tongue tied or somethin'?"

"Hey, silly girl, where are you going?"

"I'm on my way to Campbell for a coffee date."

"Can I come along?"

"Helll Nooo!" she said laughing. "Niecee ain't havin' it and I wanna stay on her good side, 'cause I got to live with the Be-atch. And, speaking on that, she's been worried about you."

Troy cocks his head to one side. He has no idea what that means.

"Are you all right, Mister Troy?" inquires Tahoe with a little more sincerity this time. Troy smiles and throws her a peace sign. Tahoe backs the Mercedes into the street, honks twice, and drives away.

Troy turns his focus back towards the house and Niecee is posted up on the front porch banister with arms folded across her bosom. She's wearing a pink, white and red floral kimono and Japanese clogs. Her blond extensions are tied in a bun. Troy gawks at her but holds his position along the foot path. He's looking at her nose job. He was trying to imagine what it looked like before she got it fixed.

Niecee started yelling, "Why have you been hiding from me, Troy? Weren't you supposed to call me and let me know you were coming? I thought you said you would be stopping by on Friday!"

Troy hadn't been scolded like that since he was a boy. He wanted to smile because Niecee reminded him of his mother. He had no immediate reply so Niecee continued with her rave.

"Troy, have you lost your voice? If you're not gonna say nothin' then the least you could do is come give me a hug. Whose car is that?" she said, pointing to the Lexus.

Troy walked up to her as if he didn't care. He pushed her out of his way and walked by. When he pulled on the screened door, Niecee grabbed him by the seat of his pants, jumped on his back and forced him to give her a ride. They wobbled inside.

The spotless living room's furnishings were done in shades of burgundy, gray and black. There were a pair of burgundy red felt sofas dotted with black silk fringed pillows, and the coffee and end tables were made of glass and polished chrome. The walls were light gray with a white ceiling. A black iron chandelier hung from the center rafter. The windows were draped with gray laced curtains and plum venetian blinds. A large limestone fireplace was in the corner of the room. With Niecee still on Troy's back, he spun around so he could check out everything.

"Keep it movin' buster. Mush!" teased Niecee. She guided him to her bedroom and he dumped her on a round queen sized bed. Across from it was a dresser, mirrors and walk-in closet. The room held an antique oval tub and marble vanity with an ornate porcelain pitcher and bowl. The ceiling had a four foot square skylight and two ornate glass mobiles dangled from its rafters. The walls were papered in a bird and forest scene, and the carpeting was Lincoln green.

Troy remembers how the old carpet had mushrooms and mold growing in it. He wore a big smile as Niecee tried to make him tumble onto her bed. He flipped her onto her back. She posed for him. She looked salacious in her kimono. The belt had come undone. Troy was staring at her red laced panties and see thru bra.

Looking back at him, Niecee claps her hands and curls her right index finger "Come to Momma, Bubba," she clowns.

"I need to take a quick shower, Peanut."

"See my tub over there? I'll fix your bath water and you can get naked. Hit that number five button on the panel by the door, please."

Troy followed Niecee's lead and flicked the number five switch. The last verse of 'Stay' by Tyrese came through speakers, heard but not visible. By the time Troy got his clothing off, Niecee had scented candles lit and the bathtub was steamy. Troy eases into the water and Niecee follows and snuggles up against him. The CD comes to an end and begins anew with R. Kelly singing 'Share My Love.' Their lips meet. The kiss is tender and slow. Niecee pulls away momentarily to catch her breath. Then she pulls her hands out of the water and claps twice. The sound system's volume is raised another octave. The music fills every room in the house. Niecee applies her plush lips to Troy's hairy chest and leaves a trail of wet kisses as she works her way down to his navel.

When Frank Dean parked his pickup behind the Lexus, he assumed it belonged to Aliya. He knew that most realtors own several autos. He walked up to it and peeked through the window and grinned. "Nice," he said aloud. Walking toward the home's screened door he could hear the stereo music. It was not jazz, so he didn't recognize the artist. It was a little before ten. The temperature had risen another fifteen degrees and was steadily climbing. Frank Dean rang the doorbell, but the loud music prevented him or anyone else from hearing it. The screened door was not latched. He called out a couple times before stepping inside.

He took a moment to admire the living room's decor. He shuffled past a coffee table and took a seat on the couch. He relaxed because he knew that sooner than later someone would show. After a five minute wait, he rose from his seat, "Aliya! Princess! It's me, Frank! Anybody wanna answer?"

He thought about leaving and coming back later, but something urged him on. He didn't even know which bedroom was Niecee's. He was trying to determine what room the music was coming from. He knocked on the first door, but it was only a linen closet. Trying the next, his first knock caused the door to swing wide.

Troy caught the glimpse of a shadowy figure dressed in black. It was blocking the sun rays from the skylight. Niecee was napping. Her head was nuzzled against Troy's chest. When the bathtub water erupted, Niecee was flung violently from the tub. The first bullet missed and Niecee shrieked. The second bullet tore through Troy's left forearm. Yet Troy was swift, he had moves like a cheetah as he lurched at Frank Dean and slammed him down on the carpet. Frank hadn't a chance to fire the third shot. The old man was strong, but Troy got his bloody forearm around Frank Dean's neck. Troy tried to crush Frank's trigger hand just as Frank was trying to keep the pistol's barrel pointed at Troy's head.

Another shot rang out and that bullet missed its mark, as Troy flipped Frank onto Niecee's bed.

Niecee was screaming for the men to stop. She tried ducking into the walk-in closet as another bullet zipped past her and splintered the closet's door frame.

Even though Frank Dean was determined to break Troy's choke hold by flailing like a fish, Troy held him in a vice like grip. Both his hands and elbows were clamped around Frank's skull. He was trying to bust Frank's neck. Frank hollered once, then his body went limp. Down on one knee, Troy was growling words that Niecee couldn't understand. He continued applying the pressure and refused to let go until the porcelain water pitcher was bashed upside his head.

Niecee hit him three times.

Frank Dean's head was covered in blood and so was Troy's forearm and chest. Troy was breathing heavily. His green eyes were bloodshot. His face was gnarly. Niecee hardly recognized him.

When Tahoe returned from her coffee date, Hull Street looked like a Hollywood movie set. The sidewalks were filled with onlooking neighbors. One ambulance was blocking her driveway entrance and men and women in navy blue uniforms were posted in the front yard. Troy was sitting on a porch chair. His top half was nude, his feet were also bare and a medical tech was applying a bandage to his head while another was taking his blood pressure. Tahoe walked past him. Troy's eyes remained closed.

Inside, Tahoe found Niecee sitting on a living room couch talking to two plainclothes detectives. One of them walked up to Tahoe and flashed a shield in her face. He explained what he understood had happened and asked her to answer a few questions.

Frank Dean was rushed to the Los Gatos Municipal Hospital. There was hemorrhaging in his brain and a severe injury to his neck. He flat lined momentarily, but a team of doctors and nurses were able to bring him back. Once he was stabilized, they placed him in isolation on the third floor. There were tubes running through his mouth, nose and arm. It would be another day later before the doctors would allow him to have any guests.

Troy was arrested but released the next morning. It was the .22 revolver that was in question. Niecee helped to clear the detective's confusion. She was angry with Troy but she also credited him with saving her life. She wasn't sure what Mista George would have done next, if he would have succeeded in killing Troy.

The George brothers, Bob Wayne and Billy Bear, wanted Troy Dominique charged with attempted murder, but Troy had a clear case of self defense. If Frank Dean died, the Georges could file a wrongful death suit and an expert criminal lawyer could probably get a jury to agree that Troy went too far, but in this case, Frank Dean was the aggressor. Billy Bear felt that part of the blame rested on his shoulders. He was the one who found the .22 revolver and returned it to his brother because he thought it was the .22 his father had given Frank. But it wasn't. No one, not even Frank, knew that it was truly lost.

Niecee was torn between two lovers. She didn't want Frank Dean George to die. She felt it was her fault and that she was the cause of him going crazy. She was the first to visit him in the hospital other than his family. He recognized her but he wasn't yet able to talk. Her plan was to spend an hour or two every day with him until he fully recovered. She had respect and compassion for him, but her heart belonged to Troy. Everything had happened so fast that she never had a chance to ask Troy about the Merced investigation and the alleged missing girl.

Lieutenant Joe Tomaino and Sergeant Fred Morillo interviewed Keith Jio once again. They only wanted to know if he made a second phone call to Frank Dean's cell before ten-thirty p.m. on that Saturday night, when Frank was supposed to be his ride from Eleventh Street to Cottle Road. Keith told the detectives that the call he made wouldn't go through, but Frank just showed up. He was surprised because he had already made plans to get a ride with someone else. The detectives had already checked Frank Dean's phone record and the phone was apparently not in use from ten o'clock that Saturday evening until the following Monday morning at nine.

The Cottle Road murders lab reports didn't turn up any identifiable fingerprints except for the nurses. There were traces of male DNA found, but it was indistinguishable and couldn't be determined whether it was Keith's or Frank Dean's.

When Lieutenant Tomaino heard about the Los Gatos Hull Street shooting, he and Sergeant Morillo rushed to the hospital to visit Frank Dean. Frank was unable to talk to them. His larynx was severely damaged. The doctor advised it would eventually heal, but not before two to three weeks would he be well enough talk. With the aid of the Los Gatos crime lab, Lieutenant Tomanino now had access to Frank Dean's mystery .22 revolver, a gun he never mentioned owning when the detectives visited his home. Having access to the weapon didn't solve anything because the ballistics report wouldn't be complete until the end of the week.

Sunny and Rob were also privy to the Los Gatos crime lab reports, and they were anxious to receive a copy from the ballistics team as well. Even with Newman's influence, Lieutenant Tomaino would not agree to allow the Sunseri case to take precedence over the Cottle Road case. Although Rob and Sunny had compiled a log of evidence, the Lieutenant wanted full credit for any collar if it came down to that, because it would guarantee his promotion. He wanted the captain's job more than anything else.

Down in the city of Merced, there was a massive search going on for a missing detective. Sergeant Valdez knew something foul was at play. Detective Marcus had been his comrade and best friend during the course of both men's careers. They knew one another's habits like they knew their own. The detective had never missed or been late for work without calling in. It was an undeniable fact the detective never reached the city of Mariposa where he was supposed to pick up the tractor parts. A highway intersection's signal light camera would help narrow their search. The Chevy Suburban was clocked traveling at fifty in a forty-five mile per hour zone at five-fifty a.m.

The search for Detective Marcus began along frontage and back roads, right outside the city of Mariposa, then the search team worked their way towards the city of Merced. Nearly a month had passed before they discovered the killing field. It was on a Friday at three in the afternoon when a trooper found a human bone. Cadaver dogs were brought in. By six p.m. they had collected 150 bone fragments as well as bits of shredded cloth with colors that resembled what the missing farmer's daughter had worn.

Night fell and the search was reconvened at the crack of dawn. More bones were recovered as more forensic anthropologists were brought in. By nine a.m. Saturday the Chevy Suburban was discovered by a separate search team, and by ten another team found the twin corpses in the sewer. It wasn't until a hour past noon that they were pulling Detective Marcus' remains from a well.

PEANUT

TWO WEEKS BEFORE the discovery of the Merced killing fields, Frank Dean's lawyer had gotten his client's initial charge of attempted murder dropped down to an assault. He used Dr. Denardo's report to show that Frank Dean George was a certified manic depressive and was dealing with a serious disease. Although it was still too early to predict how the judge would decide, his lawyer assured him that he'd get no more than a lengthy probation and would be required to wear an ankle bracelet tracking device. Based on his good standing in the community, he wasn't going to do any prison time. The gun he used at Hull Street didn't match the bullet and cartridge striations with those used in the Sunseri nor the Cottle Road murders. Frank Dean's military records showed that he had some alcohol problems, but he'd achieved the rank of corporal and had received several good conduct accommodations. He was a standout soldier.

Each day Frank Dean was hospitalized he received more flowers and visitors than the Los Gatos Hospital would allow. He was still suffering from a certain amount of pain. Although his neck and larynx were healing just fine, he was only able to talk for short periods of time.

Niecee was visiting him twice daily and she was present on the day that Rob and Sunny paid Frank Dean a visit.

"Frank, wake up, honey. You've got company," said Niecee as she closed the novel she was reading and placed it in her lap.

Frank Dean opened his eyes with a flutter. It seemed like only a moment ago Niecee was feeding him soup and crackers for lunch. His body was a quick heal, but he still couldn't get around without someone's help. He was wearing a neck and back brace and was wrapped in four layers of hospital sheets and blankets. The room smelled hospital clean but was just a little cold. Niecee helped him put on his glasses. His pupils looked magnified and the whites of his eye were garnet red.

Frank looked back at his visitors and spoke in halted speech, "Aliya called," he said with a yawn. "She told me you were coming. Find them some chairs, Princess."

Niecee gave up her seat to Sunny and left the room. She returned with two more chairs but Rob chose to stand directly behind the women who were scooted up close to Frank Dean's bed railing.

"I understand you've got some questions to ask. I'll try to answer, but you'll have to be patient because this pain medication has me going in and out.

"Mister George," said Rob, "we're not going to take up too much of your time, sir. Did my sister tell you we were hired by the Sunseri family to investigate the murder of Joe Sunseri?"

"Yes, she did. I read about that case in the newspapers. He was killed near some tract homes in Manteca, as I recall. I don't think they ever found out who did it."

Sunny was looking directly into Frank Dean's eyes. She wasn't blinking. Rob hesitates and glances at Sunny. "Ah, that's correct, sir.

"Mister George, we found this," injected Sunny, holding up a Cherokee tie clip that's fastened to a silver chain. "Does it belong to you?" She hands it over to Frank and he fondles it.

"Why, yes. This is mine. Where did you get it?"

"It was found just a few yards from the Sunseri crime scene, Mister George."

"Oh."

"Do you have any memory of how it may of gotten placed there?"

Frank Dean looks stunned. "I...I don't even know the Sunseris, so I can't tell you how that is possible."

"Mister George, please try and think back for a minute. It was Saturday, April the 16th. What do you remember doing that day?"

Frank Dean returns a blank stare. He's puzzled by the question. He knows his memory is unreliable and he's not exactly sure why.

"Mister George, we spoke with Doctor Denardo," said Sunny. "She said you suffered with blackouts. She also said the blackouts occur after you've had a certain amount of alcohol in your system. Is that true?"

Frank looks at Niecee and she looks back at him with big sad eyes. "Please Daddy, try and remember. Please."

He shakes his head from side to side. His glasses look too big for his face. "I don't remember going to the Cinnabar that evening. I always do that on Saturday evenings unless I have a date with Niecee. Princess, you had something else to do that night. I think we had a date. I don't know for sure. You were real busy or something."

"That's right, Daddy. You must remember, because we talked about all of this once before, after it all happened. That's the day Tahoe and I got our insurance money from the lawsuit. And later we got caught up running around with Miss Aliya looking at homes to buy. The day ended badly because we got arrested when the neighbors called the police about a friend who broke into our cottage. I remember that you did text me several times, but I was so caught up that I was only able to text you back a couple times."

Niecee takes a breath and Sunny gets her questions back on track. "Mister George, do you remember what you did after you left the Cinnabar?"

"No, but after a few drinks, I usually go for a drive."

"Well, like where, any place in particular?"

"No, I just get on the freeway and drive."

Rob is quiet. He's taking full notice of Frank Dean's demeanor. He realizes Frank's absence of memory while drinking is not going to help his cause. Rob reaches inside his jacket pocket and pulls out a silver bracelet. The same bracelet he snatched from the ankle of the female corpse in Frank Dean's warehouse. Rob toys with the chain where Frank can see it. "Mister George, a few weeks ago we trespassed onto your Summit Lake property."

"Why?"

"Well, sir, we were following up on a lead. The dead fish you turned in to the game warden were poisoned by puffer fish."

"Puffer fish?"

"Well, it's not common in this area. They are usually found in tropical or warm water climates. The point is, someone planted them in your lake."

"For what purpose?"

"Well, there's several unsolved murder cases where the victims were killed with poison from the fish."

"Oh no!" Frank Dean's tan complexion suddenly pales. "Princess, pour me a glass of water, please." Niecee pours water from a pink pitcher and holds the cup while Frank drinks. "That's enough, baby," said Frank pushing her hand away and clearing his throat as best he could.

"First, I have something to tell you. I wasn't going to tell anyone." Frank looks directly at Niecee. "Princess, please forgive me, but I guess I should have told you first and maybe you nor I would be in this hospital today."

Niecee's face was filled with dread. She wasn't sure she wanted to hear what Frank Dean had to say.

"The doctors have told me I have a brain tumor and that it's part of the reason for my blackouts. Alcohol does not help. And yes, I've known about this before I started seeing Doctor Denardo. The doctors want to do an operation, but the tumor has grown in such a way that once it's removed my motor skills will be impaired for life."

"Oh, my God!" cried Niecee. She clutched Frank Dean's blanket and began sobbing into it. She wanted to hug him but there was no part of him she could touch without bringing him more pain. Frank stroked her hair to try and calm her.

"Mister George..." Frank hesitated several moments before acknowledging Sunny. "Mister George, do you plan on going through with the operation?"

He smiled and shook his head from side to side. He didn't want Niecee to hear his answer. He raised his hand and held up three fingers. Rob and Sunny read his lip sync. He had three months to live.

The nurse entered the room. "Mister George, you have five minutes remaining for visiting. I'll be back in a while to bring you the pills for your nap." The nurse smiled, Frank waved and she left. Rob and Sunny glanced at one another. They looked defeated as they stood next to each other.

"I have one more thing to say before you go. Please sit. It hurts my neck to look up at you." The couple took a seat and Niecee, kneeling next to him, raised her head from the blankets to look up at Frank. "I know you found a dead woman's body on my property, and I saw the two of you leaving from the well that day. The body is no longer there. I returned it to its rightful owner."

"Its owner?" replied Sunny with a frown of disbelief.

"Yes, it belonged to that Haitian, Troy Dominique."

For the first time in Troy's young life, he realized he did have a conscious and he needed to pay attention to his gut. It was time to move on. He had to put all the chaos and destruction he caused behind him. He'd saved more than enough money to sustain himself for several years. For now, he would abandon everything and everyone, his father, grandmother, home and Niecee.

He packed a backpack and said no good-byes. He took a Greyhound Express from Santa Cruz to San Francisco and hitched a ride with a trucker and crossed the Nevada state line. He purchased eighty acres of wasteland in Washoe County. He got a price that was literally dirt cheap, minus mineral, water and construction rights. He was allowed to place a mobile trailer home on it. He couldn't dig a well, but the land contained streams, several ponds and plenty of wildlife for hunting and fishing. He bought himself a secondhand Jeep from a rancher, and every couple weeks he made a trip into Reno, usually out of boredom or just to pick up supplies.

During his absence, Troy Dominique became a major person of interest in the case of the Merced killing fields. Maple Hill Cemetery and Summit Lake are invaded by a team of C.S.I.'s. They set up camp for close to three weeks. Their attempts to find evidence to link Troy or Frank Dean to a list of missing people and unsolved murders failed. When the murders stopped, it seemed as though the forensics went cold.

In the first week of September, Frank Dean died. His brothers, Billy Bear and Bob Wayne George, held an open casket memorial. Hundreds of Silicon Valley residents came to view the body. Many were just curiosity seekers whom had read or heard of his possible link to a series of murders. Frank Dean George's body was flown back to a Cherokee reservation in Oklahoma where Indian burial customs were still being practiced. Before the family's departure, there was a reading of the will, one which Frank Dean had amended hours before his death.

I, FRANK DEAN GEORGE, LEAVE MY JAZZ ALBUM COLLECTION, MY TRAILWAYS RV, AND THE DEED TO SUMMIT LAKE TO MY PRINCESS NIECEE EDWARDS

LOVING YOU FOREVER

DADDY FRANK

Niecee, who had been diligently trying to nurse Frank Dean back to health, was traumatized. She suffered a severe nervous breakdown. Tahoe, Aliya, Brenda, and Karrene rallied to lend her strength and their support, but it's too much for Niecee's heart to bear. Frank Dean was gone forever, and even though she was still deeply in love with Troy

Dominique, no one knew where he was and he made no attempt to contact her.

Tahoe visits Niecee daily. The hospital courtyard is not large. It holds two park benches, a grassy knoll and a rose covered trellis. Two visitors are sitting with patients confined to wheelchairs. They're drinking juice from cartons and eating snacks from a fruit basket.

"How you doin, Boo?" said Tahoe, hugging her lifelong friend.

Niecee returns the big hug but doesn't reply. The doctors had her on Zoloft, an anti-depressant, as well as medication to help her sleep, but the side-effects are not good. It's taken away the sparkle from her big grey eyes and her energy level has dropped. She's very low key. Tahoe doesn't like what she sees in her girl and it's breaking her heart. She wants the old, silly and vicarious Niecee back.

"Look what I brought you!" Tahoe removes two gift wrapped boxes with a large pink bow from her Gucci bag. Niecee unravels the packages carefully, trying not to tear the paper. It takes her a total of five minutes to get the first one open. The box contains a flannel robe with rows of tiny red hearts running through like pinstripes. The collar and front is ruffled. Tahoe gets Niecee to stand and helps her remove the hospital gown and replaces it with the new one. Niecee smiles and sits down. All her attention is now focused on opening her next gift. It's a heart shaped box filled with three layers of chocolates. Most of them have soft centers, but a few are almond clusters, which are Niecee's favorites. Tahoe watches with delight as her friend carefully chooses three as though there's a dozen choices and stuffs them in her mouth. "Hmmm," is all she can muster.

With a napkin, Tahoe dabs chocolate that's dribbling from the corner of Niecee's mouth. The medication she takes has numbed her sensitivity. She's not aware that there's goo smeared on her lips.

Suddenly something in her old hospital gown vibrates. Niecee doesn't respond to it, so Tahoe searches the garment pockets and removes a cell phone. She reads the text.

SILLY GIRL
NEED A RIDE?
I MISS THEM PIGGYBACKS
CLIMB ME BACK?
HOLLAR!

Tahoe replies:

WHERE ARE U?

Troy answers:

TOMORROW NIGHT

FLEISHMANN PLANETARIUM

Tahoe replies:

I DON'T KNOW WHERE THAT IS

Troy relies:

LOOK IT UP

Tahoe switches to Google Search and comes up with the location.

NO CAN DO

HOW ABOUT SATURDAY NIGHT

SAME PLACE

EIGHT O'CLOCK

Troy replies:

IT CLOSES AT EIGHT

HOW ABOUT PARKING LOT?

Tahoe answers:

OKAY

Troy asks:

WHAT ARE YOU DRIVING?

Tahoe replies:

TRAILWAY RV

GREEN AND WHITE

As soon as Tahoe powers off, Brenda, Aliya, and Karrene arrive, each bearing a gift for Niecee. They exchange a series of hugs and kisses and Tahoe decides it's a good time to step out for a cigarette break, so she heads for the front entrance. Yet, the visit was cut short because Niecee was scheduled for a group therapy session. They said their good-byes and the foursome reconvened in the parking lot, and Tahoe told them about Troy's text.

"So you replied to his text but didn't tell Niecee?" inquired Aliya, making sure she heard it right.

"That's right, and I don't intend to ever tell her about it."

"She needs to forget about that creep and the sooner the better," erupted Brenda.

"Ya damn skippy!" cosigns Tahoe. "He's evil and he's robbed Niecee of her spirit. He's stolen my girl's heart and I'm the one who's going to get it back!"

"I don't know," said Aliya. "I'm not so sure he could have done all that they're saying about him. Nothing has been proven. He's just a person of interest."

"But you're forgetting that as soon as Frank Dean told Rob and Sunny where the body in his warehouse had come from, Troy did a Houdini Act and vanished," added Brenda.

"I'm standing by my sister on this, said Karrene. "Despite Aliya's weakness for getting caught up with foolish men, we can't just go out and crucify this dude based on media hype."

"I wouldn't give a rat's ass about his criminal mind or portfolio!" screams Tahoe. "I'm the one who encouraged Niecee to go after that jerk!"

"Yes, but that was before he showed his true nature, Tahoe," said Brenda. "You mustn't blame yourself for what's happened to your girl. I'm convinced that he is the shit-bird they say he is. I own a gun and I'd like to hunt him down and take his punk-ass out!"

Tahoe takes the last puff of her cigarette, drops it to the pavement and crushes it. "Ya damn skippy, and that's exactly what we should do."

"We?" said Aliya.

"Yes, we, and especially you," scoffed Tahoe. "Just think for a minute. He probably wouldn't have hesitated to toss your ass into his daddy's furnace or cut you to pieces and drop you in his wood chipper. Besides, even though your brother couldn't find enough evidence to put him away, why did you break off your relationship like Troy was toxic waste?"

"That sucks! Why do you have to make it sound so gross, Tahoe?"

"It is gross," added Brenda. "Okay, so let's stop picking on each other and decide on something. Miss Tahoe, whatever you've got planned, you can count me in," vows Brenda.

The two women bump fists and turn their focus on Aliya and Karrene.

Aliya sighs. "So where are we supposed to met with that fool?"

"And when do we leave?" prompted Karrene.

It was misty all day in Reno. Moisture laden rain clouds had snuck past the Sierra Mountains. The sky was murky grey. It drizzled, then stopped, then drizzled some more. Brenda Bonesteel had so many entertainment connections in Reno that she had to avoid the downtown area in case someone recognized her. The women settled on a Travel Lodge in the nearby city of Sparks.

Towards the day's end, they caravanned into the desert. Tahoe drove the green and white Trailways RV. Niecee was still embroiled with depression. She stayed in the RV's bed. Aliya and Karrene rode together in their brother's Chevy Stepside and Brenda followed in her husband's Hummer.

At six p.m. they took a gravel road that led them five miles off the main highway and set up a minicamp in the sagebrush wilderness. They were shielded from the evening's desert wind by two rocky hills. Aliya and Karrene unloaded two cords of firewood from the truck and set up a huge bonfire. Brenda brought refreshments, marshmallows, franks and beer. She also brought blankets to help keep Niecee and everyone else warm.

At seven-thirty, Tahoe cranked up the RV and headed back to town.

By seven forty-five, Troy pulled into the planetarium's parking lot. He circled the huge space and building twice. He couldn't locate the RV, so he found a vantage point and parked. At approximately eight-oh-five, he spotted the RV rambling down Main Street. Tahoe was driving. Troy assumed Niecee was somewhere inside. For a good ten minutes it was stop-and-go traffic because a crowd of people streamed out of the planetarium's twin double doors. Troy waited until the RV circled past and he beeped his Jeep horn on the second trip around.

Tahoe stopped and signaled for him to follow. She meandered through several residential streets before finding the freeway on-ramp. Troy was confused by her maneuvers. He expected her to park. As she breezed down the freeway, she frequently checked her side mirrors to make sure Troy was still following.

After about five miles into their trek, Troy got in the passing lane, pulled up beside her and signaled her to pull over. Tahoe held up three fingers indicating three more miles. Troy eased his foot off the pedal and fell back in line.

When the clouds burst, a blanket of rain fell for ten minutes and everyone within a six mile radius got drenched. Brenda, Aliya and Karrene were working furiously to keep the bonfire going when the RV and Jeep pulled into their private camp. Tahoe got out and jogged over to join her sisters.

Troy remained seated behind the Jeep's steering wheel. His headlights were still on. His vehicle faced the bonfire at a distance of no less than a hundred feet.

The girls stood huddled, except for Niecee. She was wrapped in two blankets and sitting on a sandstone boulder. All the women could see was Troy's silhouette. They wondered if he was just going to turn around and drive away.

Suddenly, Niecee stood up and, without saying a word, strolled past the women for about fifteen yards, then stopped. The stars peering through a patch of clouds illuminated her as they seemed to touch the ground.

Troy climbed out of his vehicle and posted up in front of the Jeep's grill. He wore an army green trench coat that came down to the top of his work boots. He stood perfectly still then raised his arm and motioned for Niecee to come.

Niecee halted. Then she turned around and headed back to camp.

"PEANUT!!!"

Niecee froze, as Troy's primal scream echoed through the vast desert space. The girls were urging her to hurry and not to turn back, but it was too late.

Troy pulled a coiled rope from under his trench, and when everyone heard it crackle the cord had already smacked Niecee's cheek and was strangling her neck. She reached for her throat with both hands. Troy yanked and Niecee tumbled. Just as Troy tried to rush her, a gunshot whizzed past him and blew out his Jeep's windshield. Troy didn't relent. He grabbed Niecee by the hair and jerked her to her knees.

Another gunshot rang out. It singed Troy's right shoulder.

Brenda was going for a head shot, but she was aiming her Glock .40 a little wide.

Troy pulled Niecee to her feet, held her in front of him and continued forward. The next lash from his whip caught Brenda's wrist. Troy yanked and the Glock was flipped into the heart of the bonfire. Brenda scrambled for the gun and the whip lashed across her forehead and cut a gash into her face.

Niecee fought to break Troy's grip. She almost came out of her clothes, but Troy held on. He drug her away from the fire and retreated back towards the Jeep.

Aliya came out of the cover of darkness and grabbed Niecee's right arm in a feeble attempt to pry her from Troy's grip. Then Karrene attacked Troy's left flank. She had a ten gallon can with a hose-pump. She doused his trench coat in gasoline.

The rain of petrol didn't faze Troy. Once it began to run down his neck and saturate his undershirt, he released his hold on Niecee, slammed his boot heel into her spine and crushed her to the ground. From inside his trench, he pulled out a short-handled sledge hammer on a rope and he slung it like Thor.

Karrene screamed. Her kneecap was busted on impact, and with a sweeping backhand, Troy crushed Aliya's shoulder blade. During the melee the gas can got tipped over and within seconds Troy was standing in a liquid pool.

Aliya tried to crawl away and he smashed her in the ribcage. With his attention diverted, Niecee escaped. She sprinted back to the bonfire.

"PEANUT! DON'T RUN FROM ME, DAMMIT!"

Suddenly, Niecee spun around and began a slow march towards Troy. It was as though Troy had her under some kind of Haitian spell.

Brenda was going berserk. She was screaming at the top of her lungs for Niecee to get out of the way. She'd retrieved the Glock from the fire and had wrapped a rag around the handle. She was aiming it at Troy's head, but Niecee was blocking her line of sight.

When Niecee got within five feet of Troy's reach, he snatched her by the waist and every creature in the desert heard Brenda Bonesteel's scream...just as Niecee dropped a burning ember into the pool of gas.

There was a rush of hot air that buckled the crisp cold snap...and the fiery flames engulfed both of them.

Troy flailed at the flames that raced along his legs, arms and back.

Niecee tumbled and rolled out of the fiery pool.

Aliya and Karrene hobbled over with blankets and smothered the flames that ravaged their sister.

And Brenda emptied a barrage of bullets into Troy's torso.

Troy wouldn't go down.

He stood with a shocked and bewildered expression.

Brenda reloaded and continued to fire the weapon.

A bullet ripped through Troy's neck.

Another bullet shredded his groin.

The final shot split his skull.

Ten seconds passed before Troy let go of the sledge hammer.

His mangled body gave way and he fell face down in the blackened patch of desert sand.

Brenda ran over and handed the gun to Tahoe, who smiled as she emptied another clip into the burning man.

They destroyed him with fire, but he was still...Cold as Ice.

THE END

ABOUT THE AUTHORS

Alec 'Alex Briggs' Bellard hails from the heart of Silicon Valley, San Jose, California; a former electronics drafting designer and technical school instructor. In 1994, drug abuse had taken its toll and under California's Three Strikes Law received a life sentence. With time on his hands, his sister suggested he write. Bellard began with children's stories and progressed into adult short fiction and novels. Bellard is the winner of the Oakland Bay Area Writers of Color and Distinction Award (2007) and was awarded New York's Dawson Prize (2010).

Eugene L. Weems is the bestselling author of *United We Stand, Prison Secrets, America's Most Notorious Gangs, The Other Side of the Mirror, Head Gamez, Bound by Loyalty, Red Beans and Dirty Rice for the Soul, Innocent by Circumstance, Cold as Ice, and The Green Rose.* The former kick boxing champion is a producer, model, philanthropist, and founder of No Question Apparel, Inked Out Beef Books, and co-founder of Vibrant Green for Vibrant Peace. He is from Las Vegas, Nevada.

RED BEANS and DIRTY RICE FOR THE SOUL

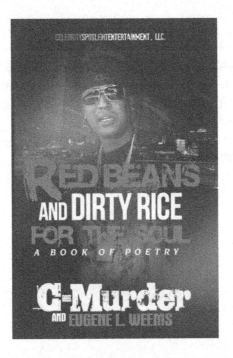

COREY 'C-MURDER' MILLER
EUGENE L. WEEMS
CLARKE LOWE

Tread the gutta' life with **C-MURDER** in this gripping compilation of poetry that is deeply rooted in the streets and behind prison walls.

WARNING! May cause a severe reaction or death in people who are square to the game. If an allergic reaction occurs, stop reading and seek emergency counseling from your local priest.

$14.95   103pgs   6x9 Paperback   ISBN: 978-0991238019
Celebrity Spotlight Entertainment, LLC

BOUND BY LOYALTY

COREY 'C-MURDER' MILLER
EUGENE L. WEEMS

The novel that critics across the nation are raving about and people are eager to read.

C-Murder and Weems constructed an elaborate contemporary urban thriller full of twists and false starts. Bound by Loyalty is absolutely chilling and bursting with surprises.

$14.95   278pgs 6x9 Paperback   ISBN: 978-0991238002
Celebrity Spotlight Entertainment, LLC

PRISON SECRETS
2nd EDITION

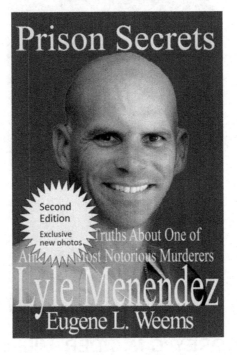

EUGENE L. WEEMS

Once recognized as a ruthless killer and remorseless criminal, Lyle Menendez remains housed in a maximum security correctional facility with other notorious murderers and gang members. In this level 4 maximum security prison, even one of America's most notorious murderers could be victimized. This novel will unlock the doors to all the prison secrets; weapons manufacturing, drug smuggling, prison rapes, gang politics, officer corruption and much, much more.

$14.95   183 pgs   6x9 Paperback   ISBN: 978-1500934873
Celebrity Spotlight Entertainment, LLC

UNITED WE STAND

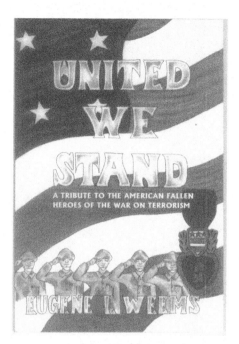

A TRIBUTE TO THE AMERICAN FALLEN HEROES OF THE WAR ON TERRORISM
Eugene L. Weems

United We Stand is a beautiful collection of inspirational artwork and passion-filled poetry created as a living tribute to the American troops who have made the ultimate sacrifice for our country in the war against terrorism.

100% of the proceeds from this book will be contributed to provide care packages for the active duty troops who remain engaged in the war overseas and provide college scholarship trust funds for the children of our American fallen heroes.

$14.95   95 pgs   6x9 Paperback   ISBN: 978-1-4251-9130-6
Celebrity Spotlight Entertainment, LLC

3 STRIKES

Crucifix

Growing up poor, abused and surrounded by violence, Tito Lopez dreamed of becoming a cop. But as fate would have it, his dreams became a series of nightmares and the treachery of life in the hood overtakes him.

When the water gets too deep, gangsters pull Tito out, embrace him and become his family. Unfortunately, Tito is drawn into a life of crime and gangsterism, which involves the Mexican Mafia and corrupt cops.

This gripping reality takes you on a journey leading to betrayal and a Three Strikes life sentence.

$14.95   187 pgs   6x9 Paperback   ISBN: 978-0-9912380-3-3
Celebrity Spotlight Entertainment, LLC

INNOCENT BY CIRCUMSTANCE

C-Murder
Eugene L. Weems

The day of his grandmother's death was the day Boo began his quest for survival in the fast-paced, treacherous and wicked streets of Las Vegas, Nevada. The grieving child is forced into hustling, larceny, burglary, robbery and even murder just to maintain the necessities of life. Boo, Jewel and the rest of the kids exact revenge for the brutal crimes committed against them. They find unconditional love, commitment and loyalty within each other and become a family unit.

This action-filled story will surprise the reader with sensitive and all too real situations. A compelling novel with deep, complex characters guilty of horrible crimes...or are they Innocent by Circumstance?

$14.95   216 pgs   6x9 Paperback   ISBN: 978-1503355798
Celebrity Spotlight Entertainment, LLC

THE GREEN Rose

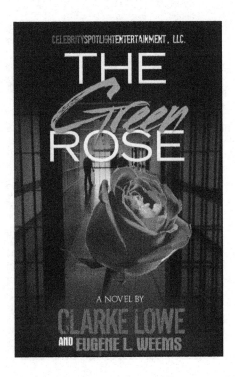

Eugene L. Weems
Clarke Lowe

MaryAnn is assaulted, but saved from harm by an heroic, stree-wise stranger. Her hero, Curtis, is not the kind of person she normally socializes with, but she can't help but be drawn to this brave and charming man. In Curtis she discovers love is blind--race, nationality and social class are irrelevant. In him she finds fun, excitement and security she has not felt in years. MaryAnn shares her experience with her best friend Amanda and suggests she meet Curtis's friend Eugene. Unfortunately, he's in prison, but sometimes true love must be sought out in unconventional places. Will they find the deepest, most exotic love of their lives? Will they find The Green Rose?

$12.95   100 pgs   6x9 Paperback   ISBN: 978-1503357044
Celebrity Spotlight Entertainment, LLC

Made in the USA
Las Vegas, NV
14 April 2022

47494033R00118